# THE
# FOURTH VICTIM

## THE FOUNDATION SERIES • SARA'S STORY

## BEVERLEY BATEMAN

Cover Design by Kelly Ferrara, KF Advertising Services
Interior Formatting by Author E.M.S.

Published in the United States of America.

# Other Books by Beverley Bateman

A Cruise to Remember

A Murder to Forget

Don't Go

By Design

Hunted

Missing

Targeted


www.beverleybateman.com

# THE
# FOURTH VICTIM

*This book is dedicated to my writing buddies*
*in my Kiss of Death Chapter*

# PROLOGUE

*18 months earlier*


The office said he'd had a heart attack. Was he alive? Did she want him to be? What if her husband had to stay home for a few weeks to recuperate? Palms sweating, Sara's breath came in short, shallow bursts at the thought.

The taxi jerked to a stop in front of the hospital emergency entrance.

Sara fumbled through her purse and counted out her meager number of dollar bills. Gordon didn't allow her to have a credit card and he only allowed her to have a small amount of cash. She didn't have enough money to pay the taxi.

"I'm so sorry. I left home without any cash. I...I... Would you take a check?" Tears spilled over and trickled down her flushed cheeks.

The driver spun around. A short stubby finger waved at the sign over the rearview mirror. "Look lady, it says right there—No Checks."

"I know, I know. I'm sorry. My husband's had a heart attack and I... I don't know what to do." Sara ran her fingers through her hair and scrunched the tight bun at her neck.

The driver shook his head. "Aw, shit. Go ahead, lady. Write the check."

Sara pulled the single crumpled check Gordon allowed her carry for emergencies out of her purse. When she touched the check a vision of Gordon floated in front of her.

She froze and rapidly blinked her eyes. She only saw the ghosts of dead people. Gordon didn't believe her and forbid her to ever mention it.

Could he really be dead?

"Gordon?" she whispered.

"Lady, are you writing that check or not?"

"Yes, sorry." Sara scribbled her signature on the bottom of the check. "Please, fill it in, and give yourself a generous tip. Thank you, thank you so much." She clutching her worn purse to her chest, slid out of the cab, and scurried through the emergency room doors.

What if he was dead? She didn't have any money. Gordon did all the finances and never shared anything with her. How would she manage?

Twenty years ago she could have handled it. Could she do it again? But he couldn't be dead. Gordon would never allow that to happen.

His face flitted in front of her, fixed in an angry glare.

He had to be dead or she wouldn't be seeing him. He didn't want to be dead. He didn't want her to be free. If he thought she could see him he'd be furious.

Sara shuffled toward the reception desk. She glanced over her shoulder, searching for some sign of Gordon, listening for his voice, waiting for him to yell at her. She couldn't believe he was really dead, even though she had seen him. She clung to the edge of the transition counter, her head down, chewed on her lower lip and waited to be noticed.

Finally a brusque voice snapped, "Can I help you?"

Sara looked up to see a heavy set, older woman in a loose blue top. The woman's thick dark brows met in a v in the middle of her forehead.

"I'm sorry, I… I'm looking for my husband. His office phoned to say he'd been brought here." Sara shrunk into her body.

"Name?" the woman commanded.

"Gordon, Gordon Peters." Sara stared at her worn black oxfords, then at the scuffed, gray linoleum with the red, blue and yellow lines that led to different areas. Maybe she shouldn't have come. Maybe she should have waited for Gordon to call and tell her whether she should be here or not. But if he was dead she would have to make her own decisions. Her pulse raced. Her head pounded. For the last nineteen years she had never made a decision. Gordon made all of them for her.

"When was he admitted?" The woman reminded Sara of a sergeant major.

"I'm not sure, less than an hour ago. They told me to meet him here. Maybe he's been discharged already?" She chewed her thumbnail. If Gordon had been discharged he'd be furious at her for spending all that money on a taxi. But she'd seen his ghost.

Tension twisted her stomach into knots. The pain caused her to clutch her purse tightly against her abdomen. She needed to get home and start dinner. She'd have to take a bus. Did she have enough money? She opened her purse.

The woman moved to a second pile of folders and pulled one out. "You're his wife?"

Sara nodded. "Yes. Can I see him?"

A sob slipped out. If she didn't find see him soon, he'd be furious. He'd think she was too stupid to even find him in a hospital and he'd be right.

His ghost floated in front of her. This time confusion mixed with his anger

"Have a seat, Mrs. Peters. I'll have the doctor speak to you." The sergeant major's voice softened. She indicated a chair near the desk.

"No, please, I need to see him right away. He'll be upset if I'm late."

The woman rounded the desk and laid her hand on Sara's shoulder. She squeezed gently for a second. "It'll be okay, honey. You just sit down for a minute. The doctor will be right out."

The sergeant major helped Sara to a chair close to the desk. Sara slumped into the seat, and dropped her head into her hands. Gordon might be dead but he would still make her pay for spending the money on the taxi, and not getting to the hospital sooner. It was another sign of her incompetence. He'd remind her she didn't deserve a man like him.

She gasped. Gordon stood a few feet away. He shook his fist. No, it wasn't him. It was his ghost. It couldn't be. Gordon said she didn't see ghosts. He'd never come to her even if he was dead.

"Go away," she whispered. Sara looked up at the Nursing Assistant. "Please, I have to see my husband. He'll be mad because it took me so long to get here." Her voice trembled.

"You sit there for a minute, honey. The doctor will be out to talk to you." The woman touched Sara's arm again, before she strode through the double doors behind the reception desk.

Tears dripped down Sara's face. She attempted to count her change to see if she had bus fare, but the tears blurred her vision. Damn. Was there someone she might call who could help her? No one came to mind. She didn't have friends. Gordon didn't approve of them. When she got to stalk to him, she'd ask him how to get home. He'd tell her what to do. Except—she'd seen his ghost and that meant he was dead.

If he was dead she no longer had to worry about what he thought or said. She tried to wrap her head around the prospect of not having him tell her what she had to do, or not. She glanced up, furtively, without raising her head. The ghost had faded away.

A sigh of relief slipped through her. Maybe it had been her imagination. That was what Gordon always said it was.

She tried to focus on her present situation, but confusion interfered.

A few minutes later a tall, rangy man with graying hair wearing green scrubs strode through the No Admittance doors at the end of the room. He paused and scanned the room before he headed in her direction.

She wondered what kind of description the nurse had provided to him that he could pick her out immediately. If she'd said, a frumpy, middle-aged woman, in a tasteless, gray cotton dress, with a developing a hump on her back from always hunching over, she would have been dead on.

"Mrs. Peters?"

Sara acknowledged him. "I need to see my husband, please."

"I'm Dr. Anderson."

"I have to go to my husband. Please take me to him. He'll be angry if I'm late coming to see him."

"Mrs. Peters, there's no easy way to say this. Your husband died. He had a massive heart attack at work. He was dead when the paramedics brought him in here."

A clamp tightened on her heart. She began shaking. "Gordon is dead?"

The ghost really had been him—and he was angry.

"Yes ma'am. I'm sorry for your loss. There was nothing we could do."

"No, it can't be Gordon. Gordon wouldn't die. He'd never leave me. Are you sure you have the right man? Gordon Peters, five feet eleven inches, forty-two years old."

"Yes, ma'am. Let me take you in to see him."

"Yes, I need to see him. I'm sure there's a mistake. He's too young for a heart attack."

"He's young, but it happens at any age. Please follow me." Dr. Anderson reached down to help her stand.

Sara jerked her hand away, stood on her own and stared into the distance. Gordon's face floated in front of her, scrunched into angry lines.

Gordon was dead. What would she do now? Dr. Anderson led her through the No Admittance double doors, past pale green curtains, to a back cubicle. Inside a figure lay on a stretcher, covered by a sheet.

A chill twisted around her spine. Her stomach seized. What if it really was Gordon?

Dr. Anderson put a hand on her back to steady her.

Sara flinched.

He pulled his hand back, reaching around her, careful not to touch her. He pulled the sheet down to expose the man's face.

Gordon's ghost stood at the head of the stretcher.

"Ohh," Sara inhaled quickly. Her hand clutched her throat. She kept shaking her head. "No, no…"

The person lying there was Gordon Peters, her husband. He appeared to be sleeping, except his face was a pale, gray color. His hair was still neatly brushed back in the new, shorter cut he'd changed to a few weeks earlier. She'd wondered why he wanted to try and look younger. When she'd asked, he'd said it would help him get ahead at work. It hadn't made sense, but you never questioned Gordon.

"Gordon?" Sara moved her hand to touch him and then jerked it back. "He's dead."

"Yes. Mrs. Peters, can I call someone for you?"

"He's not coming back?"

"No."

Gordon floated by, but this time his face had faded. His expression was hard to read.

Sara stared at the body, all life gone out of it. Fear flooded over that tiny ball of relief buried deep inside her.

As a ghost he might be angry, but he'd never be in control of her again. Now how was she going to manage?

"Is there someone…?"

"No, there isn't anyone."

"What about a grief counselor?"

"No, Gordon didn't believe in counseling." He wouldn't want her talking to anyone. She had a feeling his ghost might try to present if she tried to get counseling. Sara raised her head. "I should get home. Dinner's going to be late."

"Mrs. Peters, are you sure you're all right? Your husband won't be coming home tonight."

"Of course not, I understand. He's dead." Numbness worked its way up her body, starting at her toes. By the time it reached her face, it began to crack open A small flicker of hope crept inside. Sara met the doctor's eyes. They were baby blue. She hadn't looked into anyone's eyes for years.

"Do you have a funeral home where you'd like us to send his body?"

"Um, no, I don't…I never thought…"

"The hospital uses Woodlawn. Would you like us to call them?"

"That would be very helpful. Thank you, Dr. Anderson." Woodlawn, she'd have to remember that. "Could you write the name down for me?"

"Certainly and if you're up to it, could you stop at the desk on your way out? There are some papers that need to be signed."

"Of course." Gordon was dead. He wouldn't be coming home again. He might be angry that he was dead, but that was his problem. Hopefully he didn't plan on hanging around her for very long. She didn't usually have ghosts around her. They came when she touched people or things.

She needed to call Andrew and Amy. Andrew would be upset. He was close to his father. His sister hadn't been that close.

What did she need to do next? It had never occurred to her that she'd be responsible for burying her husband. Maybe Andrew could tell her what she needed to do. Years ago, before she'd married Gordon, she would have known how to handle it.

Gordon had a lawyer. She'd have to find his name. There would be a will.

She was free.

The thought skipped across her mind. The cage had been opened, but her wings had been clipped for so many years she had no idea what to do next.

After she signed the necessary papers, the nurse gave her Gordon's possessions in a large envelope. Sara trudged out of the hospital her mind slowly began to work. A taxi stood outside the emergency room doors. Sara slid into the back seat and gave him her home address. She looked out the back window. Gordon was still paced in the lobby. The hospital and Gordon faded into the background.

The taxi slipped through the Seattle dusk, cutting in and out of the dinner-time traffic. The rain had stopped. Slumped in the corner, Sara tried to focus her mind on the sudden change of events. Everything swirled around inside her head. It was like a piece of machinery that had sat unused for years.

Gordon was dead. No one would be coming home to criticize her and complain that she was lazy and stupid. No one would be there to tell her who she could talk to and who she couldn't. She didn't have to eat dinner at the same time tonight. In fact she didn't even have to cook. She could order take out.

The realization cut through the fog she'd lived with for a long time. She could do whatever she wanted, once she figured out what she wanted to do. It had been so long since she thought for herself she didn't know if she could manage alone.

How could this happen to Gordon? He'd been perfectly healthy. He ate better than she did and exercised regularly.

She didn't even go for walks around the neighborhood. Gordon didn't approve. But he had died.

She had a chance to become the woman she had once been, or maybe even better than that woman. She glanced into the envelope and saw Gordon's wallet. She pulled it out and opened it. Shock waved over her. She couldn't believe the amount of money inside. She started to count it.

The taxi stopped in front of the house.

Sara checked the meter and counted out a number of bills from Gordon's wallet. Thank you." She slipped out of the vehicle and hurried up to the house. The taxi sped off.

Sara fumbled with the key. She managed to open the door on the second try. Inside, she stopped. A sense of freedom overwhelmed the fear of the unknown. She could make it on her own. Couldn't she? Yeah, she could.

She headed for the basement door and opened it. A golden Labrador dog bounded up the stairs. Sara bent down and hugged the animal.

"Hey Gloria, it's you and me from now on. No more Gordon." Sara sat down on the top stair, burying her face in the rich yellow fur. The warmth and love of the animal enveloped her. Gordon didn't like animals and didn't want Gloria around when he was home.

Relief opened the flood gates. After many years of holding everything inside, the tears began as a trickle and gradually gathered force. They flowed freely down her cheeks. She sobbed into Gloria's neck. Occasionally a hiccup interrupted the crying.

Gloria whined and proceeded to lick Sara's face.

"Things are going to be different, girl. No more basements for you. You deserve better and so do I."

For the first time in years Sara felt maybe she did deserve better. The tears began to slow. Could she make it on her own? It had been so long. She'd lost touch with banking, and driving, and shopping for anything but groceries. At thirty-nine, she had her life in front of her. It would take a while to undo the last twenty years, but she would do it. She would—wouldn't she?

Damn right. She had a university degree. She'd had a brain at one time. It had been stagnant for so long she needed to restart it and get it working again. First she needed to find out about her financial situation. She needed money. She didn't even know which bank Gordon dealt with. First thing in the morning she'd go through Gordon's desk and see what she could find.

Sara pulled her shoulders back, wiped her tears on her sleeve and smiled at Gloria. "I can do it. Damn it, I can put my life back together and I'll never let any man take control of my life ever again."

# Chapter One

The four shadowy forms in black crouched low, inching closer to the Shiraz prison wall. Darkness blurred the outline of the prison and its towers. Dense clouds blocked any shard of moonlight from slipping through the ebony night, providing cover for the four. The fall rain had stopped.

The corner search lights swung slowly in a circle, cutting through the darkness. The first form held up a hand. The rest flattened onto the dry terrain. The lights swung back across the area. The total rotation took three minutes.

Two uniformed guards marched past. They followed the perimeter toward the far corner of the tower.

Several seconds after the guards past, the shadows raced toward the main road. Two dived to the ground by the side of the road. The other two raced across the road and disappeared into the bushes against the outer prison wall. They slumped down onto the Iranian soil.

After a quick survey of the area, Fareeda, the taller, sturdier figure, stood up. She checked her shoes and adjusted her harness before shooting a light-weight hook, specifically designed by The Foundation, to the top of the wall.

A thud echoed through the silence when it landed. Both women held their breath. There was no response from inside. They exhaled slowly.

Fareeda grabbed the rope attached to the hook and began her climb up the stone surface.

At the call of a heron from the other side of the road, Fareeda paused and flattened herself against the structure. Below her Assif dropped face first to the ground.

Two more guards advanced. They continued past on another trip around the perimeter and disappeared around the corner.

Seconds later Fareeda resumed her upward climb. She stopped briefly when the lights swept past. Three more minutes and it would be back again. She scrambled the last few feet to a small ledge where she swung a second large, grappling hook over the barbed wire. The hook locked onto the edge of the wall. The prisoner could slide down, once Assif rescued her from her cell.

Fareeda grabbed the ropes, swung out from the wall and rappelled down quickly. At the bottom, the shorter, smaller framed person grabbed the rope.

"Your turn, Assif. Be careful," Fareeda whispered into her headphone. "There are more guards on they said, and the search lights are shorter than reported. Our information isn't accurate. If she's not in the cell, rappel down quickly. We can come back later if we have to. We don't want to get caught in this country."

Fareeda watched Assif grab both ropes and began her upward scale of the wall. She paused at a small window fifty feet above and peered through the bars.

Another heron cry broke the night.

Four guards marched into the escape area. Searchlights flashed on, focusing on the area.

"Assif, abandon the project! Get down here now!" Fareeda whispered into her headset.

A man's voice shouted in Arabic. They ran toward Fareeda.

Assif rappelled down in two or three long jumps. She started to run as soon as her feet hit the ground. Over her shoulder Fareeda saw two guards grab Assif. They hit her over the head. Her last view was Assif being pulled toward the prison gate.

Shots rang out.

"Shoot them!" She yelled as she raced toward the road. "Shoot them!"

The two women on the far side of the road responded with their own fire. Flashes of light from their weapons shot through the darkness. Fareeda heard the bullets whiz by as she raced across the road toward her companions.

At the next volley of shots she felt a burning pain in her leg. She grabbed her leg and collapsed to the ground. Warm fluid seeped through her fingers. She crawled across the road, dragging her leg.

"Here! Over here!" Sabhita and Marley, her teammates stood up and grabbed her. With Fareeda supported between them they raced into the darkness.

Behind them more voices shouted in Arabic. Bursts of light from their guns briefly illuminated the night.

"They got Assif when she hit the ground. We can't help her. We'll do her more good if we escape. Fareeda, can you make it?" Sabhita whispered. They pulled her forward.

Sweat dripped down her back. Her pants stuck to her leg. Fareeda nodded. Nausea swept over her. "I'll need help."

"No problem. We've got you." With one woman on each side of her, they hauled her into the blackness.

Rifles blasted through the air behind them. Men shouted. More search lights flashed on. Crashes grew louder. The guards raced after them.

"What the hell happened?" Carly's voice reverberated against the metal walls. She strode through the door into the refurbished meat freezer, now The Foundation's office.

The room had been part of an old meat packing warehouse in the Bronx are of New York City. The metal outer walls kept the cold inside. Even though they'd covered the blood-stained cement floor with under padding and thick wool carpeting, and hung tapestries on the wall, a chill always invaded the room. It assaulted her body right through to the bone.

Tortoise-shell glasses framed her bleary eyes and she clutched a bundle of fur under her arm. She plopped the dog into a chair. "I had to bring her with me. She whines and I get complaints from the other residents."

Her two partners, a super model and a computer programmer, had already arrived. A slightly overweight blonde, her eyes red-rimmed and her nose pinkish, popped out from the back room, outside the freezer. She carried two pink mugs, the steam leaving a trail behind her.

"You've got another stray? How many animals does that make now?" Julie placed one of the mugs in front of Carly before she patted Phoenix's head. "Poor baby, she's going to get cold in here."

"She's wearing a fur coat. She'll be fine." Carly inhaled the rich scent of the freshly brewed liquid. "Thanks for the coffee, Julie. I could use it. So what happened?"

"Don't know. I got here a few minutes ago. Nadia will fill us in. I've checked the bank balance so we can cover whatever she needs."

"Good girl. You must have broken a record getting here this quick." Carly took another sip of the hot, black liquid. "I took a cab instead of getting Sam to drive me, and paid my cabbie extra to speed, but you still beat me. You look like hell, Nadia." She turned to the other woman who stood in the back doorway, talking into her cell.

The tall woman wore worn designer jeans and a rumpled white t-shirt. She clicked off her phone. Without makeup and black hair pulled into a pony-tail, no one would recognize her as one of the world's top super models.

"Thanks. You don't look so hot yourself. You're wearing glasses?"

"No time to put in contacts. I never expected this." Carly responded. Her gut clenched at the thought of losing one of their team. The possibility had always been there, but they spent time and money to make sure it never happened. Unconsciously, she moved her hand across her stomach.

They'd saved a lot of women and up until now, never lost a team member. Now they had to save one of their own. "How long have you been here?"

Nadia massaged her temples. "A little while."

Carly pulled her cashmere sweater tighter against the penetrating chill. "You didn't call us right away?"

"Sabhita called from the secured phone line in Iran when the two of them got back to the house where they were staying. One of our local contacts took Fareeda to the hospital. After I got the call I wanted to check out some of details. Also, maybe come up with a few ideas we could toss around. We couldn't do anything until I got more information so I didn't call right away."

"Okay, so what happened?"

Nadia's eyes glistened. "I don't know. We didn't have accurate information. We underestimated them. They set us up. All of the above."

"What do you mean, set us up?" Carly straightened up.

Nadia sagged against the wall. "From what I've been able to find out, no woman was about to be shot. It was all a fabrication. Someone planned and implemented a very elaborate scheme, including the ambush. It was a set-up. They were waiting for us. The team walked right into the trap."

"No." Julie's gasp came out more as a whisper. "How could that happen?"

"Damn." Carly pounded her fist on the oak table. Pain flashed through her hand and arm. "Who the hell knows about us?"

The dog's head shot up. She let out a sharp bark.

"Down, Phoenix." Carly patted the dog. Phoenix circled several times in the chair, flopped down, and fell back asleep.

Nadia shook her head. Tears accumulated in the corners of her eyes. She swiped at them. "I don't think anyone knows yet. I think someone is on a fishing expedition. They want to find out about us. This was the worm. We took the bait and the hook. Assif is now their hostage. They'll try and break her to get more information about the organization."

"We'll get her back. If we can do it for strangers, we can damn well do it for our own. We've got the money and the contacts. And we have women who will go to hell and back for their own." Carly stood up. "I guess after five years, and all the women we've helped, and the angry men we've left behind, we should have suspected someone might try to come after us. The idea of helping women isn't palatable for some men, especially when many of them consider their women as property. Their egos are damaged when we take someone they consider their property. We'll get both Assif and Fareeda out and quickly."

"I'm on it." Nadia moved away from the wall. "We'll get them out. Then I'll beat myself up for the screw up."

"Chill, Nadia. You didn't screw up. We got a little lax. You know, if they do break her, the only name she can give them is yours. You're her contact."

"I know."

"You need to be careful. If she breaks, they'll come after you next." Carly tapped a long, French-manicured nail on the boardroom table.

"She won't break. We'll get her before she does, but I'll keep that in mind."

"After we rescue Assif, I'll review our security. You need to check your contacts. For now, we all need to be more careful."

"I'd considered that. I thought all our bases were covered. I didn't suspect a trap. Luckily the other three escaped."

"Maybe I should check our records, put up more screens to prevent hacking," Julie suggested.

"Good idea." Carly acknowledged. "It's hard to say who planned this. The bigger we get the harder it is to stay under the radar, but I am damn well not going to let them destroy The Foundation and the good work we do."

"We won't let that happen," Julie added. "Like you said, we started out as a team. We still are."

"You're right." Carly responded. "Okay, now we know someone's after us, we'll take extra precautions to protect our agents. Right now our priority is Assif. She's in prison. They will torture her. Fareeda is in the hospital with a bullet in her leg, under the eyes of the local police. We need to get her home, too."

"I know. I accept full responsibility."

"Damn it, Nadia, no self-pity. We've been together for over eleven years. We're a team. We've helped abused women and their children for years. Now we need to focus on how to get the rest of our team home, safely and quickly. You say no woman is due to be shot as a spy tomorrow?"

"No, at least there's no one in the Shiraz prison."

"Damn." Carly slapped her forehead. "How could that happen?"

"I've got our Intel there working on details. My contacts for this assignment fed me erroneous information; set us up for this rescue mission. Whoever planned it took at least six months to set it up. They used local newspapers and reporters as well as the military. They greased a lot of palms, with a lot of money, to ensure the perfect scenario to draw us in." Nadia paced the small room. "It's got to be someone we've affected in the past."

"Probably," Carly gulped a slug of coffee. Her fingers, drummed on the table. "Okay, one problem at a time. First we get Assif out and fast. They've had her for almost four hours. Assif knows we'll come for her, but she may not be able to hold out for long. We also need to get Fareeda out of their hospital and home. Once they're both safe, then we'll look at who, what, where. They've paid big money for Assif's capture. They'll expect to get big results."

"I'm on it. Julie's checked on the available and closest teams. We have one in Bahrain. It's only two hundred and sixty five miles to Shiraz, about a thirty minute flight. They should be in Shiraz in two to three hours, max."

"I've booked a private plane from Muharraq airport. If you have enough money you can get anything. It should be ready in about an hour, enough time for the group to get there." Julie added. "I'll also book the plane to fly everyone home."

"Good," Carly tapped her fingers on the desk. "Contact the team in Bahrain and send them in. We'll work out the details and have a plan ready when they arrive in Shiraz."

"The other two members, who were with Assif, are still in Shiraz." Nadia paused. "When Sabhita called she said they want in on the action. They left Assif behind. They need to help get her back."

"Nadia, they're tired. They're emotionally involved. They might screw up this mission. We can't afford a mistake. Assif's life is in our hands, as well as the future of The Foundation."

"They won't make a mistake. They didn't this time. I did. They realized something was wrong and got away. If it wouldn't take me too long to fly to Shiraz, I'd want to be in on this one myself, because I'm angry about the set up. Trust them. Let them join the others. They know the prison set up."

Carly stared at Nadia for several seconds. "Okay, your call, your mission, but we can't afford any mistakes on this rescue. Assif and The Foundation are counting on you."

"I know. I'm on it. I'm using the back room to make some calls. Okay?" Nadia glanced at Julie.

"Sure, go ahead. Let me know if you need anything."

"I'll need money; lots of it. On this short notice we'll need to buy off a lot of officials and locals to get in and out of the country. Let me know when you finish the details on the flights." Nadia's long legs, glided across to the back room in five strides and out the door into the small side room outside the metal walls.

"We also need a plan to get Fareeda from the hospital to the airport, so we need to work out two plans." Carly called after her. "The local police will want to question her. We'll have to pay them off so we can move her."

"I agree. I'm on it. I'll work on that right after I get the teams mobilized. More money, Julie," Nadia closed the door behind her.

"She feels guilty, like she let the team down, and The Foundation." Julie moved to the door, opened it and stepped outside the metal before she pulled out her cell phone and began punching in numbers. The phone didn't work in the freezer, neither did Wi-Fi.

"She did."

"But…"

"No Julie, we're all guilty, not just Nadia. We sit here and make decisions we expect our well-trained teams to execute. They expect accurate information. We blew it. We all feel guilty." Raw emotion tore Carly's gut. She fought to appear calm. She really wanted to curl up in a corner and cry, knowing what Assif must be going through.

"You're right. I've been sick about it ever since I got Nadia's call." Julie commented.

"Me, too. For five years we've tested and adjusted our basic plan and it's worked. If we made a mistake, we need to know why, not make excuses. We're all responsible. We're a team and no one makes a mistake alone. When we get everyone home safe we can sit down and have a group cry."

"Yeah, I know, but…Hello?" Julie never finished the sentence. She talked rapidly to someone about a plane.

Several minutes later she clicked off. "You want more coffee?"

"Yes, please." Carly moved her mug in Julie's direction. "Have you forgotten what it felt like out in the field?"

Julie busied herself preparing a fresh pot of coffee. "I remember the pressure and the fear, but I knew you guys had my back. It got me through."

Carly rubbed the back of her neck with her left hand. She opened the file in front of her. "That's what we need to do for the team now. Afterward we'll make sure everyone in the organization knows about the mistake, and that it won't happen again. We learn from our mistakes. Now we know someone is out to discover who we are, we'll double up on the protection for our people. Then we'll find the bastard and shut him down. If Nadia's right, how and why did they set us up? And who were they?"

Carly glanced around the room. Maybe they needed to move, find some place more secure. She sipped the coffee to get warm.

The rough preliminary copy of the team's report sat on top of the open file. It stated the team approached the prison at midnight at the change of the guards. The pre-mission information said two guards covered the night shift and both slept most during those hours.

The two members, who escaped uninjured, said the guards didn't sleep, but made regular rounds and four extra guards were on duty. There were more search lights outside of the prison than had been reported. The guards had been waiting for them.

Carly bent her elbows, tented her fingers, and rested her chin on her hands. How the hell had they messed up this bad? Carly could only imagine the hell Assif was going through. They had to get to her and fast.

"The flights are confirmed." Julie topped up Carly's coffee. "I read their report."

Carly tapped the file. "So you know the team couldn't

find exactly where they'd imprisoned this woman, Aasera Khan. They were preparing to abandon the mission when the guards spotted them and opened fire."

"They were set up."

"Yes, but why?" Carly leaned back in her chair.

The furry mop beside her whined and Carly reached over and scratched behind her ears. "I feel like whining too, little one."

The dog stood up and licked Carly's hand.

Nadia opened the door. "Okay, I've got everything in motion. With luck we should have Assif out of the prison in four or five hours and back home in less than eighteen hours. They'll be expecting us, but I don't think they'll expect us this quickly. Hopefully we'll have the element of surprise on our side. Oh, and Intel has proof there is no Aasera Khan. She's totally fictitious. Whoever masterminded this, made the story up, developed a character with all the elements to grab our attention, and hoped we couldn't resist trying to save the woman. We played right into their hands."

"No, we did what our mission is—we tried to save a woman." Carly swallowed hard, bypassing the tennis ball size lump in her throat. "They played us. Someone has profiled at least some information about The Foundation. We'll make sure they don't get any more. That's my job. Do you need anything else right now?"

Nadia shook her head. "I'm good. I've got people checking everything over there including the prison where Assif is being held, the floor plan, the number of guards, everything. It's from people I trust completely. We'll double and triple check all the information. When the new team arrives in Iran, Sabhita and Marley will meet them at the airport. All the necessary information will be there as well. We'll be successful. We'll have her by tonight."

"Excellent, Nadia, contact us if you need anything. I'll check on Fareeda. They did surgery on her leg. Luckily the bullet missed the femoral artery. She should be able to travel. Nadia, can you arrange the payment to the police?"

"One more thing Julie, maybe arrange for Assif to visit our plastic surgeon when she's discharged from the hospital. For her protection, let's change her appearance slightly. They'll take photos when they interrogate her. We'll get her a new identity. Also run a trace and eliminate any information on her and her family. We'll relocate her."

"Sure, I can do that. It gets more complicated, doesn't it?" Julie swiped at her eye.

"I'm afraid so, honey. It was easier with just three of us, at least when it came to security. Now it's a huge organization with lots more complications, but look how many more women we help."

"You're right," Julie replied.

"Everyone back here tomorrow morning, sooner if needed. Both our agents should be on their way home by then. My cell phone is on at all times if you need me. Thanks, you two." Carly hugged each woman before she picked up Phoenix. "Limiting knowledge of the organization has been one of our safe guards. After we rescue Assif, we'll try and figure out who wants to track us down. Then we'll figure out how we take them out of the picture."

"I'll help with some computer tracing." Julie offered.

"Thanks, Julie. I'll take you up on that. It's hard to say who planned this. The bigger we get the harder it is to stay under the radar. We'll figure it out, but not this morning. If you need anything, call me." Carly strode out. Hopefully she'd find a cab at this hour.

The idea of not being able to help women tore at her soul.

Walking through the warehouse toward the front door she remembered their first training. The three of them had been the first team. When they realized they needed some professional help this building was where they had been trained.

Outside Carly flagged a cab and climbed inside. She curled up in the corner. Phoenix slept on her lap. She allowed herself to feel the pain Assif must be going through and the guilt that she hadn't prevented it. Carly swallowed rapidly. The tears would have to wait until she was in her apartment, hidden from anyone's view.

*Okay lady, pull yourself together. The other problem I need to work on is figuring out if I have a spy in CCB Enterprises, undercutting my bids. So find a spy in CCB, plus the person looking for information about The Foundation. How difficult can that be?*

Carly allowed herself a semi-hysterical chuckle. It was interesting that both things seemed to be happening at the same time.

The cab sped through New York streets in the pre-dawn. Carly stared out the window. Did she have one major problem, or two separate, serious problems?

Carly stepped off the elevator; the mop under one arm, her purse and laptop clutched in her other hand. She paused by the desk of Anna Lee, her personal office assistant on the way into her office. She rested the dog on the corner of the desk. "Can you please get Link Stone up here, ASAP?"

"Done, anything else?" Anna asked.

"No, that's it for now. How's your little sister doing?"

"She's good. She got a report card and her grades are mostly A's."

"Excellent. Congratulate her for me. Other than Link, I don't want to be disturbed." Carly picked up Phoenix and passed through the door into a large corner office. Today, the view of the Hudson River didn't even catch her attention.

She placed Phoenix in a small dog bed in the corner of the room before she marched across to her desk. First she turned on her computer. Then she flipped open her laptop. She hit the power button. She had no time to waste. She needed names.

A whine got Carly's attention. The head of the multi-colored, floppy-eared mutt hung over the edge, her dark brown eyes staring soulfully up at Carly.

"Look, you mangy mutt, I'm working. You're lucky I brought you to the office."

At another long whine Carly shook her head. "Damn dog, I should have left you in the alley. Come on, get up here."

Carly patted the turquoise DKN wool pants. Phoenix jumped out of the bed and raced across to Carly. She attempted a jump. Carly shook her head and grumbled as she bent down and picked up the dog. "You'll ruin my damn suit." She scratched behind the dog's ears.

With the dog curled up on her lap, Carly swung back to her computer. The screen came up with the CCB Enterprises logo.

It had been CB Enterprises originally, but when she'd turned twenty-one, and taken a place on the Board, her father legally changed the name to CCB, Carl and Carly Brazil Enterprises. When her father died six years ago, she'd taken control of the entire company, at the age of twenty-seven.

She scanned the emails for anything needing immediate attention, found nothing and turned back to her laptop. She only used it for Foundation business. She kept it with her, or locked up, so there was less chance anyone could access the information.

After unlocking the laptop she opened the computer file and began to scan a list of people employed by The Foundation. Over a hundred people, either directly employed or involved in the agency, compiled the list.

Then there were their contacts around the world. Most were paid spies, government employees the organization had bribed or bought, relatives and anyone else who could be bought and provide information. These connections didn't know about The Foundation. They only knew the person who directly communicated with them, usually Nadia, Julie or herself. However, they would know the type of assignments they were contacted about. If someone found them and bought that information, a person could build a file about the organization and eventually set them up.

She scrolled her mouse down the screen and absently patted the dog. She paused at each name, read the information, shook her head then moved on down the list.

Her intercom buzzed.

"Link is here."

"Thanks, Anna. Send him in." Carly swung her chair around to face the door.

A tall, broad-shouldered man, a few years older than Carly, sauntered through the doorway, his presence filled the room.

"You called, boss?" He slouched against the door frame.

"Yes, I did. Come in, Link, and close the door behind you."

"Yes ma'am, whatever you say." The broad shoulders shrugged. He closed the door. "That's a dog?"

Carly scowled. "Yes, I found her trembling in an alley a week ago, starved, covered in sores, a couple of broken ribs and afraid of everything. What could I do?"

Phoenix jumped off Carly's lap and approached Link cautiously. She sniffed at his shoes.

"If she pees on my leg I'm out of here. What the hell were you doing in an alley?"

"I didn't go into the alley. I walked by and she whined. When I looked down, I saw this ratty fur ball huddled up against the wall, almost hidden in old papers and garbage. I bent down and patted her. Not that it's any of your business."

"Agreed, but it's not a good idea. She could have bitten you."

"She didn't." Carly snapped. "She hasn't even bitten you, yet."

Phoenix sat up on her hind legs and scratched at Link's pants.

Link glowered at the dog. "I didn't think you usually brought your rescued critters to the office. Have you gone over the animal quota for your apartment?"

"No, not that it's any of your damn business. Phoenix is afraid to be left alone. She'll pee on the carpet and howl the whole time I'm gone."

Phoenix whined and pawed at Link's leg.

"What's her problem?"

"For some reason she likes you and wants to be picked up."

Link scowled at the animal and then picked her up by the scruff of her neck. He held the animal in front of his face. "Look, I don't like animals."

Phoenix leaned forward and licked Link's cheek.

"Damn dog." Link pulled her against his chest and scratched behind the dog's ears. "What did you want to see me about?"

Phoenix stretched her head back so she could continue to lick Link's chin.

"Oh good, we're finally at the reason you're here. I need you to check some things, very quietly, so no one knows, and I mean no one." Carly tamped down the anger bubbling inside. His attitude infuriated her, but she needed him for this assignment. She hated men who patronized her. If he didn't do such a damn good job, she might have replaced him. She might yet.

*What the hell is Phoenix doing? The dog actually likes the man. Who knew she had such bad taste?*

"Yeah, okay, what do I look for?"

Carly stared at the man for a minute. The sun streaked, dark hair hanging well below his ears, had started to curl at the ends. His slate gray eyes regarded her as if she were an incompetent child. He wore his tan and brown CCB uniform open at the throat with the sleeves rolled up revealing a neck, muscular from working out, arms knotted with muscles, a Montana wide chest and a narrow waist.

The surveillance left her insides feeling wobbly. Her pulse rate skipped a beat on its way up the rating scale. She couldn't help but admire his pure, male attributes. She knew women would stop and take a second look at this man, but with his attitude she'd be surprised if he had a girlfriend, or kept one for very long. His lack of professionalism, combined with his present slouch, had her wondering why she continued to employ him, except he'd been head of security for over six years, did a good job and she liked looking at him. And for some unknown reason she trusted him.

Her father had hired Link shortly before he died. Link had worked his way quickly up to head of the security department when several older men decided to take early retirement. In the last six years she'd never had a complaint about his work. He'd run security without any issues or leaks, up until now.

He stared back at her, his lips twisted into a smirk, as if he could read her mind.

Carly wished he didn't look so damn yummy. "We have a mole."

"Are you sure?"

"Yes, I'm sure." Carly snapped. "Our last two contract bids have been undercut. I don't think it's a coincidence. Someone is getting our bid information and proposals in advance. I need every employee of CCB rechecked, thoroughly. I want to know if anyone needs money, or has received any unusual amounts of money, or is involved with a competitor. Anything that looks suspicious. You know what to look for. I want you to do it personally. If we've got a mole I don't want him alerted. Also do a complete sweep for bugs, just in case."

"A routine sweep is done on the first of the month. I did an extra check last week."

"This is an order, not an option. I want another one done, now, today." Carly aimed a saccharin tinged smile in his direction. "It's possible someone bugged the offices after the first of the month or since last week."

"Yes, ma'am, I'll certainly do it again, right away." He gave her a mock two finger salute.

"Good. Is it policy to always do it at the same time each month?"

"That's been the process as long as I've been employed. I'm not sure if your father set it up or the previous security head. Why?"

"If there's leak in the company they might know our routines. They could have put a bug in the day after the sweep, knowing it wouldn't be found for a month."

"Except, I did an extra one last week and other than myself, I doubt if anyone knows about it. I will review our routine checks and policies and make sure we don't fall into any more ruts."

"Good, do that. Losing a few contracts isn't a big deal, but it is unusual. Let me know right away about the sweep."

"No problem. Maybe I should screen you as well."

"What on earth for?" Carly scowled.

"A bug might be placed in your purse or your pocket."

Carly heated up at the thought of him with a scanner close to her body. "Fine, but screen the room first, then if needed I'll let you screen me. Write up your security review. We can discuss it and see if we need to make any other changes. Let me know when it's ready."

"You want to review security policies with me?" Link raised his eyebrows. He took a step forward so he towered over her desk, Phoenix clutched under his arm. The menacing image dissolved when Phoenix licked his hand and Link scratched the dog under his chin.

"I believe that's what I said." Carly leaned back in her chair, choking down a chuckle. "It appears they're not adequate at the moment. I may have been lax in not discussing them with you sooner. Do you have a problem with that?"

"You're the boss," Link snapped. "Is there anything else?"

"You're paid as head of security. You tell me." Carly fired back.

Link glowered at her for several seconds then backed away from her desk. "I think that should cover it for a start. When do you want the review done?"

"Five o'clock tonight?" Carly met his stare.

Link's dark eyebrows knit together. "I'm not sure…"

"Okay, I need it as soon as possible. I'll pay for all overtime."

"I'll do the sweep first. It won't take long. Then I'll start re-checking personnel. It could take a few days."

"No problem. Start with those in major positions and work out from there."

"Got it. I'll let you know about the bugs and anything else I may find after I run the sweep, or if I need to check you." Link allowed a suggestive twitch of his lips before he gently put Phoenix down on the floor.

"In your dreams," Carly muttered.

He smirked. "Nice glasses."

Carly reached up and touched the square, tortoise-shell frames. She'd forgotten she still had them on. Great, she looked like a dweeb. "Thanks. Perhaps you should get to work?"

"Yes ma'am, whatever you say." Link strode toward the door.

"And Link, get a haircut. If you can't afford one, charge it to the company."

"Another order?" He swung back, his slate gray eyes dark, his lips clenched.

"Let's say a strong suggestion, for now. You're dismissed." Carly forced a tight smile to her lips.

Link opened his mouth, then closed it and stomped out of the room. The door slammed behind him.

"Well, that went well," Carly muttered to Phoenix. "Who does he think he is? A great build and a tight butt doesn't mean he can treat me like that. I'll be taking more interest in security from now on. And what's with you, making buddies with a man like that? He's a major jerk." Carly yanked her glasses off and headed to the powder room attached to the office, where she kept a spare pair of contact lenses.

Phoenix trotted over to the closed door. She whined and scratched at the bottom of the door.

"That's enough, go to your bed. He won't be back, you traitor."

A few minutes later, contacts in place, she returned to her computer and continued to check the list of The Foundation employees.

Someone was spying on CCB. And someone else wanted to find The Foundation. Could it be a coincidence?

Carly didn't believe in them. But then it meant someone had linked the two organizations. She didn't believe that either. She'd handle them as separate issues unless something turned up to connect them.

Link could handle CCB for now. She needed to find the leak in The Foundation before another mission went sour. She would not place another of their team members in danger. She'd go back into the field first.

She'd ask Julie to check The Foundation's cases for the past five years. See if a disgruntled husband or boyfriend had decided to find them and get even.

What started with the three of them and a kernel of an idea, over seven years ago, had grown to include a state of the art training facility and equipment as well as several different teams of operatives, each with different skills. The fund raisers helped finance it. Some funds were funneled from CCB and the three of them also put money into the organization.

She'd said she find whoever did this, but what if she couldn't? A sense of inadequacy flooded over her. What if someone discovered The Foundation? It would put all the women they'd helped in danger.

# Chapter Two

The cold, dampness of the cell attacked Assif. The threadbare gray pants and top she'd been given barely covered her body. The room held a small, barred window near the ceiling. She'd moved the cot under the window, but when she stood on it the window remained several feet out of reach.

She lay on the small cot, a single, ragged blanket wrapped around her shoulders, clutched tightly to her chest. Fear clawed at her. Tremors wracked through her.

No team for support now, just her own skills and strength. She'd heard the car engine fade into the distance as they'd clubbed her into semi-consciousness. At least Sabhita and the others had escaped. She knew they'd come back for her, but right now she'd hit low tide.

The first interrogation hadn't been bad. They'd dropped a hood over her head. It increased the fear. They'd shoved a small elongated object into her hand. Blind-folded, she'd grasped it tightly.

Her bare feet dragged against the cold, cement floor. Unable to see under the hood she clutched the pen-like object desperately with both hands. They'd pulled her along. This was a technique she wasn't familiar with, but it proved highly effective. She was sure it was a pen that distanced her from her captors, unable to touch them. The isolation played with her mind. It spiked her fear level. She'd desperately grasped the pen-like item as she struggled to maintain her balance. She had stumbled through the enforced darkness. Thoughts of whatever the destination might bring flooded her mind.

In a small interrogation room, her blindfold removed, she'd stood barefoot in front of three men. They'd asked basic questions; such as her name and who she worked for. She'd refused to answer.

The man in the middle, with the military uniform covered with badges, a neatly trimmed gray beard and a mustache, asked most of the questions. "You will tell us. You will beg to tell us everything."

He'd smirked at her, over his spectacles. "Take her back to her cell to consider her options."

They'd dropped the hood over her head, given her the pen. She'd gripped it tightly in her attempted to keep up with the guards. She struggled to keep her balance. Back in her cell she'd fallen onto the stone floor when they grabbed the pen out of her hand and removed her hood. She'd lain there until the guards left, before she crawled back to the cot. She'd pulled her knees up to her chest. Tears trickled down her cheeks.

*Pull yourself together, Assif. Remember the classes on interrogation. Be strong. You'll get out soon.*

Without a watch, and unable to see the sky, she didn't know exactly how long before they came for her the second time. It felt like a few hours.

They blind-folded her and gave her the pen tip to hold. She'd clutched it tightly. Again she stumbled along behind the guards, through the cold darkness.

The second time had been more intense. The interrogators sat in the shadows this time. Bright lights focused on her face. She felt naked in her thin clothing. She had to stand at attention. All three fired questions at her.

Assif stood at attention in the middle of the room. She desperately wanted a drink from the pitcher of water on the desk in front of her. Her dry throat ached. She remembered the techniques she'd learned during training. She blanked out her mind and focused on the glass.

Again, she refused to answer their questions. They shouted at her, over and over again, first one and then another. Her feet went numb, her knees sagged.

"Stand at attention."

Assif straightened, pulled her shoulders back and tipped her chin up. They wouldn't break her.

*Please Sabhita, hurry.*

"Take her back. She'll need her strength for the next time." One of the men snarled. He reached for the pitcher and poured himself a drink.

Assif could hear him swallow, after they blind-folded her. Again she clutched the pen tip, her only contact for the long trip through cold, damp corridors. The isolation and darkness effectively terrorized her. No human contact left her feeling alienated. She stumbled. Her numb feet tripped over each other. She developed a lot of empathy with the blind. She couldn't imagine a life in darkness.

She asked the guards for water. No one brought any. It was another way to break her. She had constant pain from her parched throat. She couldn't swallow any longer. Her lips started to crack.

Huddled on the cot, she stared out through the metal bars. How much longer before the guards came back? How much longer until Sabhita and her team arrived? She must have been here at least six or seven hours. How much longer could she hold out?

She wouldn't break, no matter what they did to her. If she broke she'd put Nadia, Fareeda and the rest of her team at risk. She wouldn't do that to them. It would be better if she died.

She heard the guards marching toward her cell before she saw them. She had to be strong enough to survive this one. The cell door clanked open. One guard grabbed her. The other guard dropped the hood over her face. They gave her the stupid pen to hold.

The lack of physical contact disoriented her. Their techniques worked. She resented the feeling of helplessness.

"Follow."

She shuffled after them. Her bare feet stumbled over the uneven cement floor, the roughness cut into the soles of her feet. She expected to fall at any moment. Would they grab her or let her fall to the floor? Would they laugh if she struggled to get up?

A door opened. They shoved her inside.

She fell to her knees. She braced her hands in front of her to keep from falling farther. The top layer of skin on her palms rubbed off on the cement floor. A burning pain seared through the raw nerve endings.

Someone yanked the blind-fold off and jerked her head back. She struggled to stand. Assif rubbed her stinging hands on the back of her thighs and blinked rapidly. She turned to face the three men still in the shadows. Bright lights blinded her.

"What is your name?" The man in the center leaned forward. Assif caught sight of the insignia of a Major General, two swords crossed with the republican eagle above them, on his sleeve. They had brought in high military officials to interrogate her. Someone was paying big bucks to get her information. They were not going to get their money's worth.

Assif shook her head. She'd been through this twice already. She blanked her mind and focused on her yoga mantra.

"Who do you report to?"

Mentally Assif repeated, So Hum, internally, drowning out their voices.

The man on the left nodded to the guard.

A whip whistled through the air. The lash bit into her lower back. Assif flinched.

The interrogation had escalated.

"What is your name?"

The whip snapped through the air. It slashed through the skin on her shoulders. Tears welled up. She closed her eyes and tried not to think about the pain.

Water, she really wanted a drink of water.

"Who do you work for?"

Her team would be here soon. She had no idea how long she'd been in the prison, but they would get to her. She had to hold out until then. "What time is it?"

The lash bit into her lower back twice.

"You don't ask the questions. We do. If you don't want to suffer any more pain, tell us your name."

"Jane Smith."

This time the lash cut across her thighs. She stumbled forward. She righted herself.

*I will not cry. I will not cry. It's only pain. It will stop soon.*

"We are not stupid. You will not lie or attempt to deceive us. Believe me when I say you will beg to tell us everything you know. Again—tell us your name."

Assif shook her head. The whip landed again. She felt the blood soak through her clothing and stick to her back. The intensity of the pain spread throughout her body. It left her weak and dizzy. She fell to the floor, the coppery scent of her own blood in her nostrils. Warm blood on the floor rubbed against her cheeks.

A guard dragged to her feet.

"Take her back. We'll prepare for the last interview. It will be the last interview, my dear, one way or another."

Someone dropped her blind-fold in place. They yanked her arm and pulled her through the corridors. One foot dragged across the cement. More skin ripped from the side of her foot. An overwhelming throbbing and severe pain blanked out any thoughts.

The stench of sweat and stale urine reached her nostrils. She staggered and dropped to her knees. Without slowing down, they grabbed her arms and hauled her along, her knees rubbed against the cement. They jerked her bind-fold off before throwing her back in her cell. She felt a stab in her arm. The guards left. Crumpled on the floor, she lay in a lump and heard the footsteps faded away. What had they given her?

If the next interrogation escalated Assif didn't know if she could handle it. Would she break and tell them what she knew—and put the whole operation at risk? No, she couldn't do that to the team. Would she die?

Tears welled up. Blood trickled from her cracked lips. Her throat ached. They still hadn't left any water. Assif crawled across to her cot. After three tries she managed to pull herself up. She flopped down on her stomach.

She let the tears flow. The pain burnt her back and thighs. The material, soaked with her blood, dried into the wounds. It didn't matter. If her team didn't get here soon, nothing would matter.

Her eyes closed, she visualized her home in Pennsylvania; the lush green trees in the summer, the glistening snow in the winter. She could even smell the earthy, smoking scent of autumn. Would she ever see it again?

At a low whistle, barely audible, Assif tried to sit up. Dizziness swirled around her. She must be dreaming.

Her heart pounded. She forced her blurry eyes to scan the cell. She stared up at the small window. A rope ladder slipped through and dropped down the inside of the wall.

Assif swayed on the cot. Dizziness enveloped her. She leaned forward and tried to scan the area for guards. The corridor was empty.

She stumbled across the few feet to the darkest corner of the cell. Assif shook her head in an attempt to clear the fog. She bunched the thin blanket into a lump on the cot.

*Come on Assif. You need to climb to the window. That's it. You'll be safe.*

The rope slid farther down. Assif grabbed it tightly and forced her feet up each rung of the ladder. Dizziness spun around her. She couldn't fall.

The team had originally picked her to rescue Aasera because her small frame could slide through small spaces. Her size proved a blessing, for her escape. When she reached the window she wriggled her shoulders through the opening. She twisted in one direction and then another, until her upper body popped outside the window.

"So tired," she mumbled. She clung to the ladder on the outside. Whatever they had injected into her was working. She fought the desire to close her eyes, for a few moments. Squinting, she saw Sabhita on another rope, just above her.

"You okay?"

Assif shook her head. "Gave me a shot, so sleepy, I'm going to fall asleep."

"No, you're not. Listen to my voice." Sabhita raised her whisper slightly. "You are not going to fall asleep. You are going to pull yourself the rest of the way through the window"

Assif gripped the rope tighter and swung her legs through the window.

"Good girl. Now pull up the ladder. Bring it with you." Sabhita whispered.

Assif fumbled for the hook holding it in place. Eventually it fell away.

"Good girl, stay with us. Slide down the wall. You can sit down when you hit the ground."

Assif started down, her eyes closed. She could sleep when she hit the ground.

"Guards?" She mumbled. She sat down.

"They're on a break," Sabhita whispered. She hit the ground. At the push of a button the claws of the hook clinging to the edge of the roof telescoped tightly together.

The hook and rope fell to the ground. Sabhita grabbed everything, including Assif's arm, and pulled her up. "Put your arm around me. I'll get you to safety. We need to get to those scrubby shrubs over there."

Rough twigs scraped at Assif's legs and bare feet. She barely felt it. The darkness reached for her. It tried to pull her in.

Sabhita reached the bushes, Marley stood up, hugged Assif quickly before she pulled her into the shadows. Assif tried to force open her eyes. For a second she saw another woman. One she didn't recognize.

"We need to run about half a mile down the road to the car. Can you make it?" Marley whispered in Assif's ear.

Sabhita shook her head. "She's been drugged. She can't stay awake. We'll need to carry her."

"No problem." Marley stepped up on the other side of Assif and wrapped her arms around her waist. "Let's get out of here."

The four women ran quickly and quietly through the deserted streets. Assif felt herself moving but her feet didn't touch the ground. The tendrils of darkness dragged her into the black pit.

Her pain increased, the blackness ebbed. Semi-consciousness allowed her to hear, still unable to focus. She heard a moan.

"It's okay, we've got you." Sabhita whispered. "You're safe."

Marley glanced over her shoulder. No one had sounded the alarm yet. "It's only a few more minutes. You can make it. After that it's a piece of cake."

The blackness beckoned her again. The sound of voices reached Assif through a long tunnel. She needed to lie down. She had to sleep, just for a few minutes.

"There, there's the car." Sabhita said into Assif's ear. "You made it, girl."

Through the blur Assif made out a dented, rusted car,

sitting by a ditch. As the women approached the engine roared to life.

Sabhita shoved Assif into the back seat and jumped in herself. "Okay, go."

Marley climbed in the other side and the unknown woman slid into the front seat.

The car sped off down the road, a cloud of dust in its wake.

"Where…?"

"Shush, sleep. We're going to the airport and we'll get your back treated. Was it bad?"

Assif shook her head. The darkness spun its clouds around her and she descended into the blackness one more time. "I knew you'd come."

Shots cracked through the air. The car swerved off the road and continued to travel parallel to it in the murky shadows.

"Hang on." The driver shouted.

Each bump accentuated the throbbing in her back, but then blackness wiped out the pain. Assif thought, even if we don't make it, I'm no longer alone. They came. She slipped into obscurity.

The car raced along on and off the road to avoid bullets and outrun the guard's vehicle.

❧

The dark oak shelves gleamed with lemon polish, showcasing the leather bound books that filled the shelves. His shoes left indentations in the thick burgundy carpet when he walked across to the oak desk that stretched across a quarter of the room. Antique brass lamps and fixtures accentuated the wood. Heads of deer, elk and moose hung above the wainscoting on three walls. Original oil paintings were interspersed along the embossed wall paper. Money and an interior decorator presented the image he wanted portrayed.

He chortled and rubbed his hands together, pleased at his own brilliance. The large bay window opened on to his ranch. He admired his property. He could see miles in three directions and he owned it all. He could be at the Pacific Ocean in an hour.

It took years, and an unsavory past, but gradually he'd built his empire. Besides the ranch, it included a real estate business and a partnership in a B movie company. He'd bought the ranch to be close to Hollywood, the beautiful people and the excitement.

He'd bought and built his wife, too. He'd found her waiting tables in a fast food restaurant. After several plastic surgeries, regular beauty salon visits and designer clothes, he'd transformed her into a gorgeous woman. He'd taught her how to talk and walk, and paid to give her a Hollywood career. Admittedly it had been B movies, but she became well known in some circles. That's when he married her, and made her his decoration and hostess. He only wanted the best of everything. He'd waited until she proved worthy of him.

Stupid bitch never appreciated what he'd done for her. Then she went and left him. Nobody left him.

He stomped over to a sideboard and picked up a bottle of forty-year old scotch. He poured a shot, straight up, into an antique crystal high ball glass. He took a quick drink and enjoyed the burn down the back of his throat.

He dabbed at one corner of his mouth with a finger before he put the glass down.

It had been five years today since his wife had disappeared. Five years, the best detectives he could hire, and he still hadn't found her. She had completely disappeared. None of them could find any trail after she left his house that night.

He'd received a phone call a week or two before she'd left. Probably a woman, but her voice had been altered. She had discussed his physical abuse of Kathleen and suggested he get counseling and stop beating her.

He'd told her to go to hell. No one told him what to do with his property. She'd asked if he loved his wife. He'd told her it was none of her fucking business. Two weeks later, in the middle of the night, Kathleen took her jewelry, left the house and disappeared. In the morning a woman had entered the bank with a note from his wife and emptied all her accounts, joint accounts and safe deposit box. That was the last he'd heard of Kathleen. The detectives said she'd probably left the country and taken a different name.

It took several years and a lot of money to finally figure out his wife hadn't escaped on her own. A group organized her disappearance. After he figured that out he'd started to follow any stories about women being rescued or disappearing.

Someone, or some group, was behind it. His gut told him he was right, but he couldn't find anything on them. He'd paid more detectives, but again they'd come up empty. It had been a fucking waste of time and money.

About two years ago he'd stumbled upon two cases. One in Europe, someone, or some group, rescued a woman from a firing squad. In the second case they rescued another woman from a husband who wanted to kill his wife instead of divorcing her. It was none of their fucking business what a man did with his wife.

He'd kept researching and found two more cases, one in Arizona and one in Maine. He had no proof, but his gut told him the cases were related. His wife hadn't been about to face a firing squad, but someone might have felt she needed rescuing. Not that it was any of their fucking business. She belonged to him. He'd paid for her. He could do what he wanted with her.

How had she found a way to ask for help? He'd kept her under observation twenty-four hours a day. His private guards were well paid and knew what would happen to them if they allowed her to talk to anyone without checking with him first. She never went out alone. Even at parties, he made sure someone always stayed at her side.

No one touched his property, ever. Years ago someone had stolen a pair of shoes from him. He'd found the kid. Before he killed him, he cut off his hands.

When Kathleen disappeared, he'd been embarrassed when people asked about her. He saw the pity in their eyes. He wanted his property back, and the money she'd stolen. No one walked out on him and no one stole his property— no one.

He also wanted whoever helped her to escape.

With the information he'd uncovered, he'd carefully set up a plan to bait them into his trap. It took over a year, and millions of dollars, to buy off government officials and set it up, but they'd entered his trap. If not the same group who abducted his wife, this one might have information on other groups involved in similar activities.

He'd formulated his plan so he could capture and interrogate them. The money he used for the trap was siphoned from an off shore account where he could move it around without leaving a money trail. The trap worked. His paid contacts in Iran were interrogating one of the members of the group right now.

A derisive snort escaped.

They captured a woman. He hadn't expected it to be a woman. How could any woman be part of this?

He wanted to witness her torture, but it would take too long to fly over. His own plane didn't fly that fast. Someone might try to rescue her if they waited for him to arrive, so he'd told them to start immediately. He didn't want to take any chance at losing her and the information she might supply.

He'd made arrangements to fly to Shiraz in the morning. He wanted to see this person, find out if she knew his wife.

Until then he'd have to be satisfied with a detailed report and the information they got from her. They'd sent him a report of the first interrogation.

He glanced at his watch and figured with the different time changes she should be in interrogation now. A woman—how could a woman infiltrate a prison? A sneer curled the corner of his mouth.

If there had actually been a prisoner in Shiraz, the woman might have got away with it. She had to be part of a larger group. A woman alone couldn't have managed it. Once he got that information, he had them. He'd negotiate to get his wife back and then he'd take great pleasure in making them pay for what they had done to him.

He raised his glass, took another sip of scotch and enjoyed the burn. He found it intriguing that a group could stay completely under the radar. No one, anywhere, had ever heard of them. The group had to be large and well-trained, so they could infiltrate any home, or even government, and remove people at will, without leaving any clue behind. It intrigued him. He needed to know how they infiltrated prisons in foreign countries and what they did with those they rescued. How did they arrange for people to completely disappear? The information could be helpful to him one day.

They had to have money behind them. He should know. He'd spent millions trying to find that bitch of a wife over the last few years. No one, absolutely no one, got the best of him. When he got his wife back, and he would, she would suffer. He allowed a smirk at the thought.

Besides the money, the group had to have skilled operatives, an enormous number of high powered contacts and the latest technical tools and skills. Yet no one had heard of them. Not a ripple through underground sources.

The mouse caught in his trap wouldn't take long to crack under extreme torture. She was a stupid woman. After he found his wife he might consider taking over the group that could administer such massive plans, and use it for his own purposes. He could develop a large west coast organization.

The antique white and gold phone on the corner of his desk rang. He took another quick drink of scotch. Glass in one hand he picked up the phone.

"Yes?"

"The prisoner, she has escaped."

"What?" His fist hit the desk. The glass shattered. Amber liquid ran across the desk and dripped on to the carpet. "How the hell did that happen?"

"I don't know, sir. I am so sorry, sir. She disappeared from her cell, sir."

"No one disappears. Someone must have taken her." He snarled. They got to her. They went in and rescued her right under the fucking guard's noses. "Don't expect to get paid for failure."

He slammed the receiver down with his right hand and reached for the bottle of scotch with his left. He took a swig straight from the bottle.

How could she have escaped from their prison?

They'd shut down the airport and all exits from town, but he knew they'd never get her back. Somehow the group managed to act quicker than anyone expected.

The interrogation team had taken pictures of the hostage when they first caught her. He'd have them faxed to him, along with any information they got from her interrogation. He might be able to find out her identity and trace her that way.

He'd have to start all over. They would pay for this, all of them.

The organization had screwed with him twice now. No matter how long it took, or where he had to go, he would find them. They would pay, painfully.

He'd put more people on. He'd pay for them to turn over rocks, look for clues. Someone had secrets that money could buy. Everyone had skeletons and would do anything to keep them hidden, like Bobby Mac. That secret could get him murdered, or the death penalty.

❧

Link stormed into the bar. The door reverberated behind him. Several of the guys at the bar glanced up. Then they returned to the TV and their beer. The Knicks were playing the Lakers in the playoffs on the TV.

His workout at the gym down the street hadn't burned off much of his anger. He'd didn't work out at work tonight. Who the hell did Miss Carly Brazil think she was, ordering him to get a haircut?

He pulled himself onto a barstool and motioned to the middle-aged blonde behind the bar. "Bourbon, neat."

The glass slid down the bar and stopped just to his right.

"Thanks, Shirl." He downed the amber liquid in one gulp and signaled for another.

This time the busty blonde brought the glass and set it down in front of him. Her low-cut red top, covered with sequins, showed most of her enhanced breasts. Long, fake eyelashes fluttered. She leaned her elbows on the counter. "Need to talk about it?"

Link shook his head. "No, thanks, it's a work issue."

"If you need a woman to talk to…."

"It's a woman who caused my problem," Link grumbled.

"Ah, women problems, I should've guessed."

"Not like you think, doll. This one's my boss and a real bitch."

One of the waitresses put her tray down at the end of the bar. Shirley hastened over to complete the woman's order.

Link sipped at the second scotch, He debated whether he should have another one. He knew better than to drive after too many scotch's. He'd pounded the punching bag at the gym, pretending it was Miss High and Mighty, but in reality, he knew he'd missed something. It hurt his professional pride. The fact she'd been the one to notice irritated the hell out of him. He'd hoped to get rid of his anger at the gym, but it kept boiling, ready to spill over.

Shirley returned with a smile on her bright red lips. "Okay, big boy, tell little Shirl all about it. I gather women in power annoy you."

Link shook his head. "Yeah, it's been a problem for a while. You don't understand."

"You've been hanging here a long time, sugar. I have a pretty good history on you. Try me."

"It's...she's thinks she knows everything. I mean just because Miss Brazil has her big, fancy, company office doesn't mean she's qualified to give me orders. It's not like she'd started the company or even worked her way up. She got it handed it to her on a silver platter when Daddy died. All she does is sit up there on her great butt, with her damn dog, and let the Board run the business."

"Uh huh," Shirley topped up his scotch. "That doesn't sound like the whole story to me. What are you leaving out?"

"Dammit Shirl, you're supposed to be on my side; listen to me and sympathize. That's what a good bartender does."

Shirl parted her flame red lips and let go with a belly laugh. "Sugar, you know you're angry at yourself, not your pretty boss lady. I'm guessing you embarrassed yourself in front of her and you're trying to put the blame on her."

Link glared across at the expanse of breasts in front of him. "You women all stick together." He downed the rest of his scotch and motioned for another. "She collects dogs, even takes one to the office with her."

"Oh migawd, she brought an animal to the office. Why does she collect them?"

Link took another drink. "I shouldn't have said anything."

"No, now I'm curious. Why?"

Link refused to meet Shirley's gaze. "She rescues dogs."

"Sorry?"

"She rescues stray dogs, or abused dogs, and tries to find homes for them. If she can't, she ends up keeping them herself."

Shirley stared at him and bit her lower lip. She poured another shot into a clean glass. "You're not planning on driving are you?"

"No, ma'am, I know better. You can pour me into a cab when I'm ready to crawl home."

"Good man. Now accept the responsibility of whatever you did wrong and quit trying to pass the blame to someone else. Be a man."

"I screwed up. She noticed it. She inherited the job. I'm the professional. She could fire me for sloppy work. She made me feel like a fool. When she figured out how I'd missed it, you know what she said about it—nothing. That makes it even worse. She said to fix it and recheck our policies. She's right about rechecking the policies, too. We've been using the same ones for years. God, I hate it. I feel like I'm sixteen again." Link took a long drink, savoring the burn. He planted his elbows on the bar.

"Sounds like a pretty decent boss lady to me."

"Yeah, well, it's just…, this woman thinks because she inherited a big company she can tell people what to do, like telling me to get a haircut." Link snarled.

"Oh, I see. So she expects you to look professional. I mean, I like that long, rakish look, but if you're working in a professional atmosphere…" A smile played with the brightly painted lips.

"Yeah, well…"

"I'm sure all the other security people wear that same style." Shirley chuckled.

"Yeah, yeah, I get it. She's probably right about that, too. Up until now, she's let me do my job and left me alone."

"It sounds like you didn't do your job, at least not as well as you thought. If you can't apologize for your screw-up, the least you can do is get that mop trimmed before you see her again."

"Aww, Shirl…"

"No sugar, one of these days you're going to have to grow up. This could be a step in that direction. You're a great guy, but you've got a lot of issues to resolve. This is an easy one. Now finish your drink, take a cab home and tomorrow do what you have to do."

The waitress showed up again and Shirley hustled down to fill the orders. She pulled a few draft beers and slid them down the counter. Then she mixed the orders for the waitress.

Ms. Carly Brazil could use some of Shirley's smarts. Shirley understood men. She knew how to treat a man— well most of the time. Carly Brazil might be one damned good-looking woman, but she sure as hell lacked people skills.

She did keep herself in great shape, and those long legs of hers—he'd like to see them without those designer pants. A picture of her naked, with those legs wrapped around him, sweating from exertion, had him thinking he better not stand up. Not until he reduced that hard-on those thoughts had caused. Mentally, he slapped his own face for even thinking like that. You didn't think that about your boss, even if she did have a killer body.

Shirley plopped another scotch in front of him and he drank half of it.

"Can you call that cab for me?"

"Where's your truck parked?"

"It's in the gym parking lot. How'd you know I owned a truck?"

"All you muscle guys drive trucks. It should be safe down there. I'll have the cops do the occasional drive by for you."

"Thanks, Shirl. What really pisses me off is she got lucky. She guessed right about a couple of things."

"Happens to even the dumbest of us, hon." Shirley laughed, a deep belly laugh, before she returned to several other guys at the bar. "I'll call that cab in a few minutes."

When he did the damn sweep he'd found three bugs, one in her office and two in the boardroom. She'd been right about that, too. It pissed him off even more. She'd been lucky, he told himself. He did his job and did it well. At least he thought he had, up until now.

He gave her credit, she hadn't gloated when he gave her the news about the bugs, just asked if they'd been removed. Okay, so maybe she had a small brain. She still shouldn't be the head of a company like CCB. Shit, they made computer parts. What did she know about selling computer parts?

He downed the rest of his scotch and slapped several twenties down on the counter. He'd flag a cab outside. "Thanks Shirley, a pleasure as usual."

"You take care of yourself, handsome."

He stood up and swayed dangerously before he grabbed the edge of the bar.

Shirley hustled around the corner. "Hold on sugar, I'll help you out to a cab."

"I'm fine, just fine." Link mumbled. He fell against the barstool.

Shirley appeared at his side. "Sure you are, sugar. Come on, we'll get you a cab. Tip him well and get him to help you to your door. It will be less embarrassing in the long run."

"Hey, I'll take the guy out for you." Johnny, the six foot six bouncer, strode toward Shirley.

"Naw, it's okay. I'll look after this one. You keep an eye on the bar. I'll be back in two seconds. Let's go, handsome."

With Shirley holding him around the waist, one of his arms over her shoulder, Link stumbled to the door.

He leaned against the wall while Shirley hailed him a cab. He kept thinking of Carly Brazil. Maybe after he finished her damn security checks he'd look for another job. He had no idea what he'd do. Maybe he'd take a few months off and travel. Yeah, and then she couldn't tell him to get a haircut, or how to do his job.

Okay, maybe he should have realized doing a safety check routinely on the same day could prove ineffective. She'd been right. That really pissed him off. He started to slide downward but managed to grab the door jamb.

A cab slowed. Shirley opened the door and helped Link to manipulate the sidewalk and slide into the back seat. He managed to give the driver his address, before he closed his eyes.

His last thoughts as the cab pulled away were that he'd show Ms. Brazil, but he couldn't quite remember what he was going to show her. Hopefully he'd remember in the morning.

# Chapter Three

Sara sat upright in bed. Cold sweat dripped down her back and between her breasts. In the dark, her hand inched across the sheets of the new queen-size bed. A sliver of moonlight slipped through a crack in the thick drapes and landed on the empty pillow.

For a second she could smell his aftershave. She shivered, yanked her hand back from the pillow and pulled her knees to her chest. She clutched the covers tightly to her body.

*Don't be ridiculous Sara. He's not here. He's dead. He can't hurt you anymore.*

She'd cleaned the room enough times, over the last eighteen months, to get rid of any scent of him. She'd even bought a new bed, mattress and sheets.

He was dead. But in the dream he came back. Even in the dream Gordon had the power to return her to that pathetic, abused woman she'd turned into over the years of their marriage. For almost a year and a half Sara had worked to break the chains of abuse that kept her from living her own life. She'd come a long way. She hadn't had the dream for months.

She swung her legs over the side of the bed. Her feet landed on Gloria's soft, furry back. Sara reached down and patted the dog's large head. "Good old Gloria, always there for me."

The dog raised her head and licked Sara's hand with a short whine, before she flopped back down to sleep.

Sara pulled on her robe before she crept downstairs. *Hot chocolate would go good right about now.*

She grabbed the milk carton from the refrigerator and took a swig from the container. Two years ago she could never have done this. Gordon would have punished her if he'd caught her.

"Here's to you, you bastard, wherever you are." She toasted the milk carton before she took another swallow.

It ticked the hell out of her that she'd been so stupid. He'd made her a victim and she'd allowed it. She couldn't believe a woman working on her college degree would let any man to turn her into a pathetic doormat, but it had been subtle and over a period of time. She had been a classic case.

Sara shook her head. Once he'd made her a total victim, he'd cheated on her, and not just once. How could she have been so dumb to not pick up on any of the signs? Even that stupid haircut he got should have twigged her.

It was because doormats weren't allowed to think.

The day after his death she'd tackled his office. She wanted to find the lawyer's name and the bank accounts and eradicate the last signs of him from the house. She'd found the pictures and letters.

She remembered the physical pain; a gut wrenching stab that doubled her over followed by waves of cramps. She tried to swallow but her throat constricted and locked in a vice like clutch. Then anger engulfed her. Walls of red flashed in front of her eyes. Fury raged through her body. She'd torn the pictures into pieces and then she'd got herself a good lawyer to handle the will.

She'd had someone come in and paint the room a rose pink. The new carpet was a deeper rose. Gordon would have hated it.

She poured milk into a mug and zapped it in the microwave. She stirred in the hot chocolate, grasped the mug in both hands and warmed them. She strolled into the living room, enjoying the rich scent of the chocolate.

She still couldn't believe how Gordon humiliated her, how she'd let him humiliate her. Even now he continued to infiltrate her dreams. Less and less, but he still had some influence on them.

It would never happen again. She would never give a man power over her life. She had the control back, finally, and she intended to keep it. The dreams would eventually stop permanently.

She sipped her hot chocolate. On the mantel were several pictures of her son, Andrew, and daughter, Amy. Andrew at nineteen was at Portland State studying computer engineering. Amy was older by two years and working on the Oregon coast. Neither were involved in any serious relationships yet. She hoped Amy had more smarts than her mother and didn't follow Sara's example when she chose a partner.

Hopefully the example of an abused wife and mother, wouldn't leave permanent scars on their lives. Shame seeped through her pores. She could only imagine what they must have thought. Could she redeem herself in their eyes?

She placed her mug on the coffee table and picked up the book she'd received yesterday afternoon; Women Helping Women: Opportunities around the World.

She had no idea who might have sent it to her. There had been no return address. When she picked up the book many images flooded over her; a tall, dark woman, a chubby clerk behind a computer, a slightly over-weight blonde woman. None she recognized.

She didn't get any strong feelings about any of them. It felt different from her usual visions. Was it important?

Gloria licked her hand. Absently Sara patted her head. "Good girl. You're up, too. It's okay. Maybe we'll take a little trip and drive down to see Amy, and then Andrew, in a few weeks. It's been awhile."

Sara turned the book over and read the back cover about how, when women worked together to support each other, they became stronger. She flipped the book open and started to read about women together could accomplish anything.

Who would send her book on helping women, and why?

Did it have anything to do with her life with Gordon? Could anyone have helped her prevent that? Who knew her history?

"Assif?" Carly shivered when she entered the freezer. She deposited Phoenix in a chair and buttoned her jacket to protect against the warehouse chill seeping into her bones.

"Mission accomplished. Nadia phoned to say they've got her. They went in this afternoon, our time. No one expected us to act this quickly. Assif has been tortured several times and has lash marks on her back. She blacked out from the pain, but they didn't break her. The team took her straight to the airport where the private plane stood ready for takeoff. The local police chased them. They got close enough to shoot, but the team managed to out run them, make it to the plane and take off, with seconds to spare. She's safe."

Julie grabbed Carly. They clung together for several seconds. Assif could have died. Carly closed her eyes for a second. "Good work Nadia," she whispered before Julie let her go.

"What about Fareeda?"

"The Iranians didn't want to discharge Fareeda. I think they wanted to question her about her bullet wound, but the second part of the team slipped in and whipped her out of the hospital before the local police or the military got a chance to talk to her. It cost a few bribes, quite a few actually, but it went smoothly." Julie allowed a slight smile to play with her lips. "Money works miracles. They were all on the plane when Assif arrived."

"When do they land?"

"In about four hours."

Carly let out a long breath. "Arrange for them go right to the hospital for a check-up."

"It's already done. I've got an ambulance for both of them, and hospital rooms. The doctor is standing by. I've only told them we have two women, one with a leg injury and the other abused by her husband."

"Good work. Thanks heavens we have the money. Let me know if there's any change in their arrival time. I want to be at the airport when they arrive."

"I'd like to be there, too." Julie said.

"We'll go together." Carly squeezed Julie's hand. "I haven't been that scared for a long time. I feel so damn helpless, not being able to be there."

"Me, too, I think we all did. I'm just glad all our people are safe and heading home."

"I agree. You and Nadia deserve thanks for your part, too."

"All part of our job," Julie shrugged. "Have you found anything more about the leak, yet?"

Carly shook her head. "Not yet. It has to be one of our contacts. Once I get the names of everyone involved in the original plan, from Nadia, I'll trace it back and check everyone on the list.

We'll have to be extra cautious from now on and assume every mission is a set up until we find out who wants us. Have you checked any of our past cases to see if any of them looks like they might be good for this?"

"Not yet. I will."

"Good. I'm also having problems with CCB. We appear

to have a mole there as well. I've had my last two deals undercut and we've lost business. Nothing major, but it's annoying. I'm having it checked out. Because of that, I'm also cross-checking all The Foundation employees with CCB employees to see if there's any overlap. It could be the same person sabotaging both organizations, but why?"

"If you get a motive you could probably find the individual selling you out." Julie started to shove folders into her briefcase.

"That would be too easy." Carly grinned. "We found bugs in the CCB board room and my office. Don't know for how long, probably just a few weeks, but that's how they got their advanced information. I have no idea who got in and placed the bugs, but Link is working on it. It won't happen again. At least we never discuss Foundation work there. While I check our Foundation employees, I'm letting him work on CCB. I don't think there's a connection but I'll be damned if I let any of our other teams run into this kind of trap again."

"Link, the hunk, how is that gorgeous man?"

"You think he's a hunk?"

"Hey, those smoldering, gray eyes are very sexy and then there are those full lips. I wouldn't say no if he asked me out."

Carly shook her head. "He's so arrogant."

"Really? I hadn't noticed, but then I've never got passed ogling the solid muscled arms, abs and butt, especially his butt. Can you imagine running your fingers over that gluteus maximus, and feeling his response?" Julie rolled her eyes.

Carly couldn't control a chuckle. "Nope, I admit I hadn't imagined that. I have no idea what you see in the man, but I may not be able to get that picture out of mind."

"You know exactly what I'm talking about. You just don't want to admit it." Julie gathered her binder and briefcase. "I'll phone when I'm ready to leave for the airport and have the cab wait out front of your office. Will that work?"

"Sounds good, until then I'll head back and work on finding that damn leak. Something tells me this is not going to be as easy as I'd first hoped."

"I'll lock up."

"Thanks." Carly grabbed Phoenix and marched through the icy warehouse. She thought about what Julie had said regarding Link. She had been right. Carly had looked at the man, and speculated what it would be like to run her fingers over that massive chest. She'd also noticed his nicely shaped butt.

Maybe she'd challenge him to a workout in the gym and see what he had under that uniform. A little sweaty, body contact might break through that snotty attitude of his, especially if she could take him down.

Link rolled his chair back from his computer. The chair hit the wall of his small office in the basement of the office building. He liked the quiet. No one ventured down to bother him.

He locked his hands behind his head and stared at the screen. He'd been at it for about eight hours. He'd woken up early with a helluva a hangover. When he couldn't get back to sleep he'd taken a handful of pills for the headache and come in early. So far nothing had turned up. Either he'd missed something or the mole had covered his, or her, tracks well. He needed to find that bloody mole just to prove his competency to Carly, and maybe himself.

He didn't usually give a damn what people thought. He lived life on his terms; wine and women; beer and women actually. He had no expectations of himself other than a fun weekend. This time something grated at him. He hated feeling inadequate at his job, especially in front of Ms. Carly

Brazil. He'd been angry when he found the bugs. He was head of security. He should have been on top of it. It wasn't only that, but it made him look incompetent to Ms. Buckets of Money Brazil.

Now he needed to figure out who the hell had installed them, and how they did it. At least that might raise his professional image a notch or two. He'd talked to Anna Lee. She said no one had gone in except Carly, the Board members, and the cleaning company. He'd checked the cleaning company. Nothing stood out. No one had a criminal record.

He hated to admit it, but he had let Carly and CCB, down. He felt like he'd been sucker punched. He'd make up for it and find whoever did it.

A vision of Carly, tall and lithe, with those piercing emerald green eyes, flashed before him. Okay, so once he'd got over his initial anger at her comments, and had his haircut, he'd decided she wasn't too bad, especially in the looks department. Shirley might have had something to do with a realignment of his thinking. If Carly wasn't his boss, and one of the world's wealthiest women, he might consider making a play for her. Unfortunately, she didn't play in his league. He could change that if he wanted but he didn't want to so until then he could still dream and fantasize about her.

*No fantasizing on the job, Slick. You've already screwed up. Get back to work.*

Link leaned forward and started another search, using a different list. An hour later he stopped. He stared at the screen. He backed it up, checked another entry and then another one. It looked like a lead. He hit print.

At least now he had something to check, maybe even a trail to follow. He could start doing a little footwork; watch a couple of people and assure the safety of the company.

He'd update Carly later. By then he might have more information, and the hangover should be completely gone.

He grabbed the sheaf of papers, glanced at his watch and strode out of his office. He had time to do a little visiting before he reported to Carly.

Two hours later, Anna Lee announced him. He swaggered into the CEO's office. "The one thing I didn't do. I didn't check you out."

"What are you talking about?" Carly spun her chair around.

Link swallowed a grin as he stepped forward with a wand. "Stand up."

"I will not. You don't give me orders."

"I do if I'm doing my job. I got to thinking, they may have bugged the Board room and your office, but ideally if they bugged you, they'd always be on line, no matter when or who you talked to."

Carly glared at him.

He stood beside her chair and waited. He glared right back at her, but the corner of his mouth twitched.

"Fine." She flounced to her feet and jabbed her arms out in the same pose used for going through airports.

Link waved the wand over her and listened to the steady hmm. "Well, damn, you're clear. I thought for sure they'd bugged you. It made sense. Sorry about that."

"You should be." Carly sat down stiffly in her chair, her lower lip extended. She continued to glare at Link. "Now what else have you got to tell me?"

Phoenix jumped up on Carly's lap. She attempted to stand up and place her paws on Link's chest.

"Phoenix, down." Carly wrapped her arms around the dog.

The wand started to buzz.

Link stared at the dog for a second, before he moved the wand over Phoenix. He paused at the collar. The sound grew louder.

Carly's eyes widened. She looked up at Link.

"Damn, it's not you. They bugged your bloody dog."

Link undid the collar and ran his hand over it. He pulled

out a small black dot. "I was close. Who would have thought of the dog? Doesn't she bark at people or something if they take her collar?"

Carly stared at the tiny dot. "It depends on the person and whether she likes them or not. You were right, except they didn't bug me. They bugged my dog, who I take everywhere. How did they do it?"

"It has to be someone very close to you. Someone you trust. Write down everyone who has access to the fur ball. I need to compare it to a list I'm working on." Link picked up Phoenix who proceeded to lick his face. "Damn dog, she's probably got disgusting bacteria in her mouth."

"It's cleaner than yours." Carly shot back. She stood up, took Phoenix, and gently placed her on the floor. "Go to your bed."

Phoenix sent a pleading look in Link's direction.

"Sorry pal, she's the boss."

Phoenix slunk across to her bed.

A thought hit Carly in the gut and a small gasp escaped.

"What?" Link frowned.

"These bugs, how far do they transmit?"

"It depends. The ones in the room maybe two hundred feet; the one in the collar..." Link shrugged, "maybe seventy-five feet."

"Do they transmit through anything, walls, brick, clothing...?"

Link wondered what she was getting at. "Pretty much through most standard things; metal can blur it, or interfere with transmissions. Again it depends on the thickness. A car or truck in the area might still pick it up."

"So a thick wall, like maybe a freezer room, could block transmission?"

"Probably."

Carly released a breath.

"Once we figure out who put the device in the collar, we'll figure out everything else."

"I'm writing the list as we speak." Carly sat down and picked up her pen. "I have this feeling I'm not going to like what you find out."

White satin clung to her pudgy body.

The groom swallowed a grimace. *Fat cow.*

The bride gazed adoringly up at him.

The couple took the floor for the first dance of their wedding reception. He pulled her close and bent down to peck her on the cheek. Mary blushed. She slipped her hand up his neck, under his dark curly hair. He fought the impulse to pull away.

The scent of the white roses and gardenias permeated the room. The small orchestra played traditional, romantic, waltz tunes.

"It took her awhile, but Mary finally found the perfect man," Iris, one of her co-workers, murmured to her neighbor at the table, as she licked icing off her fork.

The groom smiled inwardly at the comment when he danced past the table.

The plain looking woman in her forties, wearing a gray linen suit, brushed a wisp of her graying hair behind her ear. "And he's yummy looking. It gives the rest of us hope, even if we don't look like supermodels. Mary's only a few years younger than I am."

"Mmmm." The two women continued to drool over him for a few more seconds before they scanned the room for any single men.

A chuckle escaped. Those plain, old hags weren't going to find a man. Unless he wanted something more than marriage from them.

Mary smiled up at him at the chuckle. "I'm glad you're as happy as I am."

"Of course, my sweet. Tonight is special. I'll remember it always."

Other couples joined the wedding couple on the dance floor.

A few hours later Mary's husband struggled to pick up his new bride. She wanted to be carried over the threshold into their hotel penthouse. He stumbled slightly and quickly deposited her inside the room, before she slipped from his grip. He kicked the door shut and locked it.

The sound of waves rolling against the shore roared through the partially open balcony door. He strode over to the balcony and stared out at the dark, California Ocean. Small white caps were visible in the inky darkness.

"It's a very romantic evening, my dear, you'll have to come outside and see the ocean." He stepped back inside, took his bride's hand and turned it over. His lips caressed her palm. "But first we need to drink a toast."

Mary wrapped her arms around his neck. "Come to bed. We're married. I want to make love to my husband."

"No, first we have to celebrate our special day with champagne." He ducked under her arm and strode to the ice bucket. He picked up the bottle of champagne he'd ordered it from room service earlier that day. It had been delivered before the wedding ceremony so he would have access to it before they left the suite to go down to the hotel chapel.

"Sit down. I'll bring you a glass." He popped the cork. It hit the far wall. He filled two, crystal, champagne glasses. One in each hand, he carried them carefully toward his bride.

He handed one glass to her and made a toast. "Here's to my bride, the most beautiful woman in the world, and to a lifetime of happiness."

Mary clinked her glass and took a sip.

"After a toast you're supposed to down your glass, darling. Drink up."

Mary laughed. "Whatever you say, my husband. Oh, I love the sound of that." She downed the rest of the champagne.

She put her empty glass on the coffee table. "I'm feeling a little dizzy, too much champagne."

"It's okay." The drugs were taking effect.

She swayed and tried to stand up, but fell back on to the couch.

"Oh, I feel dizzy." She giggled, grasped the arm of the couch, planted her feet solidly on the floor and pulled herself up to a standing position. She started to fall back.

He reached out and took her arm, smiling. "It's okay, my sweet, I'll take good care of you. Let's go out on the balcony. The ocean view from the twenty-ninth floor is unbelievable."

Mary stumbled. "Wha… I can't…" Her eyes closed. She slumped forward.

He caught her, held her tightly and guided her pudgy body to the balcony.

"This way, darling." He grimaced, his arm tightly around her waist. He dragged her over the door jamb, onto the balcony. Her head lolled against his arm.

"Sorry our wedded bliss and lifetime of happiness has to be this short, but I really couldn't stand to be with you any longer. Ugly, fat, stupid women annoy me. You're all really only good for one thing." He chuckled.

He struggled to pick up her dead weight. He finally managed to hang her head and upper body over the balcony railing. He grasped her legs, lifted them up and shoved her over the railing.

He leaned forward so he could watch her body float downward. Her wedding dress acted as an awning, slowing the descent. Her head toppled back. Her face disappeared from view.

He glanced at his watch as the seconds ticked by until she finally splattered onto the rocky beach below. He stared at the broken body. His lip curled in disgust.

"Stupid bitch," he muttered. He sauntered inside, poured himself another glass of champagne from a second bottle and headed for the shower. It would be morning before anyone found her. He'd contact the lawyer after they discovered the body.

# Chapter Four

Carly deposited Phoenix in her chair before she returned to close the door to the warehouse. She observed the room. What if the person who bugged her dog, had picked up transmissions from the warehouse? If they got information about The Foundation...

The walls looked solid. She remembered the inside wall was some kind of metal. Hopefully nothing got through.

"What are you doing?" Julie asked.

Carly shook her head. "I'm checking the walls of this deep freeze. They keep it frigid in here, but they should also muffle sound."

She took a sip of her coffee and placed the disposable cup in front of her.

"She's having another bad day and cried when I tried to leave her at home." Carly rolled her eyes. She moved Phoenix to the chair beside her.

"You realize you're spoiling her." Julie said.

"I know, but she's had a rough time. Okay ladies, before we get started I want to say good work, Nadia. I heard from the doctor and Assif's injuries are superficial. They must have been testing her resilience before they started the heavy duty torture. I'm sure they felt they had a day or two before we came after her. Thank heavens."

"The drugs they gave her are wearing off, but they won't be completely out of her system for another seventy-two hours. Assif said she hadn't told them anything, not even her real name. She knew we'd come for her." Nadia let a long sigh escape into the room. "I don't ever want that happening again."

"Agreed." Carly and Julie said in unison.

"At my request, Nadia asked Assif's team members to take turns guarding her room, as a precaution. Not that I think anyone will try and get to her, but I'm not taking any chances. She might have heard something while she was captured they don't want her to share." Carly cupped her hands around the cup to warm her fingers. "Even with a sweater and a jacket that damn cold still sneaks through to the bones."

"There are a couple of blankets in the back if you need one." Nadia slid into a chair and stretched out her legs. "I'm going to talk to Assif in the morning when she's feeling better. We'll see if there's anything she learned that might help identify the person who set it up."

"Good idea. Can you give me a list of everyone involved in Aasera Khan's rescue?"

"Sure. I have it in my file. I'll photocopy it for you before you leave."

"Thanks. I'll trace every single person on that list. I'll find them. They'll pay for what happened to Assif and Fareeda. And speaking of Fareeda, she was discharged today. She's doing well and will start physio Monday to strengthen her leg muscles. I've debriefed her. So let's get back to regular business. What do we have on the agenda today?"

Julie opened her always-present pink notebook. She had her smart phone and electronic notebook, but liked to hand write some things. She pulled out two sheets of paper and handed one to each woman. "I've drawn up an agenda. It's the one from the other morning. Nothing's really changed. Check it over. See if I've missed anything."

"Thank heavens we have you to keep us organized." Carly scanned the items. "Nope, I think you've covered everything."

Nadia slowly tapped a long, slender finger on her agenda. "I'd like to add one more item, please. I have another potential volunteer."

The other two women penciled in the addition.

Carly took another drink from her disposable cup. "Okay, let's start with the budget. Julie, how are we doing?"

"Our recent gala affair raised over sixty million dollars."

"I don't suppose anyone from our fund raisers appeared suspicious or asked lots of questions?" Carly asked.

Nadia shook her head. "I didn't notice anyone."

Julie Frowned. "Not really, just Percy York, but he's always weird. He cornered me and, between trying to put his hands everywhere he shouldn't, he talked about women's place and how they shouldn't try to compete with men and run businesses. I think he's just a male chauvinist jerk."

Carly clasped her fingers, putting her thumbs under her chin. "Percy York? Did he say anything else?"

"I don't think so. I was busy trying to escape without causing a scene, in case he might make a donation. Although he's never made one yet, even though he manages to attend all the fundraisers."

"Why do we send him invitations then?"

Julie pulled her eyebrows together, squinting at Carly. "That's the strange part. We don't. He's not on any of our lists of people we usually invite, yet somehow he manages to show up for the free food and alcohol."

"Really?" Carly sat quietly. "So he gets invited to all the fundraisers, but not by us, and never gives us any money. Anyone know if he has money? Is he in debt or just cheap?"

Nadia shrugged. "I have no idea. I try to ignore the creep. Like Julie said, he stuffs his face with food and alcohol, and then looks for a woman to hit on. What a parasite."

Julie shook her head. "I don't know anything about his finances either."

"Julie, check out his financial record. I'll check Mr. York out, if only to find out how he gets invited to all the fund raisers." Carly tented her hands, tapping her fingers together. "What's next, Julie?"

"Our expenses for the last month, with missions and administration costs, are fifty seven million. We also made several good contacts, including legal or government help in other countries."

"Excellent, Julie. Any questions?" Carly glanced at Nadia over the rim of her coffee cup.

Nadia gave her head a half shake.

"Okay, next agenda item; The Foundation's missions for the past month. Nadia?"

"Wait, I do remember something else." Julie interrupted. "Sorry. I was trying to escape from octopus arms when he mumbled something about women who disobeyed should be punished and not allowed to escape."

Carly leaned forward. "Interesting. I definitely think our Mr. York needs a further look. I wonder why he's interested in The Foundation."

"He's not smart enough to be the brains. Even if he put on that act of piggishness, he's not that bright. Someone else has to be behind it." Nadia responded.

"I agree, but if he needs money and hates women, he could well be brought in as a paid informant. He attends our functions and tries to find out information on us."

Julie shook her head. "He drinks too much, womanizes, and he' a total dork. If you wanted to get information, wouldn't you try and schmooze the people?"

Carly laughed. "You'd think, but I'll still check him out. I'm getting a twitch in the back of my neck about him. Maybe I'll get Link to put a tail on him for a few weeks and find out just what Mr. York does with his days. Thanks, Julie. Nadia, our other missions?"

Nadia leaned back in her chair, the pink silk pants rustling as she crossed her long legs. The soft material clung against her skin, accentuating their muscular shape. "We had a good month. We rescued eight women. We picked up Ashad, from Turkey before her husband managed to kill her; transported her to the States and gave her a new identity."

Nadia poured a little water from her Perrier bottle into a glass and took a sip. "Another team contacted Shalla's husband. They talked to him, trying to convince him to quit beating her. He refused to listen and attempted to kill one of our operatives. I think he underestimated our team. They had to take him out, in self-defense. It left Shalla to raise five children on her own. Naturally both families are upset over his death, but his family is making plans for the younger brother to take her as his third wife."

"Oh, for heaven's sake," Carly rolled her eyes.

"It's their culture. They haven't abandoned her." Nadia smiled. "On the positive side, The Foundation has provided her with a generous monthly income so she can care for her children. We've also provided her with training and start-up money for her to open and operate a small store selling local produce to her community. It will bring in additional funds. She now has options. She can remarry or be self-sufficient and take care of herself and her children on her own. She's safe from any further physical abuse."

"That's good. What's with men who think its okay to beat women to death? We're not chattel. We're human beings." Julie shook her blonde curls. "I mean, really."

"Not to everyone and not in some cultures." Nadia shrugged.

"If anyone understands the Middle East culture, it's you." Carly said. "If she chooses to marry are we sure the brother won't beat her?"

"He hasn't hit either of his other two wives, but if she does choose him, we'll monitor her."

"Good." Carly finished her coffee and tossed the cup into the wastebasket. She listened closely to Nadia's report on the six other women The Foundation had helped in the past month.

"Good work everyone. The teams are working well? No problems?"

Nadia gave a half nod. "They're all good."

Carly grinned. "Make sure everyone gets at least two weeks' vacation somewhere nice. What about next month's missions?"

"Here's the list I've vetted. I felt these were the highest priorities we're aware of and would work with the teams we have available." Nadia passed a black folder to each of the other two women. "I've penciled in one more because I just heard that her father is looking for a hit man to take her out, Elizabeth Hargreaves."

"No kidding. How can a man kill his own daughter?" Julie chewed in her lower lip.

Nadia glanced across at her. "For the money, of course; greed is often the reason when it's an American, although greed tends to be a universal motive. According to my sources, I think the man also killed his father."

"That's disgusting." Julie picked up the list. "Isn't there some way they can get him on his father's murder, if he did it?"

"The coroner ruled normal causes, but I'm looking into it. If we can prove a murder it might be a way to assure Elizabeth's long term safety." Nadia responded.

The next few minutes were quiet as each woman read through the folder.

"Anyone have any questions?" Carly leaned forward, her folder still open.

Julie closed her folder. "I agree with the choices. And the teams you've suggested."

"I have a question." Carly pointed to an item on the top page. "The President's wife in South America; you're going to make a fool out of him in public. He'll lose respect and have to resign in disgrace. I like that. He's made fools of several mistresses and his wife. It fits the crime, but what about his wife? I don't see that you're removing her."

Nadia smiled. "No, I think she will want to stay in her country. We hope that people will nominate her to run for President to replace her husband. That's the plan. We have people in place to suggest it. If it doesn't play out and there's a rebellion we'll airlift her out and bring her to the States until she decides what she wants to do."

"Damn, I like that. Hopefully people will recognize her as an intelligent woman who would be good for their country. Perfect." Carly clapped her hands. "And you've got a team in mind for Elizabeth?"

"I didn't have time to contact them yet. I'll run it by you right after I set it up. They'll take her to our place in the Caribbean for a few days. I'll fly down and explain her risks to her. I haven't figured out how to keep her safe yet." Nadia said.

"Keep us informed. This one could cause a few problems. Her father isn't going to let her go without a fight, not if he's desperate for the money, and already killed for it. You wanted to bring up another volunteer?"

"Yes. Will we be having a training session soon?" Nadia asked.

"Probably in about three months."

"Good. I have someone in mind for the next session. I think she's ready."

"Remember this time our candidates will have paranormal talents that will complement each other. Fill out the form for your person and put it on my desk. We'll arrange interviews in about three weeks. Are there any other items?" Carly closed her folder.

Julie shook her head and shut down her laptop.

Nadia gave a half shake.

Carly stood up and brushed dog hair off the legs of her Albertino designed, off-white pantsuit. The short jacket emphasized her narrow hips and long legs. "I've considered moving this office, but I'm not sure we'd find anything better. What are your thoughts?"

"Except for temperature, it's great; at the back of an abandoned warehouse, usually no one is around the area. I wouldn't bother looking for another place. We don't spend that much time here. What do you think, Nadia?" Julie tucked her laptop into a carrying case.

"Unless someone finds out about us and finds this location, I'd say let's stay here. We're liable to attract more interest if we start looking for another place."

"Good point. Okay, we stay, for now. Let's drink to an excellent month. Meeting adjourned. Arturo's for lunch. Martinis are on me." Carly picked up Phoenix and led the way out of the room into the warehouse.

Nadia and Julie trailed along behind.

Outside Carly flagged a taxi. The three women piled in. Carly paused to do a quick survey of the area, checking for any strangers hanging around or anyone who might be watching.

Except for the body repair shop down the block, which she secretly thought was a chop shop, everything looked quiet.

The taxi pulled away. Carly tried to focus on her two main concerns, who wanted to take over CCB and who wanted to destroy The Foundation.

He dismounted from the Appaloosa, handed the reins to his stable hand and strode toward his million dollar ranch house. Losing his prisoner without gaining any useful information, after spending millions of dollars to capture her, felt like a burr under his saddle. He always expected to get what he paid for. He headed for his office, poured two fingers of scotch over ice and took a long drink. He appreciated the burn of an old and expensive bottle of liquor.

After the prisoner debacle, he'd changed direction. He'd decided to try and focus on charitable agencies that funded organizations involved in causes to protect women. He could then expand the search to those organizations. He'd get information their operation and focus on those that might be delusional enough to steal women away from their husbands.

He'd found about a dozen charities. He had someone working on their backgrounds and who they might have funded. He checked his computer. There was nothing yet.

He dropped into a chair and pulled off his riding boots and left them beside the chair. Once he found agencies that matched his requirements he'd send in spies to provide inside information about any under the radar operations. He'd spent a year planning the capture of that woman in Iran. He could be patient.

He'd had to move to South America for seven years after his failed plot to eliminate the number three in line for head of the Mafia. He and patience were close buddies. He would find the people involved in his wife's disappearance. They would pay.

Located about four miles from the White House, the private investigator office where Diane worked covered the main floor of a narrow, converted house. In the back corner of the room, Diane took a quick break from entering the data from her latest case. She rolled her chair around to face the front of the office. Gerry, the owner and her boss, had the larger desk in the middle of the room. Dolores, the receptionist, sat up front, hidden behind a small information counter. Dolores had been there forever. She had to be older than Diane's vintage, second hand desk and looked about in the same condition.

Barely five feet, Diane guessed the woman had to tip the scale at somewhere around two hundred and twenty-five pounds. She wore her white hair in a tight finger wave and knew every one of the clients by their first names. She answered the phone, made appointments, filed and made coffee. She did not clean.

An antique, wooden, ceiling fan creaked slowly overhead, jerking once on every rotation. Diane felt its only purpose was to stir up the dust in the office.

She glanced at her watch, sighed and turned back to her computer. Diane hunched over the keyboard, scanned her notes and punched in more data. Screens flipped, she hit print. She placed the papers from the printer in a folder. A few more minutes she should have all the information on the case. She could leave it on Gerry's desk and head home.

"Hey, Diane, how's it coming?" Gerry strode into the office, a porcupine hat shoved on the back of his head, covered his bald spot. An unlit cigar was clamped in his mouth. He stopped by Diane's desk, rested his large palms on the edge and towered over her, at six feet three inches. He liked to do that. It gave him a sense of power over the little people.

Diane rolled her chair a few inches backwards and regarded him slowly. He had on the same suit he wore day in and day out. He didn't change his shirt more than once a week and the lime green Mickey Mouse tie had permanent grease spots on it. Despite all that he acted like women couldn't resist him.

"I'm almost done. Give me two more minutes." Diane said.

"Good. You know you do good work." Gerry straightened up and strode to his desk. He plopped down and swirled his chair so he could watch her.

"Thanks." Diane's stomach clenched.

Here it comes. She'd been expecting it for weeks. The time had finally arrived.

"Look babe, business isn't what it used to be. I'm going to have to lay you off. I can't afford someone fulltime and at your salary. It's for your own good. You're getting too old for this kind of work."

"Yeah, that's what you said before, but at thirty-nine, I'm hardly over the hill. Besides, I can still take down any man around here." Diane shook her head. It had nothing to do with business. He'd already hired her replacement. She'd seen him interviewing a blonde, about twenty-one years old, with breasts that almost tumbled out of her low-cut sweater. Gerry's tongue had been hanging out of his mouth most of the time the bimbo had been in the office.

"Sure babe, but one of these times you're going to hurt yourself and we don't have medical coverage. Look, I don't want to do this, but it's either you or Dolores and without Dolores I can't find a damn thing in this office. And she makes better coffee than you."

"I see." Diane shrugged. "Whatever. So when do you want me out?"

"Come on, babe, don't take it like that. Look, I can probably keep you on for another month or so; give you time to look for something else."

"You're all heart, Gerry, all heart."

"It'll give me a chance to see if I can find someone younger, who's starting out and won't expect much money."

God she hated it when people lied. The extra month would be to train blondie with the big boobs.

"Take it or leave it, babe." He took off his hat, exposing a receding hair line with greasy, dark brown salt and pepper hair plastered down on his skull. He ran his fingers over his head and shoved the hat back on again.

"I'll take it, for now. Here's the information for the Wingate case. I'm taking off, if that's okay. I'll be in tomorrow morning. If there's a case, leave it on my desk. I'll work the office tomorrow. The rain will make anything else difficult." Diane grabbed her jean jacket, hooked it over her finger and slung it over her shoulder.

"It's not going to rain tomorrow. The weatherman didn't mention it." Gerry frowned at her.

Diane shrugged. She picking up her over-sized backpack and strode toward the door without looking back.

"Women! Christ!"

She felt Gerry's eyes following her. Dolores smirked when Diane strode past.

*So the bitch could make coffee—big deal.*

Dolores had mentioned playing bingo with her girlfriends tonight and then going for a drink, at least five times. Diane had a quick vision of Dolores falling on the wet sidewalk outside the bar, twisting her ankle. "I'd stay home tonight, Dolores. It's safer. If you have a drink and then try walking in the rain you'll sprain an ankle."

"Huh?" Dolores frowned.

Well, she'd warned the wicked witch from the office. If she showed up with crutches tomorrow it wasn't Diane's fault. She hadn't sunk so low she'd let someone get hurt unnecessarily.

Although…she considered casting a simple spell that would make Dolores develop a wart on the end of her nose, just for fun.

*You're above that, lady.* She gave her face a mental slap and hurried toward her older, black truck. She wanted to get home, pour a glass of red wine and slide into a bubble bath.

Witches knew that if you used a spell to be vindictive, it came back to bite you, usually twice as strong.

She shoved the truck into gear and peeled away from the curb. Thank heavens her condo was paid for, and she didn't have a mortgage. She didn't owe anything on her truck either, so she'd be okay for awhile. It wasn't fair that a jerk like Gerry had control over her life. It just wasn't fair. Diane swallowed hard. She forced tears back and choked on them. She would not cry until she got home.

Gerry would expect her to train that bimbo, too. Damn, if she could just find another job and walk out on him without any notice. That would feel good—like she'd ever get that lucky.

She considered making the rounds of the other PI firms, or maybe opening her own firm.

Neither idea appealed to her. She'd like to do something more proactive than chasing after cheating husbands and wives, although in Washington there were enough of them that she could make a decent living. She edged into her underground parking spot, grabbed her bag and headed for the elevator.

Okay, she couldn't put a spell on Dolores or Gerry, but she could do a spell to get herself a new job. That might work.

Inside her condo she dropped her bag on the ancient, carved, wooden chest and tossed her jacket on top of it. In the kitchen she pulled a bottle of Merlot out of the cupboard. After pouring a glass she moved quickly around the kitchen. She pulled out drawers, opened cupboards and assembled a number of items. She placed them on the corner counter, pulled up a bar stool and took a sip of wine. She lit a gold candle and repeated the words:

*A good job awaits me I know.*
*For thine brilliant light scans and searches a place for me.*
*A good job awaits me, for thine goodness is great.*
*My faith in thee is complete. A good job awaits me.*

After taking another sip of wine, she left the candle lit, and began to mix the rest of the ingredients into a search incense. She hummed a piece of a song she'd heard playing on the drive home. She'd get a great new job and tell Gerry where he could go.

She mixed one part of Frankincense, one part Basil and

one part Sandalwood and stirred the mixture in the small bowl. She proceeded to add a half part Vervain, Mugwort and Pansy, and finished with a quarter part cloves.

She carefully carried the candle, the incense and her wine into the bathroom where she ran a strawberry scented bubble bath. She lit the incense before she slipped into the tub. The scented water gently moved around her neck. It soothed her stress. Her body relaxed. She contemplated the question—*What am I going to do with the rest of my life?*

Hopefully the spell would help answer that question, and quickly.

He watched her from the shadows. He'd been there for the past two weeks. The plan was important for his success. He'd learned that when he was eleven.

She left the University library, scurried down the walk way to her older model, compact car. Her key was always in her right hand, ready to put in the lock. She opened the door, quickly slid inside and locked it behind her.

Like that would actually stop someone who seriously wanted to attack her. Women were so stupid. She drove out of the parking o lot. He strolled to his late model Jaguar and pushed the remote. He didn't need to hurry. He knew her schedule. Today was Tuesday. She'd stop at the Market Basket and pick up a large bottle of Diet Seven Up, two or three boxes of no name macaroni and cheese, lettuce and two pounds of lean hamburger. Then she'd stop at the Cluck and Chips for take-out chicken, with a side of coleslaw. She'd go straight home, turn on her twenty-one inch TV, curl up on the couch and eat right out of the cardboard bucket.

He'd wait near her apartment. He'd be there when she arrived, just like he had for the last five days. He needed to make sure he had her schedule down perfectly.

Amy Peters fit his profile of a single woman with low self-esteem, few friends, no close family and no life. She hoped for a Prince Charming to sweep her off her feet and take her away from her mundane life. Her father had also died two years ago, so she probably wanted a father image as well. He'd fit all her requirements.

Women were so predictable. Sluts—only good for sex and money. He'd learned that before he turned twelve. He'd also learned cops were stupid and lazy.

A few more days and he'd put his plan into action. He'd run into her at the Market Basket. He would be her Prince Charming. At least until they were married. Then he'd dispose of her and collect the insurance. It kept him living the life style he deserved.

A smile slithered across his face. He loved everything about his job; the planning, the implementation and particularly the climax. Death could be as exhilarating as sex.

He planned each one so carefully no one even suspected, or connected any of the deaths. He was smarter than any cop. He'd never get caught.

# Chapter Five

The knife shot through the air and landed dead center in the target nailed to the tree. Mac marched forward to the tree. He needed to keep his skills upgraded. Never know when he might need them again. He yanked out the knife, returned to his throw line and flicked the knife quickly back at the tree. Dead center again.

Sweat trickled down his back. A drip raced down his nose and fell to the ground. For early April the weather had been unseasonably warm. The heat didn't touch the steamy temperatures of some of the jungles he'd crawled through, but the humidity was fucking close.

The murmur from the black flies buzzed in his ears. He hated flies.

He glanced at his watch, walked back to the target, pulled out the knife and tucked it into the holder inside his boot. A small plane circled overhead. It flew lower. A breeze swished the shrubs and grass, but had no cooling affect.

He headed back to camp. The Commander would want a report on the latest trainees. Carly had given him a list of potential missions for his input on those he thought would best fit the newest team.

The plane landed and rolled to a stop. Mac approached the door. She'd probably want a date for the next training session. He'd been thinking about whether he wanted to do it again. It had weighed on his mind all through this present session. He felt something was missing from his life, but he hadn't figured out what.

After his injury he'd taken this position Carly had offered to him. He couldn't turn down more money than he knew what to do with, cutting edge technology and equipment, some still in the testing phase, plus a hand-picked staff. Still, after five years training women for special missions, he felt restless. Maybe he needed to look for something different.

The door opened. Carly stepped out, wearing a designer fatigue suit in greens and browns with a matching brown t-shirt and brown heels, Manolos, or some other weird Italian name. Amazingly, she didn't look out of place.

She removed her helmet. He saluted and swallowed his grin. She bounced down the steps. Something furry was clutched under her arm. She held her helmet in her other hand. She approached him and handed him the helmet before throwing one arm around his neck, "Good old Mac Langston, still trying to be so professional. Give it up, Mac."

He couldn't contain the smile that sneaked out. He hugged her back. "Good to see you, Carly. You look fantastic as usual."

She stepped back and spun around on her four inch heels. "You like the outfit? I had it designed for you, so I'd look professional."

Her spontaneous laugh burst forth at the expression on his face.

"You're incorrigible. I'm sure the staff would love the outfit, except of course, they're all busy with our trainees. It's too bad they can't appreciate their Commander in Chief."

"It's part of our security. We're going to need to talk about that, too. Someone is trying to get information on The Foundation. We were set up on one of our last missions." Carly pranced through the dirt and gravel behind Mac.

"What? Who? How?" Mac stopped and twisted around to face Carly.

"I don't know. I'm working on it, but we can't rule out a leak from up here."

Mac shook his head. "I don't see it."

"I don't either, but we need to check out every angle. We almost lost one of our agents."

"Who?"

"Assif."

"Oh, shit. Is she okay?"

"She will be. Anyway, that's why I need to review everything, and keep an even lower profile." Carly let out a sigh.

"No problem, except—what is that exactly?" He gestured to the furry bundle, teeth now exposed, sending a low growl in Mac's direction.

"Shush, Phoenix. He's a friend. This is Phoenix. I found her a few weeks ago and she doesn't like to be left alone. She doesn't appear to like you."

"What exactly is it?"

"I'm not sure. The vet said a Maltese, Yorkie, Chihuahua cross with maybe something else thrown in. Basically she's a mutt."

Mac shook his head, took Carly's free arm and continued toward the building that held the cafeteria and Mac's office. At one time he'd considered getting involved with Carly, but decided against it. She was his boss and had more money than he did, but the biggest reason, was he liked her. He didn't love her, or want a permanent relationship with her. Sex would have ruined a good friendship.

He kept a firm grip on her arm in case she tripped in those ridiculous heels. "How's the work going?"

"We keep busy. I hope you made decent coffee."

They reached the top step. Mac opened the door and moved to one side to let her pass.

"Yes, ma'am, I got your special brew and made it fresh before you landed." Mac ducked his head when he passed through the door.

"Good man." Carly slid behind his desk, Phoenix curled up on her lap.

Mac placed her helmet on the edge of the counter before he filled two mugs with the steaming liquid. He added a dash of cream to one.

"Here you go." He placed it close to her right arm.

A folder sat in the middle of the desk. Carly flipped it open and skimmed through the pages. Unconsciously she picked up the mug and took a sip. "Very good, thanks Mac. Training is finished. This team is ready for their first assignment?"

"They're ready."

"I sent you some options for their first mission. What did you suggest?"

"I marked my first two choices." Mac handed her a sheet of paper.

Carly glanced at it. "I agree."

She placed the paper inside the folder, closed it and picked up her coffee. She held the mug with both hands. "Our next group of volunteers is going to be a little different this time. They are women with paranormal talents. The plan is to meld their individual paranormal talents. We're hoping the merged talents will make a more effective team. Along with all the other skills you'll teach them, this team will be available for some special missions. Are you okay with the idea?"

"Like, what are we talking about, reading crystal balls?" Mac rolled his eyes but struggled not to say anything derogatory.

"Not quite. They may see or talk to ghosts, things like that."

"For real?" Mac stared at Carly, looking for a sign she was joking.

"You're not a believer in the paranormal, huh? It's for real, believe it or not. I'm also going to add one more training session for these recruits. A Dr. Mogee will join you. He's a paranormal specialist. Don't bother rolling your eyes again. His job will be to work with the women on their special skills and pull them together to strengthen the effect." Carly shrugged. "It's an experiment. You know me, I always want to try something new and see if we can improve."

Mac shook his head. "I think this one sounds off the wall, but hey, it's your money. I can work with it. It might provide us with a few laughs."

"Mac," Carly fixed him with a stare. "No making fun of the candidates, or the instructor. The next session starts in nine weeks, after everyone gets back from their two months off."

"Are you all right?" Carly studied his face. "You look off. What's wrong?"

Mac's lips twisted into a semi-smile. "Nothing gets by you, does it?"

"If it did I wouldn't be a very good CEO or Commander. Spill it." She leaned back in the chair.

Mac paced, across the room then back to the desk.

Carly took another sip of coffee.

"I'm thinking of leaving."

"Leaving? You mean the whole program? The Foundation? What brought this on?"

"I don't know. I'm tired. I feel like I'm missing something in my life. I'm thinking about a trip around the US on my motorcycle."

"Okay, a motorbike trip? You could take a leave of absence. You don't find the work satisfying anymore?"

"Yes and no, but no, it's not that." Mac scratched his head. He searched for the words. "It's a great job. I couldn't ask for a better one, but I don't have a balance. It's all work.

I don't have a life outside of it. The staff is my family. They're a great family, but I want more. I haven't seen my brother or his family for three years, because it's always awkward. I can never discuss what I do with them. When I was in special ops it was the same. I'm tired of the secrecy and the risks, should I let anything slip." Mac slumped against the wall, his eyes on Carly. "I don't know what I want, but I need more. If I even had someone I could talk to without worrying I might let something slip."

Carly put her coffee down and tapped her fingers together. "I understand. The secrecy is hard. Look, you've got eight weeks leave coming when this session is finished. We'll fly you wherever you want. Pick a nice Caribbean island, or a Greek Isle, and relax, or go on a motorbike trip. Think about what you want to do when you grow up, and what you'd do if you left this place. Then we'll talk."

"I don't know, maybe. I may stop off in Seattle and see my brother and nephews first. They've probably forgotten me after all this time."

Carly kicked the chair back and uncoiled from the seat. She clutched Phoenix to her hip, moved across to Mac and gave him a hug. "I do understand what you're saying. Part of me also has some of the same stuff, but I have Nadia and Julie. I care about you, Mac. If you really want to leave I won't stop you, but think about it. You may find leaving isn't the answer. It's been a part of you for so long. For the next two months, pretend you aren't coming back. See how you feel about that possibility."

"I will, and thanks Carly. You're a good person."

"Shh, don't let anyone hear that. Nadia will be here for the graduation ceremony. She'll give the recruits their first mission. Can you also rerun background checks on your staff, check their bank accounts, family, whatever?"

"I'll get on it right away. I don't think we have a leak, but I'll do a thorough check." He hoped Carly was off base on this one.

"Good. Let me know as soon as you finish the check. Then we'll figure out where to send you for some R & R. Don't give this up until you figure out what you want to do to replace it."

Carly was right. What would he do if he left?

The plane coasted in for a landing. Nadia checked her seatbelt and opened the message she had received before she'd boarded the plane. She reread it while she waited for the stewardess to open the door. There were only a few people in first class. The door opened. She shoved the note in the pocket of her DKNY sweater jacket, grabbed her carryon bag from the overhead rack and edged down the aisle. She ducked through the door onto the stairs.

She loved Paris in the spring and arranged a shoot here once a year. The city put on a fresh coat for the New Year; trees dressed in their fresh green coats, flowers sprang up with bright colors, people headed for the outdoor cafés.

Outside the airport she flagged a taxi.

"Hotel Georges V, *s'il vous plait.*"

Forty minutes later the taxi pulled up in front of the elegant, old hotel.

"*Bonjour, mademoiselle,* welcome back." The doorman held open the taxi door.

"*Merci, Francois.*"

"How long will you be with us?" He took her bag and walked her inside.

"I plan to be here about a week, this time."

The desk clerk handed her a key. The elevator whisked her to the top floor and minutes later she entered the penthouse suite to the ringing of the phone.

"*Bonjour.*"

"*Bonjour chérie. Comment-allez vous? C'est Elmo.*"

"Elmo, how are you? How did you know I was here?"

"I have spies everywhere, darling. I knew when you walked into the airport. Are you available for dinner tonight? Taillevent's?"

"Perfect. We need to talk. I need some information. We'll see you at eight?"

Instead of a leisurely soak in the extra-large, marble tub, Nadia pulled out her laptop, and placed it on the antique desk. She unfolded the message and booted up her computer. The note referred to Nooria, the eighth wife of an Afghanistan warlord. She'd been replaced by a younger wife, but instead of being sending her off to retire with grace, he had her locked in a prison. It said she was due to be executed within the week. It was unusual but not unheard of. She wondered what wife number eight had done to make the warlord mad. Then again, this could be another set up.

The information she found online validated the possibility of the woman's imminent death. Nadia scanned her teams and found one who could be there within twenty-four hours. She needed information on the prison and a plan to get her team in and out safely. Emailing Carly and Julie she passed on the information she'd compiled so far and the team she suggested could accomplish a rescue. She also asked them to double check the information with a few different people.

She checked the time, shut down and locked her laptop. In the opulent bedroom she grabbed one of the designer dresses that had been left for her in the closet. She stepped into it. The deep gold, color made her skin look even darker. She added gold heels and a gold cobra necklace with matching bracelet and earrings. After a quick glance in the mirror she grabbed her bag and hurried downstairs.

At Taillevent's, the maitre d' ushered her to a quiet corner table. Elmo rose and took her hand. He was tall and distinguished with an iron gray goatee and mustache. After kissing her palm he smiled at her.

"Darling, you look ravishing as usual. It is good to see you again."

Nadia touched her cheek to his before she slipped into the chair the waiter held for her. "Elmo, you're looking well."

"Ah, well, life is good to me these days. It's more peaceful, although lately it appears there's an escalation in the spy industry. I ordered a Perrier on ice for you."

"Thank you."

"Your uncle, do you see much of him?"

"No, we don't keep in regular contact with the king. I did see several of his sons the last time I visited Saudi Arabia. Are you travelling much?"

"I was in Afghanistan five months ago and Iran last month."

"Excellent. I need some information on Afghanistan." Nadia sipped her Perrier.

"You're still involved in whatever you and your friends do?"

"Of course, we have no choice."

"What do you need this time?"

"I need a floor plan of the prison in Herat, and a list of security check points so we can circumvent them. That's all."

Elmo shook his head. "You don't ask for much do you?"

"If it's too difficult..." Nadia shrugged.

He glowered at her. "You know it's not. For you, I can get it in a few days."

"A few days?" Nadia pursed her lips. "I really need it within twenty-four hours, at the most.

"Tomorrow?" Elmo frowned. "I'll need to start right away. I might be able to get what you need by then."

"I realize it's not much time, but I only found out about this case when I boarded the plane."

"I understand. I hope you're not going there. The countryside is not safe. There are IED's everywhere."

"The Improvised Explosive Devices, I know about them. No, I'm not going there, be we'll be very careful. Thank you, Elmo." Nadia glanced up at the waiter and ordered two of the chef's special vegetarian dishes.

"How long are you in Paris?" Elmo leaned across the table and took her hand.

"Just a week this time, for a layout of the fall line of one the couture designers."

"And you are still alone?"

"If you mean, am I still not married, the answer is yes."

"Tch, tch, I hope you are considering finding a mate soon."

"Is that an offer?"

"Ah, if I were but twenty years younger, it would be. I know some nice Muslim men."

"Thank you, Elmo, but I can find a man if I want to. Besides, I don't want any man. He has to be a very special man who meets all my requirements and accepts the things that I do to help other women."

Elmo kissed her palm. "You are too complex a woman for me. Let's enjoy our dinner and talk of less serious things."

"Perfect," Nadia agreed. She needed to finish dinner and get back to the hotel. She had to work on the new mission. Nadia suspected wife number eight knew something political that the warlord did not want to get out. They had to get to her quickly or she'd be dead.

The best team had just come back from Iraq and was missing at least one member, if not two. She had scanned her lists, but there wasn't another one that was that fluent in Arabic so they wouldn't be at risk in a prison. It came back to Sabhita and Marley. Assif was physically healthy but Nadia questioned if she would be ready to go back into the field yet. She might be okay if she stayed outside as the support. She'd email them tonight, to see if Assif wanted to participate, so they could prepare. She needed one more person to fill Fareeda's spot. She hadn't finished the physio on her leg.

She needed Elmo's info, hopefully by the morning, because two of the team were going to have to go into the prison to get Nooria, the eighth wife out. It would be tricky and dangerous.

The timing had to be perfect and the right people bought off.

# Chapter Six

Carly sat in her office and scanned lists on her computer. A beep alerted her that a message had come in on her personal and encrypted computer link. She punched in a code. A message popped up, from Nadia. Carly read it quickly.

At the tap on the door Carly switched screens. "Come in."

"I'm here with the update you wanted." Link strolled into the room, looking sexier than any man should, in the beige and brown uniform.

Carly held contact with his dark gray eyes a second longer than she should.

Link handed her a couple of sheets of paper with a wink.

A ridge of warmth began to spread at the base of her neck. She reached for the papers and leaned back in her chair. She skimmed over the papers.

Link strolled around the office, checked out her bookshelf and bent down to pat Phoenix asleep in her bed.

"So Minnamar is trying to undercut us?" Carly lowered the papers. "They're the ones who placed the bugs?"

"Yes."

"Sit." Carly waved to a chair beside her desk.

Link folded his long legs under him as he slid into the padded office chair. "I think they're looking at a takeover."

"A takeover, isn't that a little presumptuous for a new and smaller company?"

"Yeah, they're either ambitious or desperate. I'd say desperate, and revengeful. A man by the name of Fred Remple heads the company. He formed it just over three years ago. From what I've been able to determine he has limited resources."

"So how does he plan to initiate a takeover?"

"I'm not sure yet. It looks like he hopes to cut your credibility by taking a few government and other large contracts away from you. He probably hopes that will also affect your financial bottom line. Then he can make a buyout offer."

Carly tented her fingers and tapped them together. "Not a bad plan, but it's not going to work. Keep checking for more bugs. How about employees? Have you discovered any high risk ones?"

"There's a couple, maybe. I have over a dozen on a list that I need to do one more final check. The one I'd be most concerned about is a man by the name of Frank Reed."

Carly pulled her forehead muscles together. "Frank Reed? He's one of our newer employees. Works as an assistant in the computer lab with Arnie?"

"That's the man."

"Why do you suspect him?"

"Do you remember a Frank Rempler?"

Carly shook her head. "No, I don't think so."

"Eight years ago your father took over his small company. They had a few contracts in Asia your father wanted, so he instituted a hostile takeover. It left Rempler broke. A year later the man committed suicide."

"Right, I think I do remember something about that. I tried to talk my father into buying the man out. It would have left him with some money and his dignity. As usual, my father preferred to ruin him."

"That sounds about right. Anyway, Fred Remple, head

of Minnamar, is Frank Rempler's son. He dropped the r to change his name. Frank Reed is Fred's son, really Frank Rempler."

"Ouch, that explains a lot, including why he wants to takeover this company. Okay, let's keep an eye on the situation. Make sure no new bugs get planted and inform Arnie that our little Frankie only gets the boring daily stuff, nothing that could give him any information on the company. I need to think about how I want to handle this."

"No problem, I can do that. I'll keep checking the rest of the names on the list as well. Anything else you need, Carly?"

Carly stared up at Link, her body felt hot under her cool, lemon yellow, linen suit. Oh yeah, there were a lot of things she needed from this man. His body heat radiated off him. She could smell his musky aftershave. It reminded her of the outdoors and hot, sweaty nights.

Afraid to look at him she felt his masculinity and wanted to feel his naked body moving against her own. Too bad he was her employee. If she slept with him she'd probably have to fire him. Besides, he wasn't interested in her. He always kept his distance, accompanied by that damn cool, professional attitude.

"No, I think that's…what do you know about Percy York?" Carly stood up. Phoenix trotted across the floor and begged to be picked up. "Down, not now."

Link shook his head. "Percy York? Who is he?"

"That's what I want to find out. Maybe look into his background and his financial position and see whatever you can find. Apparently he keeps sponging off our fund raisers and he's not on our guest lists."

"We can't have that, can we? You might run out of caviar." Link chuckled.

"Get out of here." Carly punched him in the arm, feeling the rock hard bicep beneath her knuckles. Her stomach clenched and she swallowed hard.

Link grabbed her hand. "Don't hurt the merchandise or I can't keep you secure."

Carly found herself struggling for the next breath. She couldn't look at him for fear she'd give a hint of her emotions. "Let me know what you find out about York and keep me updated on the Remples."

He smiled, released her hand slowly, almost caressing her palm as he let go. With a salute he closed the door behind him.

Carly stared at her palm. She must have misread his touch. It had been so gentle. She held it up to her lips.

*Damn you, Link Stone.*

Nadia reviewed the information Elmo had sent her. If a woman was incarcerated it was usually at Herat, where most prisoners were women. To find the warrior lord's eighth wife among all those women wearing burkas, someone would have to go into the prison, probably two people. The most likely way would be to get two members of the team arrested. They would need to have a connection to the other members outside the prison. She also needed to buy off a guard inside the prison.

Once they found Nooria they would need to contact the others to arrange the escape. This one could be trickier than rescuing the ghost of Aasera.

Nadia sent information off to Carly and Julie for input. Her photo shoot would keep her in Paris for several more days so she needed to arrange everything from here with their help.

Back in her hotel room Nadia punched in plans on her laptop. She read them, made notes, deleted parts and added a few other details. She wished there was a way they could open the door so all the women held captive there could escape.

Once Nooria was free, maybe—maybe they could open the gates. There would be no plan or protection for those women, but maybe, maybe if they got free they could find ways to protect themselves. It was more of a wish than an actuality and could cause more problems for the other women. She'd stay with the assignment. She'd need a helicopter for Nooria and the rest of the team.

Nadia opened Elmo's diagram. She'd sent it off to Julie and Carly. Carefully she worked through the escape and the safest and easiest area to land. This had to work. She couldn't put another team member at risk. The guilt consumed her for what Assif had endured.

*Was someone trying to find them with this assignment, too?*

Wearing the traditional blue burqa, Marley kept her head down and followed the guard. She'd been sentenced to ten years in Herat prison for not wearing her veil in a public place. It was a different role than the last time she was in Iran. Now one of her team was injured. The other shouldn't be here, but insisted and she had a new team member.

Men raped their wives and it was appropriate. Women couldn't even refuse to have sex with their husbands. Marley struggled to keep her mouth closed. This was a mission to save one woman, not to try and reform the Muslim society.

The guard opened a door into a large, crowded prison cell and shoved her inside with the butt of his rifle. Marley stayed where she'd been pushed and studied the room. It contained far more women than it had been originally built for. All the women appeared complacent; accepting their imprisonment.

If this had been the United States there would have been rebellion and fighting.

Interesting, Marley contemplated, the difference in cultures and women's attitudes.

Two women approached her, cautiously at first. One asked if they could help her.

Marley shook her head. She responded in Arabic that she was fine.

When asked what sin she had committed, Marley wanted to say nothing, but instead said she hadn't worn her veil in public.

Several women close to her gasped and shook their head.

Marley attempted to look properly ashamed. She moved through the throng of imprisoned women, searching for the one she needed to find. She'd memorized her photo, but all the women in prison dressed alike. It could be harder than originally thought.

Marley could only guess what time it was. She couldn't wear a watch. It had to be mid-afternoon. Sabhita had been caught wearing nail polish and sent to prison to await a trial, if there ever was a trial. She should be here soon.

At the back of the prison cell Marley noticed one woman sitting by herself in the corner. The other women appeared to avoid her. Marley sat down beside her. She didn't say anything, just sat quietly.

"You shouldn't sit here."

Marley looked at the woman. "Excuse me?" she responded in Arabic.

"I am marked for death. It is bad luck to sit near me."

"Why are you marked for death?"

"I cannot say, but you should move away."

Marley moved a few feet away. Okay, she'd found Nooria, the eighth wife, now what?

Their plan had Marley take the woman to safety, but she appeared to accept her imminent death. "I've found her." she whispered. She hoped the tiny microphone in her ear canal picked up the message.

There was a commotion at the front of the cell. Marley watched a guard shove another woman into the over-crowded room. The woman glanced up over her veil. Her eyes met Marley's. Marley nodded and edged back toward Nooria.

"No one should die unless they've committed a crime. What is yours?"

The woman raised her head and looked at Marley.

She couldn't be more than thirty years old. When she didn't respond Marley asked, "Do you have children?"

A mask crossed the woman's face. "Yes. I have four children."

"Won't they miss their mother?"

"The other wives will take care of them. They will be safe."

"But you will not see them grow up."

She shook her head. "Even if I lived, I would not be able to see them grow up."

The bare-bone sorrow of the woman's despair grasped Marley's heart. Even if they saved her, this woman had lost her children. No wonder she didn't appear to care about dying.

Sabhita moved through the throng of women. She stopped to answer a question or make a comment. A different guard entered the cell. He carried water for the women. He noticed Sabhita and slowly made his way toward her. He leaned forward and whispered something in her ear.

Marley struggled not to smile. Whatever he said would be heard by at least five other people.

Sabhita indicated Marley. The guard followed her direction.

He must be one of the ones they'd paid off. Marley turned back to Nooria. They had to be quick. The guard wouldn't be on duty for that long.

Marley sat down beside the woman and said quietly. "You don't deserve to die. Please come with me."

The woman stared at Marley, "You don't understand…"

"I don't understand your culture, no, but I understand a mother's love for her children."

The woman scanned Marley's face.

Marley offered her a hand. After a long pause the woman took it.

Together they worked their way to the side of the cell and a small door. Sabhita and the guard worked their way toward the door from a different direction. He handed out water as they passed through the women.

Suddenly the first guard shouted for the water guard. He turned back toward the main door.

Sabhita glanced over her shoulder at Marley and shrugged. Marley nodded. She took Nooria's hand and held it.

Four more guards marched down the outside corridor.

Sabhita shot Marley a desperate look as she followed the water guard. He had a deer in the headlights look.

Something was wrong. It wasn't going down as planned. Marley could sense the panic of the guard. He bumped into Sabhita as he headed toward the main door. He was out of their plan.

Sabhita turned and slipped through the crowd toward them. She reached Marley and Nooria where they stood by the small door. She indicated a key she held between the folds of her burqa.

Marley inclined her head toward the door. Sabhita slipped her key into the lock.

The woman stared at her. "How?"

"Don't ask right now. We'll talk later." Marley stepped through the door into a garden area. She prayed the people on the other end had heard everything up until now. "Get the damn helicopter down here and fast."

"That's asking nicely." Sabhita grinned.

"They're up there nice and safe in the helo. We could get shot at any minute. I thought that was pretty damn nice." Marley turned to the woman with them, switching to Arabic. "A ladder is going to be dropped down from a helicopter, in the next few minutes. Climb up it into the helicopter. I'll be right behind you. I'll explain everything later."

The woman stared at Marley, her eyes dark with confusion.

"You don't want to die. Even if you can't raise your children you will be able to check on them."

Another door from the prison opened. Two guards stepped into the garden area for a smoke.

Marley grabbed Nooria and dived behind bushes. Sabhita flattened herself on the ground.

A helicopter whirred overhead.

The guards moved forward to observe its movement.

It hovered over the garden.

The guards shouted to each other. Drawing their guns, they aimed at the helicopter.

Sabhita reached into her boot and pulled out a small twenty-two. She fired in rapid succession and hit the guards as the helo lowered a ladder.

Marley shoved the distressed Nooria up the rope ladder. Marley put her foot on the ladder to follow and continued to shove Nooria up in front of her. Another prison door opened. Four more guards stormed out.

Nooria disappeared inside the helo. Marley grabbed the hand that reached down for her. Wendy, the temporary team member, grinned and pulled her up. Marley felt a sharp pain penetrate her thigh. She stumbled, but another hand grabbed her wrist and yanked her inside. More hands dragged her along the floor. Wendy and Assif strapped her in.

"Take off." Someone shouted and the helicopter tilted to one side and then rose straight into the air.

"Sabhita? Where's Sabhita?" Marley yelled. "We don't leave without her."

A few bullets passed pass the outside of the cabin as it turned and flew off.

"I'm here." The voice came from behind Marley. Another body was pulled through the door. "Let's get out of here."

Through the veil of pain Marley saw Nooria strapped against the opposite wall, terror registered on her face as the helo shot through the sky, tears streamed down her face.

"It will be all right." Marley stuttered in Arabic, trying to concentrate on anything but the pain. "You will be safe. You can keep track of your children."

The woman shook her head. "No good, no good, should have died."

"It doesn't look too bad." Sabhita crawled across to Marley and knelt to check the wound. "The bullet went right through. Assif, hand me the first aid kit."

Assif dug out the kit and handed it to Sabhita.

"Hang in there, Marley. Once we stop the bleeding we'll give you something for the pain. You did great." Sabhita applied pressure.

"I'm f…f…fine, r…really." Marley chattered. "You made it up?"

"I was right behind you. I was still hanging onto the ladder when they took off, but Assif and the others pulled me in. The guard's guns weren't powerful enough to get a good shot off. The only injury from the mission is you. We'll get you patched up."

"Glad you're okay. Worried." Marley felt herself fading with the pain. "Oh shoot, I'm going to pass out."

# Chapter Seven

Sara opened the window and took a deep breath of the fresh air. "Hey, Gloria, maybe we need to go for a walk and enjoy the day."

Gloria barked and galloped off to find her leash.

Seattle could be fickle this time of year, frequently gray, cold and rainy. Early to mid-June acted as a transition between the usual cool spring and the time when the sun finally burst forth with some warmth. In the garden the purple and white of the lilacs presented a hedge of color, their heady scent filled the air. Delicate pink droplets were hanging on the bleeding hearts. The tall fir and pine trees reached toward the sky. Their lacey, artistic branches, formed intricate designs against the brilliant azure blue.

Like the coming of spring, the last year or so had been her rebirthing. This was the first spring since college she'd felt alive and excited at her options. Maybe she could find a job. She had almost finished her Bachelor's in Business Administration, maybe move to a new area, or even get a new wardrobe. Her options left her exhilarated.

Gloria bounded back with her leash in her mouth and skidded to a stop on her butt.

Sara laughed. She clipped on the leash and opened the front door. She chased after Gloria, down the street, toward the park.

Gloria chased a squirrel up a tree. She charged around the corner, sniffed at the ground, pulled her extension leash to its limit and disappeared from sight. Sara caught up with the golden retriever and jerked to a stop. A slender, dark haired woman bent over Gloria. She patted her head. Gloria wriggled with delight.

The woman straightened. She must be six feet tall, Sara thought. She stared at the woman. Her face had high cheek bones, an aquiline nose and large mink, brown eyes. Her deep, emerald green tunic and loose pants looked exotic and expensive. She could be a model. In fact, Sara thought she may have seen her in a magazine.

"You have a beautiful dog. She's very friendly."

Sara grinned. Damn dog, she was no protection as a watch dog. She loved everyone. "Thanks. I think she's a great dog. She's my best friend. In fact, for years, she's been my only friend."

"Some women aren't lucky enough to even have a dog. Nadia Nassif." The woman extended a hand.

Sara noticed the long, slender fingers, perfectly manicured with green tips that matched her outfit. She was conscious of her broken nails and those she had chewed to the quick. She hesitated before she slowly extended her own.

"Sara Peters. Aren't you a model?"

Nadia slowly smiled. "Yes. I do some modeling."

Their hands touched. Sara felt the jolt. She saw the woman standing in an office, a woman in a prison cell in the back ground.

"I've seen your picture in some of the magazine ads. One's a shampoo advertisement, right?"

"Yes and a few others."

"What are you doing in this neighborhood park?"

"I'm looking for you. You walk your dog here every day. I took a chance I'd run into you. I wasn't sure, but I know where you live, so if I'd missed you I could have contacted you there. I thought this might be a better place to talk than your house. Did you get the book?"

Sara pursed her lips. "I don't understand."

"We've followed you for awhile. We've watched you since you lost your husband, gradually regained your confidence and became that person you lost when you got married. You look great in that outfit by the way." The woman reached down to pat Gloria who was nudging the woman behind her knees.

"But why would you watch me?" Sara jerked on the leash and pulled Gloria to her side. She started to turn away. People had followed her since Gordon's death? Confusion and vulnerability seeped through her at the thought that people knew all about her and how pathetic she had become. She felt personally invaded and began to hyperventilate. "I'm sorry I need to get my dog home."

Sara hastened down the park path. She dragged Gloria behind her.

"We want to offer you a job."

Sara slowed to a walk. She turned back to the gorgeous woman. "A job? What kind of job? And why would you do it here in the park?"

A mixture of concern and curiosity overwhelmed her. Why had they followed her and what did it have to do with hiring her? *Did it have something to do with the woman in prison she'd seen in her vision a few minutes ago?*

"Let's say we prefer to maintain discretion until we actually have a mutual agreement. The job is one where you can help other women. These are women who are in abusive or even life and death situations."

Sara thought of her own life and where she'd be if her husband hadn't died. She'd been in an abusive situation for almost twenty years. It would have been nice if someone had come along and helped her. She wouldn't have wasted that large chunk of her life. She'd looked into volunteering for a shelter for abused women. Maybe fate had finally decided to smile on her.

"I don't understand. Are we talking about counseling? How would it work? Abused women wouldn't be allowed to attend regular counseling sessions." She knew that for a fact.

"That's true, as you well know. No, I work for a large company called The Foundation. The office is located in New York." Nadia gestured toward the path. "Shall we walk while we talk?"

Sara's mind swirled. She nodded. Gloria took off to sniff the grass and bushes.

"So what would I be doing? I'm brushing up on my clerical and computer skills."

Nadia slowed her stride so Sara could keep up. "That might come in useful, but it's not a clerical position. The first step in our process is to ask people to come in for testing and an interview. If that works out I share more information and answer questions. Can I book you in for next Monday, about ten?"

"Do you mean in New York, next Monday?"

"Yes. I have booked a conference room at one of the hotels in Manhattan, overlooking the water. I'll arrange for you to fly out on Saturday and back Tuesday. It will give you a day and a bit to explore the city. We cover the cost of the flight and the hotel. Can you arrange for someone to care for your dog?"

Sara ran her tongue over her lips. The old paralytic fear that accompanied something new washed over her. Gordon had done a good job, but eighteen months later she'd done a better job of compensating for his regimental, isolation techniques. Even Nadia had said so. *To hell with you, Gordon Peters, I'm moving on. I'm not going to let you stop me from a new experience.*

"You'll fly me to New York for an interview?"

"Yes, of course and we'll arrange for a hotel in Manhattan while you're there."

"What if I don't qualify or don't take the position?"

"No strings attached, we still cover expenses."

"I can put Gloria in a kennel for four days. She won't be happy, but she'll manage. Okay, I'll be there. It doesn't mean I'm agreeing to anything until I know more about it."

"Of course not, and we're not offering you anything at this time. It's a chance to exchange information and see if there might be a fit. I'll be doing the interview. It should take about four hours."

"That long?"

"It's a very thorough process. We want to make sure you understand the position and will be happy with us. Here's my card with the address on it. Take a cab, get a receipt and we'll reimburse you for the cost."

"Really?"

"Of course, it's a business interview. We don't want you spending any money if it's not going to work out. I think you're ready though. Are you still practicing the self-defense you learned in the class you took at the community center?"

"You know about that?" Sara took the card. She noticed Nadia avoided contact with Sara's hand this time.

"Yes, that's when I figured you might be ready to take the next step."

"I'm still practicing. I've moved up to the next level. I'm a green belt."

"Excellent. I'll see you Monday." Nadia held out her hand.

Sara took it. Flashes of Nadia in expensive costumes being photographed, a child everyone laughed at because of her height, and a man making her kiss his feet, all flashed before her.

"What do you see?" Nadia asked.

"I don't understand,"

"Yes, you do," Nadia replied. "You have a sense others do not. When you touch my hand you see things, things about me. I have no idea what they may be, but I am sure you see something. That is one reason why we want to interview you."

Sara put her hand to her mouth. Until Gordon's death she'd had to pretend none of what she saw existed. Now someone wanted her because of it. The thought that people knew about her visions and wanted her because of them, left her dizzy. She tried to adjust to the switch in attitudes.

"I see, sort of." Sara tried to organize her thoughts. "Mostly I saw bits of your childhood. Is there anything I can do to prepare?"

"Read the book." Nadia strode down the path toward the exit. A few seconds later she swung back to face Sara. "Wear something dressy, but comfortable, and bring another outfit, something you might wear to your defense class."

This time she disappeared around the corner. Sara stared after her, absently patting Gloria. What had she got herself into? She should have asked more questions. Maybe she could practice tonight, but what would she practice? Nadia had said it wasn't clerical.

Sara turned the card over.

*Nadia N Nassif*
*Recruiter*
*The Foundation*

A New York address was in the bottom left hand side of the card and a phone number in the bottom right hand corner. She'd check the address in the phone book when she got home.

"Gloria, come." Sara signaled with her hand and the dog bounded across the grass and skidded to a sit at Sara's feet. "Good girl, time to head home."

Sara pulled the leash tight, "heel."

She walked down the path Nadia had taken. She replayed their conversation in her head. Why had Nadia been following her? What did they want from her? Should she even go to their interview? Then again, how often did someone offer to pay for a trip to New York?

Sara checked down the street before she crossed. Gloria jerked on the leash and pulled Sara back. "Gloria, what the…?"

A motorcycle roared by, inches in front of Sara.

"Oh, my gosh." She'd been so busy thinking, that she hadn't double checked in both directions before she stepped off the curb. If it hadn't been for Gloria she'd have walked out right in front of the motorcycle.

Breaks squealed as the Harley slowed to a stop and swung around. The rider pulled in front of Sara and stopped. He removed his helmet.

"Are you okay? I didn't mean to come that close."

"No, it's my fault. I was daydreaming and not watching where I was going."

"You're okay?"

"I'm fine." Sara stared into a pair of warm deep brown eyes. Warmth started at her toes and crawled through her body. It heated every part of her. She swallowed hard and tried to drag her eyes away from his square face with the five o'clock shadow.

"Mac Langston." He pulled off the leather glove on his right hand before he extended it.

Sara put out her fingers and immediately found them engulfed in a strong, warm, hand. She could feel a few calluses on the pads of his palm, the hands of a working man. Another jolt shot through her body. Darkness, flashes of light, loud noises—it was a gunfight of some kind. *Was this man part of it or observing it?*

That made twice today. After blocking the flashes for years her rusty senses appeared to overcome the blocks quickly. They also took a toll on her energy levels.

"Excuse me, are you all right? Ma'am?"

Sara gave her head a shake. "Sorry. Sara, Sara Peters and I really am fine. Thank you, Mr. Langston."

"Mac, please, and after a shock like that I insist on seeing you get home safely. Hope on and I'll give you a ride."

"I don't think that will work. My dog doesn't ride motorcycles and neither do I." Sara pulled on the leash and started to walk away.

"Right, of course," Mac slapped his forehead. "Then I'll have to walk you home."

"No, don't be silly."

Mac pulled on his glove, lifted his leg over the bike and proceeded to walk beside her. He pushed the bike. "Do you live very far?"

Sara shook her head. "No, in the next block."

"Good, this thing could get a little heavy if we had to go a couple of miles. So what were you thinking about?"

"Pardon me?"

"Instead of paying attention to where you were going?"

"Oh, about a job interview I have coming up."

"A career change?"

"It's something like that. This is my house. Thank you, Mr. Langston." Sara turned into the yard.

"Have dinner with me?"

"Excuse me?"

"Have dinner with me. I've just arrived in town. I don't know any good places to eat around here and I hate to eat alone. Please? It's my treat."

"No, I..."

"I'm not taking no for an answer. I'll sit out in front of your house and rev my bike until you say yes."

"You can't. The neighbors..."

"Exactly." Mac grinned.

She stared into his twinkling eyes. Heat rose through her body. Emotions she hadn't felt since college surfaced.

"An early dinner, then I'll bring you home and be out of your life. You haven't eaten yet, I know that."

"No. I...okay. There's a little Italian place a few blocks from here. Let me put Gloria inside and you can park your bike in front of the garage. We can walk."

"I was going to ride down."

Sara shook her head. "No. I'll have dinner with you, but we will walk there and back."

Mac shrugged. "Okay, fair enough."

After giving Gloria fresh water, Sara ran a comb through her tangled hair and touched up her lipstick. She closed the front door behind her and locked it.

Mac had parked his bike and removed his gloves. He stood grinning like the bad boy people always warned you against. His military style hair cut had developed a few dark curls around his neck, a thin scar down his left cheek showed white beneath his dark tan. His patriarchal nose had a bump on one side. Probably broken in a fight, Sara figured.

*Oh yeah, he wasn't a church choirboy.*

What was she doing going to dinner with a stranger who looked like he slept with danger? Excitement scooted along her spine. Her sex life had died almost twenty years ago, but her libido had just received CPR. She hadn't dated anyone except Gordon since her last year in college. She hadn't wanted to, until now. While she had no intention of getting involved, Mac Langston had definitely invaded every cell of her body, raising her temperature to fever levels.

Mac slipped his arm through hers. "Lead the way."

Sara took a deep breath. Feelings of fear mixed with excitement washed over her. At his touch, an image of a jungle, hot and sweaty and Mac crawling through the underbrush flashed through her mind. The danger appeared a little too real. She tried to erase it from her mind. "So what are you doing in Seattle?"

"I'm looking up a brother I haven't seen for years. I'm

not sure where he lives. He's moved since I saw him last. I'm actually lost."

"What? A man who admits he's lost?"

Mac chuckled. "I admit it. I'm going to have to ask for directions."

"Give me the address. I'll see if I can help you."

"I'd appreciate that. It's inside my jacket. I'll dig it out over dinner."

Before she knew it they reached the restaurant. Mr. Agostino ushered them to a corner table. "Ms. Peters, it's so nice to see you, and your friend. Good to have someone to eat with tonight, eh?"

He winked and pulled out a chair for her. "Mama's lasagna is our special tonight. You want some red wine?"

"A bottle of your best," Mac responded. He sat down and took the menu.

Sara stared at the man across from her. What was she doing, sitting here with a stranger; a stranger who radiated violence and had spent time in a jungle?

"So who is Sara Peters and what is she like?"

"She's a widow with two grown children, a boy and a girl, and a dog. She leads a very boring life."

Mr. Agostino poured a glass of wine. Sara took a sip. "Right now my biggest decision is whether to plant spring bulbs."

"That actually sounds nice, and normal." Mac raised his glass. "To normal lives, which are highly underrated."

"So who is Mac Langston and what is he like?" Sara noticed a veil come down over Mac's eyes. He bent his head to take another sip of wine.

"Mac isn't a very interesting topic. Seattle doesn't look like it's changed too much over the last few years."

So the jungle stories were off limits? What else about Mac Langston was off limits? Fair enough. There were things she certainly didn't want to share—like her last twenty years.

"Nope, it's pretty much the same. They built a new football stadium, Quest field. That's about it for recent changes. What's your brother's address?"

"Oh right, thanks for reminding me. I could phone him and ask for directions, but I wanted to surprise him." Mac fumbled through an inside jacket pocket.

Mr. Agostino returned with their orders and topped up their wine glasses.

Sara chewed on the excellent lasagna. She wondered if Mac would leave after they walked home. She didn't even know how to talk to a man anymore. Of course Mac wasn't any man and he didn't want to talk about himself. Dredging into her memory she vaguely remembered that most men liked to talk about themselves, to brag about all their accomplishments, no matter how stupid. Gordon certainly had and she'd simpered, smiled and encouraged it. No more. If he didn't want to talk, fine. They'd eat dinner and she'd never see him again.

Mac found the slip of paper and slid it across the table to Sara.

She finished most of her dinner and shoved the plate to one side. "That's it for me. I'm stuffed."

She picked up the wrinkled paper and squinted at the messy printing.

Agostino removed their plates. "You want anything else?"

Sara shook her head. "Not for me, thanks. Tell Rosa it was delicious."

Agostino grinned. "I tell her. It will make her very happy."

Sara tried to figure out how to give directions to the address in front of her. Another thought crossed her mind. What if he didn't leave after he walked her home and wanted to come in?

Part of her thought of how he made her feel, but the other part wasn't ready for any man, not yet. Hopefully he would he say good night and then they'd never see each other again. Sara wasn't sure she wanted that either.

Mac collapsed into the thread-bare, single chair. One spring in the upholstered cushion stuck out at the side. The basic, economy franchise motel room, had been the first place he'd seen, after leaving Sara Peters at her door. He'd turned in and rented a room because he needed a place to think.

She'd appeared so sad and vulnerable when he'd almost run into her. He'd wanted to make her smile. He'd wanted to protect her.

When he turned his bike around and took her hand he'd felt like he'd been caught in a lightning storm. She'd taken his breath away and given him a hard on at the same time. He didn't want to leave her at the door. He wanted to pick her up and carry her into her bedroom and make love to her all night. It must be because it had been so long since he'd had sex.

Her fresh, floral soapy scent still clung to his memory. He knew her bedroom would be feminine with flowers and smell like daisies, or lilacs.

Normal, he'd told her normal was highly overrated. Was it? Could he ever do normal? Maybe he could with a woman like Sara? Was that what he was searching for? But she'd never understand his work. They wouldn't be able to talk about it, which took him back to square one. What was he going to do with the rest of his life?

Maggie saw the ghost in the corner of the gym. It watched her pound toward her thirty minutes on the treadmill. Most of the time, Maggie didn't see them. She only heard them talk to her. Maybe she'd ignored this one, so she needed to show herself to get Maggie's attention.

She pushed the speed higher, moved up to nine miles per hour. Not bad for a thirty-eight year old woman who was too old for her ex. She could see the faded image of the woman in her thirties. She wore old jeans and a t-shirt. The ghost waited patiently for Maggie to finish her work out.

Maggie debated whether to talk to the woman. Then the guilt seeped through her pores. She'd pay for it for days. She'd feel like pond scum and the woman might keep haunting her. She had to talk to the woman, but Maggie decided to wait until she got outside.

She wiped the sweat off her face and slowed the speed to cool down. She'd had enough problems in her life, and no one to turn to. She couldn't ignore this woman. When she couldn't see them and they just suddenly talked to her she didn't have to think about whether to talk to them.

Half an hour later, after a quick shower, Maggie emerged from the gym into the humid seventies of New Orleans. She didn't mind the humidity, although as a local she spent most of her days inside, in air conditioning. She clicked the key fob and the door of the red, economy car unlocked. The woman appeared beside the door.

"What do you want?" Maggie asked.

The wide, vacant eyes nailed Maggie with their desperation. "Please, tell my brother, Johnny, he's in danger. He always works late. This Friday night, his partner is going to have Johnny shot when he walks to his car."

"Your brother won't believe me."

"He will if you tell him Larry, his partner, killed me because I was a silent partner. Larry wants the real estate business for himself. Johnny has insurance that goes to the company. Tell him if he's not careful I'll come back and tickle his feet until he believes me."

"Tickle him?"

The woman nodded.

"Johnny's last name and where do I find him." Maggie pulled a notepad out of her gym bag. She wrote down the address the woman gave her. "I'll tell him. That bit about tickling should convince him."

"Thank you." The woman faded into the darkness.

Maggie climbed into her car. Hearing ghosts could be a nuisance sometimes. Often the people she gave messages to didn't believe her, or got angry. Usually she sent anonymous messages about where to find the bank safety deposit box, or similar messages if she felt the wife or mother of the deceased needed to know. A message like 'you're going to be shot' was going to be a little trickier. It was a good thing she had developed a thick skin.

She drove toward the French Quarter, stopped at the corner store to pick up red beans and olive oil. She'd make red beans and rice tonight. It would last for a few meals.

A ghost passed by her, stopped and stared at her, before moving on. Sara reached her car. A second ghost in the same day was unusual. She could count on one hand the number of ghosts she's actually seen in the last few months. Something about this ghost seemed vaguely familiar. She reached for the door handle.

"I can't do it. I have to tell you." The ghost stood beside her.

Maggie shifted the bag of groceries to her other hip. "Excuse me, do I know you?"

"I was your husband's lawyer. I died a few months ago, massive heart attack."

"I'm sorry."

"Thank you, but I can't move on. I'm stuck here because of all the terrible things I did as a lawyer. I'm trying for redemption. In your case, your husband hid most of his money in off shore accounts and hidden assets. If you've got a pen and paper I'll tell you how to access them and give you some of the codes."

Maggie stared at him, her mouth hung open.

"Are you going to write the information down?"

"Uh, yeah…" Maggie placed the groceries on the hood of her car and dug into her bag for paper and pen.

The lawyer spelled the name of the financial institutions. Then he gave her codes to access them and codes for off shore accounts. Maggie scribbled frantically. She hoped she'd be able to decipher the information later.

"Thanks." She raised her head, but he had disappeared.

Maggie stared at the notes she'd scrawled. She'd known Doug had more money than he'd admitted, but hadn't been able to prove it. The bastard, it was bad enough he'd left her for a younger woman, but he kept his job, got a young woman and kept all the money.

Her mind spun in several directions. Her record with men was a failure. She sure knew how to pick them. They treated her like dirt and she allowed it. She stayed until they kicked her out. Doug had left her for a young, airhead. But Maggie had continued to work in the same bank as he did. She didn't even have the guts to tell him off and walk out. She probably could have a gotten a job at another bank. Why hadn't she done that? Instead she'd stayed, let him put her down, watched him with his blonde and then he'd laughed and fired her.

She'd turned into a doormat. She didn't respect herself. She didn't think she was worthy of anything better. How had she sunk that low?

Maybe now she could stand up and even the odds. She knew how bank accounts worked. Maggie pulled into her parking spot. She grabbed the bag of groceries and climbed the stairs to her second floor condo in an old house in the Quarter. Inside she placed the groceries on her counter and immediately fired up her computer. She took out the piece of paper and started to punch in names and numbers. Accounts opened in front of her. Her eyes widened. She couldn't believe how much money he'd moved off shore.

Where had he got all that money? Was he embezzling? That bastard had made sure she didn't get anything in the divorce.

She needed to get her self-respect back. She'd work on it. She needed to find an expert to help her figure out where the money came from, and then how to get the money out of his accounts and into hers. And it needed to be done without Doug figuring it out until everything was completed.

How would she find someone who could help her, and do it so Doug couldn't come after her? If he ever found out, he'd kill her.

# Chapter Eight

Carly sat with the four volunteer folders in front of her. She'd read them all and penciled in a few questions. Julie and Nadia strolled into together. They carried large coffee mugs.

"Sorry if we're late. Cindy, the barista in the coffee place down the street, it's her birthday and she insisted we have a piece of her cake." Julie grinned.

"So did you bring me a piece?"

"Sorry Carly, we thought you might be on a diet." Nadia shrugged.

"Bitches! You did that deliberately. I'll get you later." Carly laughed. "Fine, I hope you enjoyed every crumb and I am on a diet. Let's get down to our next team of volunteers. I assume you've both reviewed them, over cake?"

Still grinning, the other two women slipped into their chairs, dabbed at the last few crumbs on their lips and picked up their folders.

"I did the initial screening and interviews, but I've gone through them again. They all look ready. It's the first team we've had where they all had a paranormal talent. They're also older than our usual recruits, but I don't think that will be a problem. Our trainers are older. The new recruits all have a history of being vulnerable women and want to help other women out of similar situations. I'll be interested to see how it turns out, too and whether the age makes any difference and their paranormal talents add much of an advantage to the team." Nadia commented.

"It could add a definite twist to the team. And it could give them some validation for those talents most people don't believe. I can't wait to see how it plays out." Julie said.

"I agree." Carly added. "I'm planning to add an additional two weeks to cover the paranormal training. We'll bring Mr. Mogee in for two hours of work per day, and rearrange the rest of the schedule."

A twitch played with Nadia's lips. "I haven't seen old Mogee in ages. I didn't know he was still around."

"Oh yeah, he's still around. He hasn't changed. He still shows up when needed." Carly grinned and opened the first folder. "Okay, Sara Peters from Seattle; she passed all the tests and her interview. She's forty-one. She's fluent in Spanish, although she hasn't had a chance to use it for years, which could be a benefit. She hesitated when asked if she could kill someone if she had to, but after she thought about it she said she could if a woman's life was at stake. She's a sensitive, with psychometric talents, but her husband threatened to commit her if she ever mentioned it, so it's been sublimated for many years and needs some work. Any concerns?"

Julie and Nadia shook their heads.

"Good, then she's approved. Nadia, can you contact her and get her ready for the next training session?"

Julie made a note in a small spiral notebook. "She did ask to bring her dog. Are we okay with that?"

"It's a first, but I don't see why not. We're open to firsts. Maybe a dog could be part of a team." Carly inclined her head at her sleeping mutt in the corner. "Gwen, our Krav Maga trainer is a dog lover and has experience training police dogs. We'll check and see if she's willing to take on an extra task. If she is, we'll see how it works. Okay, next is Lydia Chapman from Miami. She's in her early forties, the oldest member of the team and the least fit. Her husband is a medical doctor. He's been cheating on his wife for years. She's aware of some of it but she stays for prestige. He wants a divorce, but with his ambitions to run for political office he can't afford the scandal if she ever decided to say anything about his affairs. Besides, it's her money. I understand he's looking for a hit man to take her out."

"Yes, he's been asking around. Makes you feel all warm and fuzzy when the husband wants to take out his wife with a hit man." Julia said.

"She passed all the tests and didn't hesitate in the interview. If she's off training the husband can't get to her and she'll be better prepared when she goes home. Otherwise we're going to have to make her a victim and plan to save her. We'll also inform her about his intentions. She has a telekinetic talent that needs work. She also speaks French, Spanish and some German. We can re-evaluate her home situation before she leaves camp. Anyone have any problems with her?" Carly asked.

"Nope, I think she's going to be a definite asset," Julie responded.

"Good. She's approved. Next one is Maggie Shore from New Orleans. Nadia, you've been following Maggie and interviewed her, any thoughts?"

"I think she's ready. When her cheating husband left her for a younger woman she had a lot of buried emotions. She had poor self-image, low self-esteem and little confidence. She's improving, I think our training will help her work through a lot of it. Sara might be a role model for her. She took on a guy with a knife in her past and she speaks a smattering of French. Maggie talks to ghosts, which could be really helpful in some missions."

"Okay, Maggie—approved, unless you have any concerns Julie."

Julie shook her head.

"Last one is Diane Whiteside, from Washington. Diane is interesting. She's losing her job as a private investigator because she's female and she's getting older. She's angry about it. She doesn't admit to any paranormal talents just gut reactions, but she is a witch. That could be an interesting combination. With the other members of the team and Mr. Mogee, we'll see how her powers and spells work. I think she could be a valuable asset on a mission. During her interview she spent a lot of time referring to what is legal and what is right. Is that going to be a problem?" Carly looked first at Julie and then Nadia.

"I don't think so. I think she's had to fight to make it in a man's world for so long she's still keeping up the façade. Once she bonds with the others on her team she should be all right. We can always wash her out if it looks like she's not fitting in with the team." Nadia replied.

"Agreed?" Carly asked. "But we have to make sure she doesn't tell anyone about the training."

"I don't think that will be a problem," Julie responded. "She'll want to protect the other women even if she can't do it herself. And if we had to, we have a drug and the use of hypnosis which should erase any memory of her experience. We've never had to use it, but it's supposed to work."

"Good. Ladies, we have out next team of four volunteers, plus a dog. I'll let Mac know. I'll warn him we'll be sending Mr. Mogee up for the training and it will take ten weeks instead of eight. Mac can reschedule the classes. It shouldn't be a problem for the trainers. We'll send them to some place exotic for an extra two weeks. Nadia, could you please contact the volunteers and help get them ready for the training? Have them all meet at the airport in our private lounge. You and I can fly them up on the private jet. You can introduce them to Mac and the trainers. I'll stay out of sight." Carly closed the last folder. "We'll need to keep a close eye on this group. It's a first in many areas. After the past events and close calls, I want to keep an even lower profile. This team could be valuable in cases where we need to check out our resources and sources to make sure their legit."

"Good idea," Julie closed her folder.

"I hope they'll pick up anything that looks like a plot to get us. I'm considering we might be able to use them at an occasional fundraiser to check out our contributors and see if they can spot any problems. Sara in particular might be valuable at the fund raisers. We could use them one or two at a time at the events, and rotate them, so people don't think of seeing a group of four. I'd want to think about whether that might add a risk to The Foundation. Is there anything else?"

Julie and Nadia shook their heads.

"Then let's get back to work. We've got a lot to do in the next few weeks. I need to work on who is trying to take over CCB enterprises and I'm still checking on the lists of The Foundation's contacts. I've come up with about a dozen contacts in Iran that we won't be using again. I want to make sure I get them all before I say anything. I also want to get one of our contacts to talk to them and see whether they were paid more or threatened."

The jet landed. Nadia descended followed by four women and a dog.

Mac squinted at the dog. Damned if he didn't recognize that specific animal. Of course all golden retrievers looked alike so he had to be wrong. His imagination was playing tricks on him again. He pulled The Foundation ball cap down over his recently cut hair before he strode forward to meet the new recruits. The rest of his training team were already lined up and waiting in the dining room.

Mac slid into place at the same time Nadia's elegant foot hit the ground.

*Damn place was going to the dogs.* Mac saluted. "Ms. Nassif."

Nadia extended a manicured hand. "Director Langston, these are your trainees. Ladies, step forward and form a line."

The four women proceed down the steps and fell into a straight line at the bottom. Mac strode forward to meet them. His heart pounded erratically when he stood in front of recruit Sara Peters. Heat shot through his groin area. He remembered all the feelings he'd felt when they first met, and all the erotic dreams he'd had since.

She stood erect in her jeans and a t-shirt that emphasized her luscious curves and slim hips. She'd lost a few pounds since he'd seen her, but she still look like the woman he wanted to get into his bed. *What the hell was she doing here?*

"This is Ms. Peters and her dog, Gloria. I believe you were told about the dog." Nadia introduced them.

"Miss Peters." Mac touched the brim of his cap. He wanted to grab her and kiss those perky, pink lips. He'd been thinking about her very day since they'd met. Now she shows up here. They would work close together for ten weeks. He didn't know how to handle it. He had to keep it professional, but this would be the most difficult assignment he'd ever had. He bent and patted the dog. "Yes, I was told and I understand Gwen is going to do the training."

Gloria wagged her tail enthusiastically.

"Excellent." Nadia moved down the line and introduced each of the members of the team.

Mac followed her. He acknowledged each woman, but his mind stayed on Sara. He'd refrained from touching her because he knew how his body would react. Look what the hell it was doing when he hadn't touched her.

After introductions, Nadia lead the way to the cafeteria for the recruits to meet the training staff and get a formal introduction to the training schedule and the expectations.

In the cafeteria a row of seats spread across the front of the room. The four instructors took their seats, observed the new recruits and assessed them. Nadia sat the recruits at the first table in the front of the room. An introductory packet with each woman's name on the envelope acted as a place card. The envelope contained a copy of the daily schedule and a description of each course, plus a bio of the specific instructor. Their assigned living quarters and roommates, was also listed.

Sara pulled the sheets from her envelope.

She ran down the list of the staff. Numero Uno, Director Mac Langston, ran the whole damn camp, taught shooting and driving. Driving?

The man she'd thought was a bad boy turned out to be a special ops bad boy working for The Foundation. She'd dreamed about him for the last two months and he now would be one of her instructors. How the hell had this happened and how was she going to manage a strictly professional attitude for ten weeks, when she wanted to find out how he was in her bed?

Sara ran both her hands through her hair. She stared at the people who sat across the front. Mac sat ramrod stiff and stared straight ahead. She did want to experience him. She might survive the training, but she didn't think her body could survive without sex with that man. She'd managed after that first night because she thought she'd never see him again. Besides, she thought he was younger than her. He wouldn't be interested in an older woman.

Nadia stood beside Mac and introduced him. "You met Director Langston when you landed. He's your boss for the next ten weeks. Any questions or problems take them to the Director. Now he'll introduce the rest of his staff." Nadia slipped into a seat at the end of the table.

Sara tried to take her mind off the Texas wide body with the six pack abs she was sure existed underneath and focus on the other trainees. On the flight up together they'd a chance to introduce themselves and find out a little about each other. The other three women appeared nice enough. They all had the same goal, to help other women.

Maggie appeared a little shell-shocked by her husband's desertion, but who could blame her. Men were such scum. Maggie stared at the package of information, not making eye contact with anyone.

Lydia's designer casual jeans and top were haute couture and cost Sara's monthly income, but she seemed nice and had been chatty during the flight. Apparently her husband had political aspirations and wanted her help, mostly her money. Sara hadn't quite figured out why Lydia had joined The Foundation.

Then there was Diane. She appeared the most defensive of the group. Her anger spilled over anytime she mentioned being fired from her job because she turned thirty nine. Her jerk boss had decided she couldn't do the job any longer and replaced her with a twenty-one year old bimbo. Sara could understand the anger, too. She hoped the training would help Diane work through her issues.

"Are there any questions, ladies?"

Sara pulled her attention back to the cafeteria. Nadia looked in her direction. Somehow she'd missed most of the instructor introductions. Good thing she had the bio sheet. She could put names and faces together.

"There are two people in each yurt?" Diane asked.

"Yes. Hopefully that won't be a problem. We want you to get to know your team members so when you work together there are no surprises. You'll rotate at the end of each month and get a new partner. Is there anything else?" Nadia responded.

Sara raised her hand. "There's a course called PI by a Mr. Mogee. What is that?"

Nadia smiled. "PI stands for paranormal investigations. You ladies all have special talents. We want to make sure you will use them for our advantage, as well as yours. You'll see by the bio, Mr. Mogee is a specialist in that area. He hasn't arrived yet."

They knew about her psychometric skills, which were really underdeveloped. What talents did the other women have? Sara wondered.

She glanced at Mac. He met her gaze. Damn he was sexy.

"Okay ladies, find your living quarters and explore the area for the next hour. We'll meet back here for lunch. After that I'm out of here and you're officially in training." Nadia stood up.

Sara pulled herself to her feet and followed people to the door. "Where are we going?"

Lydia turned toward her. "We're heading to our assigned yurt, honey, to unpack and get acquainted with our roomie before we meet for lunch. Weren't you paying attention?"

"I guess my mind drifted off for a second." She glanced at her assigned yurt. "I'm in yurt number twelve, whatever that is."

Lydia grinned. "So am I…roomie."

She looped her arm through Sara's. "Let's go check it out and get settled in."

"I hope you don't mind dogs."

"No, I'm an animal lover. What's her name?" Lydia patted Gloria.

"Gloria. I named her after an imaginary friend I had as a child. For the last eight years she's been the only friend I've had."

"You're one up on me." Lydia responded. "Maybe I should get me a dog. Here we are, honey." She bent down, opened the door of a large yurt and held it back for Sara and Gloria. Gloria charged ahead sniffing the area, tail wagging.

The small bags they'd been told to bring with them had been delivered to the room, one beside each of the single cots. A small closet stood on each side of the two beds, with a drawer at the bottom. A narrow counter contained a small boat-size sink. A cupboard above the counter covered the space at the end wall by the door. A single table with two chairs and a small frig completed the contents of the room.

"Very cozy," Sara commented. "This is not going to be an easy ten weeks."

"You're right. I'm beginning to questions why I signed on for this. At the time it seemed like a good idea. Why did you come?"

Sara paused. "They said we'd be helping other women. If my husband hadn't died I'd probably be one of those women you might be helping. I'd like to help other women lead a more productive life. What about you?"

"My husband is still alive, sleeping with anything under twenty five years of age. Occasionally I think he's probably committed statutory rape. The bastard is now goin' to run for political office."

"But you're still living with him?" Sara asked.

"Up until now I didn't have any place to go. I have no friends, just garden club acquaintances. If I try to leave now, he'll probably have me killed. He can't take any scandal if he wants to win an election, plus all of our money is mine." Lydia opened her bag and began to hang up her expensive, if limited, wardrobe. "That's why he married me, for my money. Too bad I didn't figure it out sooner."

"Gloria, down," Sara made a hand signal and the dog flopped down beside the bed. Sara unzipped her sports bag and took out the basic white cotton underwear The Foundation had required.

After she hung up her clothes Lydia sat carefully on the cot. "I found out, when I had my interview, that the bastard is actually trying to find a hit man to take me out, and make it look like an accident."

"Oh, Lydia, that's awful."

"Thinking he might consider it is one thing. Knowing he is trying to get you killed is a real gut punch. That's one of the reasons I volunteered. I need to protect myself and maybe, get some help from The Foundation. I also need to change my will, but that may have to wait until after training."

"I'm sure, since they know about him this is probably part of their plan to protect you. He can't get to you here and by the time you return home they'll make sure there's a plan in place to protect you."

"Honey, I sure hope so, because I really am scared."

Sara wrapped her arms around the tall, blonde and hugged. "Don't forget, when you leave here, you'll also have a team on your side."

"Ladies, lunch in the cafeteria in ten minutes." A uniformed staff person popped her head in the door.

"Thanks, Sara. I feel better." Lydia closed the closet door. "Don't tell anyone else, okay?"

"My lips are sealed." Sara made a zipper motion across her lips. "It won't take long for me to finish unpacking. Maybe we'll find more out about our training after lunch. I wonder what the foods like here."

"I'm sure it won't be gourmet, but healthy and edible. The paranormal class might be interesting."

"You have a paranormal talent?" Sara pulled out jeans and sweatpants and hung them in the tiny closet.

Lydia shrugged. "I'm not sure that it's a talent. If I concentrate hard I can make objects move."

"Really? Wow! That's very cool."

"Not unless you're using it for parlor tricks. It'll be interesting to see what the professor makes of it. What about you?"

Sara hesitated. She still remembered Gordon's threats. "I can read things about people when I touch them. I can also get readings or visions from papers and photographs. Sometimes I see ghosts."

"Now that is interesting? What can you tell about me?" Lydia put out her hand.

Sara didn't move. "It doesn't always work. I touch lots of people and don't get anything."

"That's okay. I'm not very interesting anyway, very superficial. Come on."

Sara hesitated before she touched Lydia's hand. If there was something hidden there she didn't want to know. She gently picked it up and held it for a second. "There's nothing, sorry."

When she pulled her hand away Sara got a flash of a woman crying over a very small body in some place cold and sterile.

"Well?"

Sara shook her head.

"I know you saw something. I saw your face change."

"Please, I don't want to…"

Lydia froze. "You didn't? You couldn't have."

"I saw you crying over a small body, probably a child."

"Well, I'll be… You do have a talent. No one knows about that, no one. Come on, we'd better get going."

"I'm sorry." Sara checked her bag then zipped it and shoved it under the bed.

"Not your fault. I insisted. I should know better at my age."

"I need to fill up the dog bowl with water for Gloria." The water sloshed over as she placed it on the floor. "Okay girl, there's your water. Now you stay. I'll be back shortly. Okay, let's go."

Sara stood up and brushed a few drops of water off her jeans. "They asked if I could kill someone if it was to protect a woman. Did they ask you that?" Sara asked. They sauntered toward the cafeteria.

"Yes, they did." Lydia replied.

"Do you think we might have to?"

Lydia shrugged. "I don't know. I hope not."

"Could you do it?"

"Could you?"

Sara contemplated the question. She'd said she could. She thought of Gordon and how his death had finally brought her freedom. If it came right down to it, to help another woman escape whatever abuser she suffered, could she take another person's life?

"I don't know. I guess it would depend on whether someone's life depended on it."

"If she was being physically abused and it was escalating?" Lydia pushed.

Sara frowned. *Could she?*

"Or if someone was going to kill your child?" Lydia persisted.

"I'd kill him in an instant."

The helo approached the city of Mashhad, Iran. Descending darkness helped to avoid being seen as the helo dropped toward the ground. A small plane waited at the end of the runway, in the far corner. When the helo touched the ground lights flashed on from a building farther down the runway. Assif and Sabhita jumped out and turned to help Marley, and then Nooria out of the helo.

Nooria stared at the small plane in front of them. She shook her head.

Down the runway engines cut through the darkness. Vehicles started up, headlights snapped on. Marley grabbed Nooria's arm and started to pull. Wendy stepped up on the other side. She grabbed the other arm and hurried Nooria along. Marley tried to hurry but her limp slowed her down.

Motorcycles roared down the runway.

The small plane fired its' engines. Wendy jumped inside. Assif and Marley shoved Nooria up the steps. Wendy pulled her inside. Sabhita pushed up Marley and clambered up beside her.

The plane began to taxi down the runway.

Voices yelled. Guns flashed.

Assif pushed Nooria into a seat, clicked the seatbelt and slid in beside her. She began to explain to Nooria what was happening in Arabic.

Sabhita and Marley collapsed in seats and buckled up as the plane took off.

Wendy gave thumbs up from her seat. "We made it. One more step to go." She motioned to the bags beside her and the others in the baggage compartments. "We've got our disguises and everything we need for our next step.

Exhaustion settled over Marley. "I think I'm going to pass out again."

"Nope, not this time, but you can take a quick nap." Sabhita turned to her. "Is the pain bad?"

Marley shook her head. "No, but I'm so tired."

"Being shot kinda saps your energy." Wendy unbuckled her seatbelt, stood up and grabbed a blanket from the overhead compartment. She tucked it around Marley. "Go to sleep. I'll wake you before we land. We change at our next stop. We're also going to have to convince Nooria to change into whatever they've sent for her."

Marley closed her eyes, her voice drifted off. "She won't go for it. She wears a veil, for heaven's sake."

The plane leveled off. Wendy began to open the bags and boxes. "You won't believe this?" She laughed.

"What?" Sabhita asked.

"You won't believe what they've made Nooria?" Wendy held up the new US passport.

Assif frowned. "What? I don't get it."

"They've made her a nun, a nun who has taken the vow of silence. Assif, you're her novitiate, who will talk for her." Sabhita chuckled.

Everyone burst out laughing, except Marley, who slept

soundly. The other three looked at each other and start to laugh all over again.

Nooria stared at them, eyes wide.

"You will need to change clothing, but you will be wearing the costume of a nun and you will not need to speak." Assif translated to Nooria.

Nooria nodded.

After several minutes the laughter subsided. It faded to a few more chuckles.

The women started to sort the clothing change and the documents. They read the arrangements detailed in a cover letter.

"We're headed for Vienna and then a flight on a commercial airline home." Wendy announced.

"That sounds good to me. I can't wait to get home. I'm going to sleep for a week. So who am I?" Sabhita asked.

"Looks like you and Marley are archeologists, returning from a dig. I'm a tourist." Wendy shrugged. "But at least I'm a wealthy tourist. We get into Austria early. We'll have time to change at a local motel."

Sabhita moved across to Nooria. "I know this is hard, but it will work for you, eventually. You will be able to see how your children grow. Please, trust us. We only want what is best for women. We will protect you, and we will protect what is important to you in your religion."

Nooria looked at Sabhita. "I will be living in the United States?"

"Yes. Unless there is somewhere else you would prefer."

Nooria shook her head. "I am confused. I don't know…"

"It's okay. After we get to New York, we'll talk."

Nooria nodded.

"Okay everyone, we can relax or nap until we get to our next destination. Marley's asleep. Don't wake her up." Sabhita settled down into her sleep.

Wendy closed up the bags. "I hope the nun with a vow of silence works with customs?"

Assif and Sabhita glanced at each other.

"It better or we're all in deep trouble." Sabhita tried not to think what might happen to all of them if Nooria was discovered.

He read each page carefully. There were six strong possibilities for organizations that could be involved in helping women. Two of them were in Europe and four in the United States. In the United States one was in California, one in Texas, one in Nevada and one in New York.

Now he had some definite information he could do more research. He could check the people in charge, the head of the organizations and maybe get financial statements. Armed with a little more information he'd see what areas the organizations might need help. He'd find people with appropriate qualifications and infiltrate the organizations.

He could research from the outside, but he needed inside information. A few carefully placed bugs, maybe a video camera, someone on the inside who could watch and listen. One of his contacts in the Mafia might know a few people when it came to the next step. He hesitated to call them. Someone might remember Bobby Mac.

Excitement shot through his body. He knew the trail was finally getting warmer. It might take months yet, but he had learned patience a long time ago. When he was a child he'd learned to sit quietly, watch everything and never ask for anything. Eventually he'd learned how to take what he wanted, and no one realized it. He'd been a numbers runner by the age of nine and part of the Mafia before he hit his teens. He'd killed at the age of thirteen and never looked back.

He would find who took his wife, find her and she'd pay for leaving him.

# Chapter Nine

The four women crowded into Lydia and Sara's yurt after dinner. Gloria made the rounds to get patted and then curled up under Sara's bed and went to sleep. She'd had a long day.

Lydia had invited everyone over since they were going to be a team and training started in the morning. She opened a bottle of Chablis she'd managed to get chilled.

"We need to get to know each other a little. We talked on the plane, but more about where we were going and what it would be like here. Since we're going to be a team, I know I'd like to know a little about whom I'm working with and why you're here."

"Good idea." Maggie said.

"I'd like to learn a little more about the rest of you." Sara replied.

Diane shrugged.

"With all that enthusiasm I'll go first. Lydia Chapman from South Beach, Florida, socialite. I'm being generous there. Although I actually have an unused law degree and speak three languages. I'm married to Harry Chapman, a doctor. He specializes in dermatology so he has time to play golf and cheat on his wife."

At the shocked look on the other three faces Lydia continued. "That's right. He cheats on me with anything under the age of twenty-five. I know about it and put up with it because I like being a doctor's wife and the status it gives me, socially. At least I used to like it. He's now going to run for political office. Who wants to go next? Oh, wait, I've been told he's taken a contract out on me. He's hired someone to kill me and make it look like an accident. Honey, it's your turn." With an artificial smile plastered to her face, Lydia turned to Maggie.

Maggie exhaled. "Oh sure, I get to follow that. What languages do you speak?"

"Spanish, French and a little German, I use them when I travel."

Maggie shook her head. "I speak a little French but that's it. And your husband hired contract killer to take you out for your money, that's almost unbelievable. I'm sorry. Let's see, I'm Maggie Shore from New Orleans. I'm divorced with no children. My husband also cheated on me, frequently. One of the blonde bimbos convinced him to marry her, so he dumped me. He managed to hide all his money and got everything but the house in the settlement. Ii was mortgaged to the hilt. He also got me fired because I worked in the same bank as he did. He didn't want me around to remind him what a slimy snake he'd been. He hasn't hired a hit man to take me out, yet, but I'd put a contract out on him in a heartbeat if I knew how to do it and had the money. I'd take out that bimbo too, but since he got the money, I've been doing a little computer work at home to cover food and utilities. I needed to get a job and this showed up. Oh and his lawyer died and couldn't cross over until he told me the truth about where Doug hid all his money. I know where it is, but I can't get to it. Next?"

Sara waved her hand. "Wow, I can't believe what we've all gone through or are going through. It sounds like we've all managed to get involved with despicable men. No wonder we jumped at the chance to save other women from them. I'm Sara Peters, from Seattle. I almost got my Bachelor in Business Administration and I'm fluent in Spanish. My mother was Spanish. My husband emotionally abused me and isolated me from all family and friends. He turned me into a pathetic, abused wife, unable to make a decision. I spent nineteen years living in fear, without money, family or friends. I did everything he told me to do and believed I was a useless drain on society.

I got lucky two years ago, when he died young, of a heart attack. I've been fighting to regain my confidence ever since. When I went through his off limits home office to find out about lawyers, banks, etc. I found letters and pictures from several different girlfriends. He'd been cheating on me for years. I have two children, a boy and a girl. I'm ashamed of the role model I portrayed for them. I don't know how I'll ever make it up to them, but I will try. Oh, and I can see things when I touch people and sometimes photos."

Diane slumped in the corner.

"Oh come on, honey, it can't be that bad. We've all shared our most embarrassing secrets." Lydia cajoled Diane.

Diane shrugged but didn't make eye contact with anyone. "I'm Diane Whiteside, from Washington, DC. I'm not married, well I was for about six weeks when I was twenty one, but he was a total jerk. He thought I had money and would be his 'mommy'. I left and got a divorce. I don't speak any languages, a few words in Spanish and French. I'm a private investigator, or was, I got fired because I was too old. He wanted one of those enhanced, bleached-blonde airheads. I was looking for another job when I was approached about The Foundation. I jumped at the offer. My boss had given me a month's notice. He wanted me to train Bootsie. I swear that is her name. I got to walk in and say I quit, clean out my desk and ten minutes later walk out on that creep. It felt so good. He stood there with his mouth hanging open. I heard him splutter something about training Bootsie, but I kept walking. That had to be the best damn feeling I've had for a long time."

Lydia filled everyone's glasses. "It's beginning to sound like ninety percent of the men out there are liars, cheats and general all round disgusting individuals. I'd say we need to drink a toast to all the women we're going to save from that ninety percent."

"Hear, hear." Maggie raised her glass.

"It sounds like we all have a lot of hostility we're carrying with us. I wonder if that's good or bad." Sara raised her glass.

"A good dose of anger is always good. It gets the juices flowing. To us," Diane clinked her glass to the other three.

"I think we're going to make one heck of a team." Maggie took a drink.

"Ladies, you need to head for your own yurts. Lights are out in fifteen minutes." Sergeant Bush poked her head through the door.

"I guess that's us. Better not get a penalty the first night. See you guys in the morning, in those cute uniforms we get to wear." Diane and Maggie scampered out the door, after the Sergeant.

Sara stared after them. She wondered how men managed to screw up the lives of so many women and never pay any price for it. Maybe now they would.

Marley woke when Wendy gently shook her.

The small plane cruised to a stop on a private airfield, thirty miles outside of Vienna. Marley could see the dark limo parked beside the runway.

"Okay, everybody, we're on our last leg." Sabhita unbuckled her seat belt and stood up. "It's early in the morning and still dark. Our flight doesn't leave until almost noon, so the limo will take us to a small motel that's been pre-booked. We can shower, change, grab coffee and breakfast and check our documentation."

"Oh, coffee and a shower, that sounds good." Wendy rotated her shoulders. "What—about twenty more hours and we're home?"

"About that, I think. I don't know about anyone else, but I'm planning to sleep as soon as I get on that commercial flight." Sabhita responded.

"That works for me, too." Marley stretched. "I'm still exhausted."

She turned to Nooria and translated what everyone had said.

The women gathered the bags, descended the plane and hurried across to the limo. Assif, bags in one hand, held Nooria's hand. Marley grabbed a bunch of bags. Wendy moved up beside her to act as a crutch.

A woman slid out from behind the wheel and opened three of the limo doors. "Welcome, ladies."

She stepped forward, took a bag from Assif and stowed it in the trunk. Once all the bags were loaded and everyone had climbed inside she shut all the doors and slid back into the driver's seat. Seconds later the limo slipped through the dark night.

At the motel, with cups of coffee and croissants in hand they opened the bags and handed out the clothing changes.

Marley took Nooria into the bathroom for privacy. She checked to make sure there was no way to escape. She handed Nooria the nun's costume. "If you need help with any part of the costume you ask and one of us will help you."

Marley closed the door and joined the bedlam in the other room as everyone pulled off their clothing. They pulled out various pieces of clothing from the bags, joked and laughed.

A colorful top in pink silk; a brown t-shirt; designer pants and durable cotton ones were passed about as everyone dressed for their new personas. While they prepared for the trip to New York, Marley sobered. She worried about customs, especially with Nooria.

It was several hours later, in the bright sunny June morning, everyone piled back into the limo in their new clothes. It drove through the crowded streets to Schwechat airport, eleven miles southeast of central Vienna and pulled up in front of the International departure terminal. The driver whipped out and hastened to open the doors for the women.

They disembarked into the hustle and bustle of the busiest airport in Vienna. The hordes of people immediately absorbed them into the colorful and noisy stream. Various languages and dialects reached their ears as people shouted for taxis and porters offered to help with luggage.

"We need to travel separately." Sabhita reminded everyone.

They collected their small, soft-sided overnight bags from the trunk. Wendy grabbed her bag. "See you guys in New York." Wearing bright red DKNY pants with matching red heels and a pink silk blouse, she threw her jacket over her arm, strode into the airport, her Prada sunglasses perched on her head and disappeared through the door.

"We'll go next." Assif took Nooria's arm.

Dressed as a nun, Nooria looked comfortable in the outfit. The only thing missing was her veil. She kept her head down and covered her lower face with her hand. She had a death grip on Assif's arm. Assif picked up two small bags, moved slowly toward the door and whispered something to Nooria. They disappeared inside.

"I hope that outfit and vow of silence works," Marley mumbled to Sabhita. "She must be terrified. Everything is moving so fast. We didn't have time to work with her."

"It will work. Don't worry. If it wasn't for you, she'd be dead by now." Sabhita patted Marley's arm. "Now we have to get you through customs. How's the leg doing?"

"It hurts like hell, but I took pain killers so I should be able to get through customs before the drugs start to wear off."

An armed guard strode by, checking passengers as they exited the vehicles.

Marley froze. Her stomach did a Ferris wheel spin.

"It's okay, breathe. They have no idea who we are, or even where we are. Her husband's not looking for us. As long as they don't put us together as a team, we're fine. He will eventually have many of the major airports checked, but they won't find us."

"You're right of course. The guard barely glanced at us." Marley let out the breath she was holding.

"In khaki pants and jackets, t-shirts and runners, we look like normal American archeologists. Come on, let's get our boarding passes and get through customs. Once the plane takes off we can all relax."

An hour later they'd cleared customs and sat in the boarding area.

Assif and Nooria huddled in a far corner. Nooria kept her head down, Assif talked to her.

Wendy chatted with a well-dressed man in his forties. She laughed and smiled up at him.

Marley found seats close to the gate to the plane. "Looks like Wendy found herself a man for the trip."

"It will make the trip more interesting. Me—I'm sleeping." Sabhita replied. "I wonder what Nooria knows that almost got her killed?"

"Don't know, but it had to be serious. She accepted that she was going to die." Marley stretched out her leg. "Maybe it has something to do with National defense, or an assassination plot? We may never know. Do they usually check passengers in the departure lounge?"

Sabhita turned to follow Marley's gaze. A guard wandered through the crowed area. He paused in front of Nooria.

Marley held her breath. She reached toward her boot. Sabhita put a hand on her arm. Neither one of them breathed.

He moved on.

They exhaled slowly. Sabhita frowned. "Do you think he suspects anything?"

Marley shook her head. "We need to plan a diversion in case he comes back, or comes back with more guards. I could scream and fake a seizure."

"Let's hope we don't need to do that. They're starting to board. Give us ten more minutes and she should be onboard." Sabhita stood and moved forward so she could intercept anyone approaching Nooria.

Amy sat across from the gorgeous man who had invited her out to dinner in this very expensive restaurant.

She glanced down self-consciously at her plain black cotton skirt and short-sleeved gray blouse. She wished she'd had something nicer to wear.

"Don't worry, Amy. You look fine. We'll go shopping so next time you won't feel out of place." Phillip smiled across at her.

"To a special lady and a special relationship." He raised his wine glass.

Amy picked up her glass and clinked against his. A few drops of red wine spilled over the edge.

"Oh, I'm sorry." She put her glass down and grabbed a napkin. She dipped it in her water glass and dabbed at the stains.

Phillip reached across and took her hand. "Don't worry about it. They change the tablecloth after every customer anyway. Relax. Now take a sip of wine and tell me what you'd like to eat."

"I don't know. You pick. I'm sure you're much better than I am at choosing." Amy offered a tentative smile.

"Of course, is there anything you don't like or are allergic to?"

Amy shook her head. Her stomach was clenched so tightly she didn't know if she could even eat. Here she was, in a fancy restaurant, with a tall, dark and handsome man, looking well-dressed in a sharp gray suit with a red tie and matching hankie in pocket to match. She couldn't believe he'd asked her out.

After this disaster she knew he'd never want to see her again.

Phillip ordered shrimp cocktails and T-bone steak with a baked potato. He turned back to Amy and took her hands in his.

"I'm so glad you agreed to have dinner with me. I was afraid you might not accept my invitation."

"Oh no, I wanted to go out with you." Amy blurted out.

Phillip smiled. "You're so sweet. Tell me about your family."

"Uh, my father's dead. He died of a heart attack two years ago. My mother lives in Seattle."

"She lives alone?"

Amy nodded.

"That must be very lonely for her. You should invite her for a visit. I'd love to meet her."

"Really?" Amy felt her cheeks flush at the thought of seeing Phillip again, and he was interested in meeting her family. She couldn't believe he really liked her. "She's away right now, taking some training, but I'll invite her when she gets back."

"Excellent. I look forward to meeting the woman who raised such a beautiful daughter."

Amy giggled. She put her hands to her cheeks, unable to think of a thing to say.

"More wine?" Phillip topped her glass first and then filled his own. "Let's drink to many more memorable evenings. Are you busy this Saturday?"

Amy shook her head. He'd asked her out again. She took a long drink of wine.

"Excellent. My business is closed on Saturday. We could have an early dinner and take in a movie."

"That sounds nice." Amy took another sip of wine. "What kind of business is it?"

"It's import, export, nothing you'd understand. It's not relative to you."

"Of course" She'd have to write her mother and tell her about the perfect man she'd just met. Not only was he handsome, but he was smart, well educated, older than she was and owned his own business. And he liked her.

If she didn't mess it up this might be the man she'd been waiting for her whole life.

He smiled across at her. "Don't worry your little head about little things. I'll take care of you."

# Chapter Ten

A sharp rap on the door frame reverberated through the room. "Wake up call, cafeteria at six thirty."

"Wha… Who…" Sara rolled over. A grayish light crept through the darkness, enough that she could see Lydia asleep in her cot. She checked her watch.

"What time is it?" a muffled voice rose from the covers and pillows.

"Six in the morning," Sara responded.

"They've got to be kidding."

"Nope, I don't think so. We've got less than half an hour to shower, get dressed and make it to the cafeteria." Sara threw back the covers and raced for the shower.

Ten minutes later she emerged from the bathroom. "Your turn."

Lydia jerked her sleep mask off and kicked her legs over the edge of the bed. "I didn't realize that I signed up to get out of bed at some ungodly hour. I don't do mornings. I think I want to renegotiate my contract." She staggered into the bathroom.

Twenty minutes later both women raced to the cafeteria. They shoved open the door and walked quickly to the front row.

"Ladies, you're two minutes late." Mac glared at them.

"I'm sorry." Sara tried an apologetic smile.

"Two minutes could mean your mission is scrubbed. Two minutes could mean the woman you've been sent to save, is dead when you get there. Two minutes could mean that a team member is killed, because you're two minutes late." Mac stated in a cold, metallic voice.

Sara slipped into a seat. "You're right. I'm sorry. It won't happen again."

"Good." Mac gave a crisp nod. "Okay ladies, Laura will lead you on a one hour run this morning. We'll see you back here for breakfast in an hour." Mac inclined his head toward the tall, Eurasian woman who stood by the back door. She looked to be in her mid-forties and great physical condition.

Laura stepped forward and opened the door. "We'll head out this way, ladies."

Diane groused about the hour and now the run. Lydia mumbled something about life before eleven in the morning.

Sara allowed a half smile. If Mac wanted to get even with her for some reason he certainly had the advantage. He could make her get up at this ungodly hours and run for an hour before she even got coffee. Well, she'd show him she could take it.

Ten minutes later the women were jogging through the forest, the scent of pine in their nostrils, needles crunching under their feet. The crisp morning air helped to reduce their perspiration.

Thank heavens she'd been working out at the gym and running. Sara could imagine the picture she would have made eight months ago, staggering behind everyone, gasping for breath.

An hour later the four of them straggled into the cafeteria behind Laura. They panted for air and collapsed in the chairs closest to the door.

"Ladies, it's a buffet breakfast. I'd suggest you focus on carbs and some protein. You have half an hour, then it's time for your Krav Maga class." Laura strode to the table and picked up a plate.

"What the hell is Krav Maga?" Sara mumbled under her breath to Maggie.

Laura scooped up scrambled eggs. "Krav Maga is a self-defense class taught to Israeli fighters. It evens the playing field for a smaller person and teaches them how not to die at the hands of an attacker. Krav Maga is interesting because it is easily learned and it works. There isn't a lot of technical holds or moves. People are shown how to kick, bite, gouge and stomp in the right places. You'll need your energy for the two hour class." Laura added several strips of bacon to her plate. "You might want to drag yourself up to the food."

"Boy that sounds like a fun class." Lydia dragged herself to her feet. "I can hardly wait. First I'm going to have a large mug of black coffee."

Sara struggled to her feet and followed Lydia. She grabbed a plate and piled on the eggs. "I have this feeling we won't need to watch our weight here."

"I should have studied the class schedule in more detail. I swear I didn't see the six o' clock reveille call." Maggie complained. She poured a cup of black coffee.

"I didn't see it either. I thought it would be a gradual entry type program. Obviously I was I wrong. At least we have bacon. I'm guessing they don't allow us a leisurely second cup of coffee." Sara sighed.

Diane snorted. "I'm guessing you're right."

Twenty five minutes later a short, solid built, blonde woman marched through the doors. "Ladies, I'm Sergeant Gwen Golding. We'll be going to the recreation center for the Krav Maga class. Place your trays on the empty cart over there and follow me please."

Lydia shook her head. "It's like army time. Not a minute out of sync."

Sara swallowed her last gulp of coffee. "Come on, Lydia.

You may need to learn how to cold cock that husband of yours."

They linked arms and followed the Sergeant, a woman about fifty, out into the morning air. The darkness had been replaced by a crisp, cerulean blue sky. The scent of fragrant sumac drifted through the air.

Sara felt invigorated. It was a great morning to be alive.

In the rec center the instructor faced them.

"Ladies, there are two training rules in Krav Maga. First, there are no rules in a fight and second, one must not injure oneself or one's partner when training. The training is an intense mix of aerobic and anaerobic workouts. It relies heavily on the use of pads in order to experience both delivery and defense of strikes at full force. Your pads are on the bench in front of you.

Maggie picked a couple of pads. "They look like hockey pads."

"They're similar," Sergeant Bush replied. "You'll find it can be as taxing to hold a pad as to practice against one. You will wear the head guards, gum shields, groin protectors, shin and forearm guards, during the practice of attack/defense techniques, so that a realistic level of violence may be used without injury. Sara and Lydia, would you please put on the equipment in front of you?"

Two hours later, Sara collapsed to the ground in front of the rec center. She pulled her knees up, wrapped her arms around them and laid her head against the knees.

Diane fell face first to the ground and laid her head on her crossed forearms. "I am not going to move. Just throw some dirt on me and leave me here."

"That's it. I can't do anything more today. What are they trying to do? Kill us?" Maggie leaned against a pine tree.

"I don't know, but if that's their goal, it's working." Sara closed her eyes. "Do I dare ask what's next?"

Lydia pulled a sheet from a pocket in her cargo pants. "It says pharmacy class on poisons."

"At least we don't have to expand any more physical energy for an hour or two. Where do they want us?" Sara asked.

"Classroom two," Lydia replied.

"I guess we better find Classroom two or we'll get another lecture." Sara struggled to her feet. Part way down the main path she checked out the wooden signs posted on the canvas tents.

"Over there." Diane pointed.

They tromped over to the building Diane indicated. Inside they found themselves in a small classroom with six desks arranged in a semi-circle around the lectern. A large photo screen hung from the ceiling behind the lectern. A tall, red-haired woman, about fifty, her hair pulled back into a frizzy ponytail, her large-boned face covered in freckles, stood at the front of the room. She checked her watch. "Excellent, you made it on time. We have a lot to cover today. There are notebooks at each desk. Please be seated and let's get started. Oh, I'm Dr. Agnes Normand.

We're going to start by discussing some of the poisons you might want to use if you want to simulate a heart attack and not have the drug found in the body."

Lydia and Maggie exchanged nervous glances. Sara felt a chill, like a ghost stood right behind her. That sounded like how Gordon had died. She looked over her shoulder. Thank goodness he wasn't there.

"Don't worry ladies we won't be trying them out."

A collective sigh went up.

"We've already tested all of them." Dr. Norman grinned. "Some of the possibilities are insulin, succinylcholine, oleander, foxglove and liquid nicotine. We'll start with a synthetic mixture of nicotine, succinylcholine and heparin mix we have developed. It's a drug specifically developed for the purpose of causing a terminal heart attack. It's difficult to detect in the body and works well when put in coffee or hot chocolate to hide the slight bitter taste. It's effective in about thirty minutes. That gives you time to get away and not be a suspect.

Your assignment for tomorrow will be to come up with a scenario on why you might use this drug to protect an abused woman and how you would use it. Think outside the box, because nothing is ever as easy as it might sound. Now let's look at another drug you might use."

Sara read the handout in front of her and jotted notes at the bottom.

They'd asked if she could kill someone. She'd said yes, but could she? Could she put a poison in someone's coffee, walk away and let them die? She thought about it.

Not that Gordon had been poisoned, but his death had set her free. It had given her a second chance at life. A year ago she wouldn't have enjoyed the fresh crisp air. A year ago she wouldn't have exhausted her body with exercise. All of which made her feel alive. A year ago, she hadn't felt alive.

If she could do that for another woman, give her freedom and a new life, maybe she could. No man should have complete control over any woman and turn her into a doormat.

People pushed and shoved. They dragged suitcases or luggage carts toward La Guardia's exit doors and bumped into other passengers. Constant chatter bombarded the ears. The odor of gasoline seeped into the area each time the doors opened.

Marley grabbed Sabhita's arm and pulled her back. "I want to make sure Assif and Nooria make it to the taxi before we leave."

"Okay."

Several minutes later they spotted the nun, being lead toward the door by Assif, and the waiting taxis. A dark sedan, with tinted windows, pulled up. A priest stepped out, opened the back door and the two women slid inside. The priest closed the door and disappeared into the front seat. The sedan pulled slowly out into the traffic.

"Whew! They made it. I can't believe it. I was more worried about the trip to New York than actually rescuing her from the prison."

"Me, too." Sabhita made a motion to mop her forehead. "There they go. No one is following them. Once at the monastery they'll transfer to another car which takes them to the nunnery. Let's get our taxi to the hotel. We need to make sure no one can trace us."

"They've got a car waiting behind the hotel. We walk through the lobby and out the back door. Then we drive to our apartments." Marley limped out the door. "I can't wait to get home. I'm going to bed for two days."

❧

Carly and Julie entered the freezer room. Phoenix poked her head out of the new dog carry. They gave Nadia a high-five.

"Good work, girl. You did it. Nooria's safe. Right now the CIA is questioning her. Assif is with her for translation and support. Once they're finished we'll change her identity and have her disappear completely."

"How's the team?" Julie asked Nadia.

"Marley took a shot in the leg. It went right through so the damage is minimal. She's being seen at home by a private doctor."

"That's two injuries. We need to give that team a break for a few months."

"I agree, Julie." Carly replied. "Let's hope we don't have any more urgent cases where we need people who speak fluent Arabic. Everyone made it to their homes without being followed?"

"Yes. Nooria and Assif are at the State Department.

When they leave there they'll change cabs twice, go through a hotel and an apartment building and then Assif will drive them to a local nunnery." Nadia responded.

"A nunnery?" Carly raised her eyebrows.

Nadia shrugged. "She's chosen to enter the sisterhood. We'll provide an English tutor for her. She'll take her vows and be transferred to another nunnery in a different part of the country."

"Sounds like a perfect disappearance. I'm glad she's going to be okay with the relocation. Any idea what she's going to tell the CIA?" Julie asked.

Carly hesitated. "Off the record, from what Assif said, she was in the room when two warlords, one was her husband, talked about an assassination plot of a high ranking American Military official. Once she was discovered in the room he had no choice but to have her killed. The plan was to kill her in a skirmish in prison."

"So we saved her life and some high ranking military guy? Not bad for a day's work. I'll let the team know. They deserve to have some idea of why Nooria would have been killed." Nadia smiled.

"I agree. Okay, Elizabeth Hargreaves is now the potential victim of a hit man, hired by her father. Hit men seem to be popular these days. I also managed to get a few personal articles from Graham Hargreaves's late father, who he may have killed. I'm going to send them up to training camp. Let's see if our new recruits can come up with anything to help with the murder."

"That's a unique idea. It can't hurt." Julie agreed. "I'll be interested to see what they come up with. Maybe with their talents they'll figure out how Graham killed him."

"That's what I'm hoping. Now I'm going home to my animals to spend some quality time with them." Carly picked up the dog carry.

Julie shook her head. "You should take Link home with you and spend some quality time with him."

Nadia burst out laughing.

"Come on Phoenix, we're out of here." But the idea niggled in the corner of Carly's mind. Would Link ever come home with her? Was it even a possibility?

The thought of his body, without the uniform, gave her heart beat a blip and a shot of heat. *Chill lady, focus on important things like who's trying to take over the company, either one.*

The four volunteer recruits lounged in their chairs in the small classroom.

"I can't believe the schedule they expect us to follow." Maggie complained. "I swear every muscle in this body is screaming 'get me out of here'."

Lydia rubbed her biceps. "I know the feeling, sugar. I can't believe I volunteered for this. I'm sure they never mentioned any of this in the interview. The heaviest thing I've lifted in the last ten years has been my evening bag, or maybe a double martini. That Krav Maga is wicked. I get the feeling by the end of the ten weeks we're going to be expected to take down two hundred pound men."

Sara rolled her shoulders in backward circles. "I guess they want to make sure we can take care of ourselves, if we run into any of those two hundred pound men."

Diane laughed. "You guys are such wimps. You and your soft life styles, this will get you in touch with your body."

"Right," Maggie glared at her. "Just because you're a PI and work out regularly. I heard a lot of complaints on that six-thirty run this morning and I didn't see you kick butt in the Krav Maga class today."

Diane shrugged. "I don't like early mornings without coffee. As for Krav Maga, it's a new form of self-defense. I've never done it before."

"Good, it's nice to know we're on a par at something."

Lydia commented. "Let's see how you do in the PI class, and that's not private investigations."

"Paranormal Investigations? What the heck is that?" Diane frowned.

"I guess we'll find out." Sara commented. "Our instructor appears to be late."

"No, I'm here." A falsetto voice, with hint of a Boston accent, sounded from the front of the room.

All four women spun around.

A man with bushy reddish-gray hair and thick, coke-bottle glasses and indescribable age sat behind the desk, smiling at them.

The women stared at each other and then back at the desk.

"But you weren't…." Sara started.

"You didn't walk in here," Lydia added.

"But here I am and obviously you missed my entrance. Shall we begin? My name is Mr. Mogee. I will work and assist you to develop and fine tune your special talents. You will need to work hard on your own particular talents. I will also help you combine your talents so they work together. You should be able to accomplish more if your talents complement each other. Shall we begin by each of you explaining your paranormal gifts and what you've done to develop it, or not? Lydia?"

Lydia glanced at the other women. She took a deep breath. "I can sometimes move items by thinking about them."

"That's very good, Lydia. The ability is known as telekinesis. How have you used it?"

"I haven't. It usually happens when I get angry. I've never deliberately tried to use it. My family accepted it as part of my temper tantrums. They ignored it."

"Mmmm," Mr. Mogee tapped his fingers together. "It's a shame it's been wasted all these years. Let's begin to work on it now." He placed a small pen on the desk. "Go ahead Lydia, move the pen."

Lydia stared at him. "You mean now, in front of everyone?"

"Yes."

Lydia tightened her lips, pulled her shoulders back and focused on the black ballpoint pen. She scrunched her eyes and stared at the pen.

Sara held her breath. The pen sat there.

"Damn." Lydia continued to focus on the pen. Finally it began to slide toward Mr. Mogee. Inch by inch it moved a little faster, until it reached the edge of the desk.

Mr. Mogee grabbed it before it fell. He smiled. "That was good, Lydia. You can see it's not easy. It's like any other skill. It needs to be used and strengthened every day. Work on it and we'll try again tomorrow."

"It works better when I'm really angry." Lydia mumbled. "I can throw a glass all the way across the room."

"Then maybe you need to practice harnessing that anger and using it." Mr. Mogee suggested. "Sara, you're next."

"I feel or sense things from touching. Sometimes it's a person, or maybe a photo or a letter. I haven't used it very much. My parents told me it was wrong and got angry. My husband hated it and threatened to have me committed to an institution and make sure I never got out, if I ever used it."

"Unfortunately a lot of people react that way. They're afraid of the unknown, or what you might find out about them that they don't want you to know. Take Diane's hand."

Sara glanced at the instructor, then at Diane. "I don't know. I mean if there's something…"

"Go for it." Diane shrugged.

"You don't believe?" Mr. Mogee asked Diane.

"Hell no, but I'm willing to take part in this farce." Diane stuck out her hand.

Sara hesitated, not sure if she would sense anything or if she wanted to. After Lydia this morning, Sara really didn't want to find out personal secrets of her other team members.

"Sometimes I don't feel or see anything."

"That's okay. Go ahead, Sara." Mr. Mogee encouraged.

Diane winked. "Go ahead. I'm up for a séance."

Sara reached over and took Diane's hand. "It doesn't work like that."

Waves of sadness flowed over her. Tears climbed to the corners of her eyes. Sara felt the pain. A small child cowered in a dark corner, a young woman cried in a bedroom and a man screamed at her.

"Diane, I'm so sorry. Your childhood…"

Diane jerked her hand away. "I don't know what you think you're pulling, but there's no need to feel sorry for me. My childhood was friggin fine."

"I'm sorry. I didn't mean to see it."

"Go to hell."

"That was very good, Sara. You're a sensitive and it's called psychometry. Always trust what you see, even if the person denies it."

Diane shook her head. "I'm not denying any bloody thing. Nothing ever happened. She made it up."

Mr. Mogee shook his head. "Of course, she didn't. It's just harder to accept for some people. Maggie, what's your special ability?"

Maggie hesitated. "Sometimes I can talk to ghosts. Sometimes I see them, mostly I just hear them."

"Ohmigawd," Diane groaned. "I had no idea you guys were all nuts. You see people's past, see ghosts and talk to ghosts. This is all a big hoax. I didn't realize I signed on with a bunch of nut cases. Let me out of here."

"Diane, please sit down. It may be difficult for you, but please respect your teammates."

Diane slouched back in her chair.

"So you can hear the ghosts talk?" Mr. Mogee asked.

"Like I said, sometimes. I don't hear anything right now."

"You'll need to work on being more open and receptive so the ghosts can find you easier. How often do you see them?"

"It depends. I didn't used to see them at all. Then occasionally, maybe every few months or more one would come up to me. I see them more often now."

"Ah, it means your gift is becoming stronger. Do you sense anything, like Sara?"

"Nope, suddenly they're there, in a room or on the street. They come up to me and usually ask me to help them get a message to a friend or family member."

"That's good. Stay open and continue to help them. The more you help them the stronger you will become. Now Diane, let's see what talent you have."

"I don't have any stupid talents and seeing ghosts or reading palms isn't a talent. It's a damn freak show."

"Nothing?"

"No," Diane snapped.

"Ah, what are you feeling right now?'

"What do you mean? Diane glared at him.

Mr. Mogee smiled. "In your gut, what are you feeling right now?"

Diane stared at him. "Nothing."

"Diane?"

Diane crossed her arms over her chest, sank her chin down and glared at the man. "Something's upsetting Sara. She's afraid for someone."

"Good, very good Diane. Sara?"

Diane continued to glare at the man. "Big deal, it's a gut reaction," she mumbled. "Anybody can tell when a person's worried. Read their damn body language."

Sara stared at Diane. She wanted to deny it, but if they were a team, honesty was important. "You're right, Diane. I'm worried about my daughter. I'm afraid she might be in danger."

"Thank you, Sara. You see Diane, you sense what people

are feeling or seeing. We'll work on it so you understand it better. What about the other thing?"

"What other thing?" Diane shot him an angry look.

"I understand you're a witch."

"Aw, shit." Diane tried to slide farther down in her chair.

"You're a witch? I mean a real honest to gosh witch?" Sara stared at her.

"Okay, I'm a witch. I can cast spells, big friggin' deal."

Mr. Mogee smiled. "Yes, Diane, it is a big deal. It could come in very helpful for your friends. Maybe you can explain to them how it works over dinner tonight. You know how you don't wear the hat and use a broomstick?"

"Okay, I get it. I don't understand any of this, but I'll try and explain how spells work and that there really are witches out there."

"Good and don't forget to get in touch with your gut as well. We'll work on that. Diane comes from a long line of witches. You might get her to talk about her family. Okay ladies, your assignment is to work on your talents by taking these items. See if you get any message or information from them. Share them, pass them around. Do you have any questions?" Mr. Mogee handed each woman an item.

They glanced at what they had received.

"This looks like a man's glove." Sara looked up.

Mr. Mogee had disappeared.

"We'll figure it out." Maggie stared around the room.

"Sometimes you can use a spell. It causes people to see, or not see, what is really there. I'll check it out." Diane offered.

"Cool. Let us know what you find. Now what are we supposed to do with these." Sara held the glove in her hand. A freezing breeze wafted over her. She shivered.

"What?" Maggie asked.

"I don't know. It feels like someone is here."

"A ghost probably. They tend to be cold." Maggie turned over a worn, wool sweater.

*"He killed me."*

Maggie swallowed. She closed her eyes. The scent of licorice permeated the room. "Does anyone else smell that?"

"What?" Lydia asked.

"I can smell licorice. And someone's here."

"I don't smell anything but I can sense him. He's angry." Sara rubbed the glove between her palms. "I can see a bedroom. A man drops something in a cup and offers to a man in bed."

*"My son is poisoning me."*

"I don't see him but I hear him. He says his son poisoned him." Maggie waited. "I think he's gone."

"Wow, you guys are either totally nuts or really good at what you do." Diane stood up. "If you really heard a man say that, we need to let someone know. They sent these articles of clothing up for a reason."

"I guess this is what they expect from our team. Let's go tell the director. He must have known about the stuff we were given." Sara headed for the door. "I wonder who died, and why? Is the other person going to kill again? Is that what they need from us?"

# Chapter Eleven

She'd gone to bed in her own king-sized bed, with Egyptian cotton sheets, in New York and woken up in a double bed with regular cotton sheets, who knew where. She still wore her nightgown.

Elizabeth padded to the bedroom door and opened it. She stared at the small living area of the cottage. The windows were open, the air hot and humid. She heard the roar of the ocean in the distance. She was somewhere tropical, but had no recollection of how she got here.

She padded past the wicker and floral couch and chair, the wicker coffee table and across a rattan carpet. She shoved the door open and stepped out onto the stairs and quickly shielded her eyes from the brilliant sun.

"Sorry Elizabeth, you're going to have to stay inside a few more minutes until the leader gets back." A short, dark haired woman stepped in front of her.

"And if I choose to leave?"

"Then we'd have to stop you. You don't want that. Why don't you go back inside, have a shower. There are clean clothes in the closet. Someone will be in shortly to explain everything and answer all your questions."

Elizabeth hesitated. Something in the woman's eyes said

she wouldn't hesitate to physically stop Elizabeth should she try to leave. Elizabeth grimaced and retreated back inside. She found shorts and a t-shirt in the closet and headed for the shower.

Thirty minutes later, feeling better, and in clean clothes, she found another dark-haired woman in loose silk pants and a flowing top in varying shades of oranges and greens waiting for her. The woman sat relaxed, on one of the floral patterned, padded wicker chairs in the main room. A tray with a coffee pot and cups sat on the coffee table.

"Good afternoon, Elizabeth. Would you like coffee?"

"Who the hell are you, and why am I here? Kidnapping is illegal. I'll make sure you all go to jail for it. Do you know who I am, or is that why you kidnapped me, for my money?"

"Sit down, please. Do you take cream or sugar?" The woman waved to the second chair across from her.

Elizabeth stared at the woman, prepared to ignore the request.

"Please, I will explain everything. Although I don't think you're going to like what you hear." She handed Elizabeth a cup. "There are croissants."

Elizabeth shook her head. She sank into the chair, her eyes on the woman.

The woman put the cup down. "I'm Nadia. I'm part of an organization that helps women."

"I don't need any help."

"Unfortunately you do. Someone is trying to kill you."

"I don't believe you," Elizabeth replied.

"I didn't expect you would. Your father owes a lot of money. He expected to get it when your grandfather died, when he was murdered actually."

"Grandpa died of a heart attack, natural causes. The doctor said so."

"We'll get to that. Your father is desperate for the money. He needs you to write a will that leaves everything to him. He's been trying to convince you to do that, right?"

Elizabeth paused. "Yes, he has. I don't feel comfortable doing it for some reason, but I'm not sure what else to do."

"When you write that will and leave everything to him he plans to have you killed so he will inherit all the money. He's already hired a hit man. That's how we found out about his plan. If you don't sign a will leaving everything to him in the next few days he has a forged one ready for after your unfortunate demise."

"No. Father wouldn't do that. I'm his only daughter."

"He killed his own father. He poisoned him with a succinylcholine. It simulates a heart attack. The body metabolizes it quickly so there's little evidence of its presence. It does stay in the metabolites which can prove the drug was, at one time, present in the body. We got a special order to exhume your grandfather secretly, so your father wouldn't know. An autopsy revealed residual succinylcholine."

Elizabeth felt the blood drain from her face. This was a bad dream. She'd wake up and be home and everything would be normal, except her father would be on her about a will, again. He'd made three appointments with his lawyer already.

"I think I'd like that coffee, now. Why did he do it?"

Nadia unwound her long legs from the chair, leaned forward and poured a fresh cup. "He owes a lot of money to bad people. Do you take cream and sugar?"

"Cream, please."

Nadia added cream and handed the cup to Elizabeth. "Now where were we? Oh yes, your grandfather's murder. The information is being turned over to the police for further investigation."

. "How did he do it?" Elizabeth took a sip of coffee.

"We're guessing your father talked to your grandfather about his will and when he was assured he was in the will, he felt he would get everything, or at least most of it. Then your father found a drug specialist. He got him to explain how to do kill someone with poison, so it wouldn't be questioned. If he'd hired a contract killer there would have been more of a risk the death would be investigated. The night your grandfather died your father secretly crushed several sleeping pills and put them into your grandfather's cocoa, which he always had at bed time."

"Grandpa always said it helped him sleep and he wasn't going to take any of those damn sleeping pills."

"We're guessing you father sat with him chatting until your grandfather fell into a deep sleep. The he injected him with succinylcholine. It paralyzes the muscles of the body and prevents all movement, including breathing. Death is by asphyxia. It would be fairly quick. Because of his age, the doctor assumed your grandfather had died of a heart attack in his sleep."

"He smothered to death? Did he feel any pain?"

"I don't think so," Nadia responded. "He would have been unconscious. Your father took the mug, rinsed out any sign of the sleeping pills, refilled it with regular cocoa and poured that out, leaving the cup with the residual cocoa beside the bed."

Elizabeth clutched one hand to her throat. "He sat there while Grandpa died?"

"We think so. Of course we can't prove that, yet. We don't know where he got the sleeping pills or the succinyl either, but we're working on it."

"How could he watch his own father die? Poor grandpa," tears trickled down Elizabeth's cheeks. "Are you sure?"

"Did your grandfather like licorice?"

"Yes, how would you know that?"

"For now take that as proof your grandfather knew he had been poisoned and by his son." Nadia sipped her coffee.

Elizabeth swiped at her eyes. "I don't understand it. Daddy killed grandpa and he's going to kill me."

"Money and greed does strange things to people. When the will was read and you got everything your father was furious. He began to plot how to kill you to get the family fortune."

Elizabeth shook her head. "I can't believe it."

"We can prove a lot of it. The police will do the rest. It may take a few weeks or even a month or two, but your father will be charged with your father's murder. We're trying to prevent you from becoming his next victim and making it a double homicide. You were brought here so we could tell you the truth, and figure out to what to do next. Once your safety is assured, you'll be free to return home."

Elizabeth sipped the coffee. Her mind spun in circles. She tried to get a grasp on everything she'd been told. "So what do I do now?"

"We have come up with a tentative plan. You have final approval of course. First, do you have relatives you can leave parts of the fortune to?"

"No one close, but I have several cousins, an aunt in California, my grandfather's brother and my mother's family in Vermont. I haven't seen them for awhile."

"Good, that's a start. You need to look at your family money and break it down—the business, the house, any other assets and the actual cash. Decide how you want to handle each of them and then write a will. Take your time to figure it all out and to make sure it's what you want. Would you like us to bring Todd Weber down here?"

"My boyfriend?"

"Yes."

"Oh, please. That would make it so much easier, to have someone to talk to."

"We could also arrange a Caribbean wedding if you like."

"You mean if I'm married father would then have to kill both of us." Elizabeth asked.

"Yes, but if you love each other, it's a nice place for a honeymoon."

"Todd won't marry me. I've asked him. He said it would

look like he was marrying me for my money and he didn't want that."

"He's an artist?"

"Yes, his paintings are beautiful. I wanted to get him a show at one of the exclusive New York galleries but he wouldn't let me. He said he wanted to do it on his own, without me buying his success."

"Sounds like you've got yourself quite the man there."

"Yes, but he won't marry me." Elizabeth took another sip of coffee.

"Maybe when he finds out how much you need him, he'll change his mind. I'll have someone talk to him. We could get him down here by tonight."

"You could do that? That would be so great."

"In the meantime you need to work on the will. Once you and Todd are married, and the will is written we'll send copies of both the will and the marriage certificate to your father, his lawyer, and maybe an occasional news official who might be interested in what you've been doing since your grandfather's death."

Elizabeth stiffened. "What you're saying is you'll make sure everyone knows who has the money and who it goes to."

"Yes. You'd be safe then, you and Todd."

"It stills feel like a dream, or actually a nightmare. I expect to wake up in my room back home."

"Sorry, that's not going to happen. I've got to make some calls. Have you any problem staying here for a few days?"

"No. I'm fine, now. I'll wait and see if you can convince Todd to marry me. You're sure about my father?"

"Yes and he will kill you if you return home now."

Elizabeth stared into her coffee cup. She'd wondered about her father in the last year or so. His insistence that she write a new will and leave everything to him had scared her. She hadn't said anything but she'd even tried not to be alone with him.

Now she understood it.

"I'm so sorry Grandpa," she whispered.

Carly stretched her back. She linked her fingers together, turned them around and shoved them straight out in front of her. She'd been at the computer most of the afternoon, trying to find any links between Percy and Remple, or anyone else who might be interested in CCB. She'd wasted a lot of time with no conclusive results.

Anna Lee popped her dark, curly head into the room. "It's after five. I'm heading out, unless you need me for something."

"No, go ahead. Got a heavy date?"

"I wouldn't say a heavy date, but I am meeting someone for drinks."

"Is this someone new?"

"Sort of, we've gone out a few times."

"You go and have fun. We'll see you in the morning." Carly thought how nice it would be to have a drink with someone interesting. She knew who she wanted that person to be, but as an employee he was off limits. If the man wasn't so good at his job she might fire him, but then he'd be mad at her and wouldn't go out with her anyway.

Stiff from sitting all day Carly decided a workout in the office gym would feel good. She locked her computer, and her office, picked up Phoenix and took her personal elevator to the basement. She strode into the locker room to change.

"You stay in the corner." She ordered the dog.

In the gym Carly stretched before she picked up the free weights. Half an hour later, she felt looser and more alert. She moved to the punching ball and took a few practice kicks. She stiffened, stopped, stood quietly and listened.

The door had opened.

Phoenix raced from the corner where Carly had put her.

"Phoenix!" Carly spun around.

"I thought I heard someone in here. You have a hard day?" Link scooped up the dog. "How're you doin' girl?"

"Something like that."

He stood a few feet in front of her wearing gray workout shorts, running shoes and nothing else.

She swallowed a couple of times. She couldn't take her eyes off his well-developed pecs and rippling abs. Blond curls covered most of the chest area and tapered to an arrowhead pointing directly to the shorts. Carly tried, without success, to pull her thoughts away from Link's magnificent body and say something intelligent. Her lips flapped but her voice refused to work.

"Mind if I join you in a work out?"

Carly shook her head and gestured toward the equipment.

Don't be an idiot. You're his boss. Act like it.

Finally she found her voice. A smile picked at the corners of her mouth. She looked across at the hunk in front of her. "No, unless you'd like a real work out?"

She motioned to the floor mats.

Link glanced in the direction she indicated. He put the dog down. "You want to challenge me to a fight?"

"Not exactly a fight, a joint workout. Unless you're afraid I might beat you. Go to your bed, Phoenix."

Phoenix glared at her but reluctantly crawled back to the corner where Carly pointed.

"That'll be the day. I don't usually fight women."

"Don't think of me as a woman, just a well-trained opponent." Carly stepped on to the mat.

Link watched her for a few seconds, a frown creased his forehead. He strode over to the mat. He eyed Carly and checked her out. "Somehow I'm not sure I can forget you're a woman."

"Try." Carly spread her feet apart and balanced on her toes.

He stepped on to mat. Carly immediately grabbed his arm, kicked at his feet and landed him on his back.

"Damn," Link grunted. "Okay, woman, you asked for it. No holds barred?"

"No holds barred." Carly reached out and hooked one of his hands, jerked it behind his back and flipped him onto his stomach.

Link rolled quickly to the left, gripped Carly's leg, pulled her to the mat, and anchored her legs with a scissors cut.

The musky male scent, mixed with sweat reached Carly's nostrils. She relaxed for a split second to enjoy the masculine scent. He flipped her onto her back and held her down, his body pressed against her back.

Carly wanted to enjoy the sensation, but knew she couldn't relax again. She couldn't let a man best her. With a quick motion she pulled her knees up, raised a foot and kicked hard.

"Oaf," Link groaned.

Carly yanked one of his hands free and used it to flip him to one side. Her knee came back up and landed on his abdomen. Her forearm came down across his throat.

She looked into his dark, slate gray eyes and felt his sweaty skin. She wondered if he'd sweat like that during sex.

"Uncle?"

"What?" Link hesitated.

Carly figured he had to be weighing his options.

He grinned. "Okay, uncle. Lady, you are some wicked fighter. You really can fight. I underestimated you. Where did you learn to fight like that?"

Carly reluctantly rolled off, flopped over on her back, sweaty and exhausted. She pulled her arm down slowly. She let it slide over each of his well-developed muscles.

Sweat glistened all over Links' body. It took on a golden sheen. She wanted to lick all that sweaty salt off with her tongue and then....

"Never underestimate me, or anyone else. It's not good for security. I took some training. A woman never knows when she might need to protect herself." And I need to be better than any man in my world, Carly thought to herself.

Link rolled over on his side, propped up on one elbow. He stared down at her. He didn't say anything. His sensuous lips were six inches from hers.

Carly held her breath. Her heart rate raced. She'd won and Link didn't appear threatened.

Link moved an inch closer.

Carly closed her eyes.

He pulled back, stood up and offered her his hand.

"Thanks for the workout." Regret flooded over her. Carly took his hand and jumped to her feet. "That got rid of the stress."

"Glad I could be of help. Want to catch a cold one after you shower?"

"A cold one?"

"Sorry, I guess I shouldn't have…"

"No, you should have, and I would love to catch a cold one. Give me twenty minutes."

"What about the mutt?"

"Phoenix? She can sleep in the car with Sam. She'll be fine. See you out front."

Carly hurried toward the showers. She hummed to herself. A drink with Link, even a platonic drink, made a nice end to the day. She'd worry about finding the leak in CCB tomorrow.

❧

"Okay ladies; let's see what you can do with a gun. Everyone put on their ear protection." Mac indicated Sara. "Sara, you go first."

*Why couldn't Gwen or Dr. Agnes teach Shooting 101?*

Sara picked up a full magazine from the box on the

ground and stepped up beside Mac, her body barely an inch away from his. His heat permeated through her camouflage gabardine. His woodsy aftershave wrapped itself around her head. She couldn't concentrate on what he was saying.

It was their second day and their first lesson on the shooting range.

"Pardon me?"

"I said, first you need to spread your feet for balance and stick your butt out. Pay attention, recruit. Your life could depend upon it one day."

Sara flushed and followed Mac's instructions. She felt silly sticking her butt out.

"Not quite so far out."

Sara shifted her butt in slightly.

"Good. You're right handed?"

"Yes."

"Okay, this is a semi-automatic Glock 22. Pull the slide back and drop in the magazine." Mac demonstrated first. Then he handed the gun to Sara.

Her hands shook slightly. She followed his instructions and loaded the gun.

"Good, now take it in your right hand, index finger along the barrel." Mac moved in closer and put his hand over Sara's to demonstrate. His voice, deep and warm washed over her. She tried to concentrate on the words.

"Now take your left hand and grip it over your right hand." Mac's torso pressed against her.

She could feel the sweat start to gather and drip down the middle of her back. She stared at the target twenty feet in front of her.

"Arms straight out in front and focus through the back sight. Bring it in line with the target and focus through the front sight so your target is dead center."

His cheek almost touched hers. She tried to line up the sights. Her breath hitched up a notch.

Did he have to stand so close? How the hell was she

supposed to concentrate when everything around her screamed—very sexy man?

"Got it?"

"I think so."

"Okay now, release the lock with your left hand, slid the right index finger on to the trigger, good, now pull the trigger." Mac put his hand on her back.

Sara pulled the trigger and the gun barrel of the Glock shot upwards into the air. She fell back against Mac's hand.

"Whoa, that's some kick."

"Try again and push the barrel down."

Sara repeated the process and pulled the trigger. The barrel shot upward, although not as far."

"Finish the clip. You've still got ten rounds left." Mac kept his hand on her back.

Sara refocused and shot the next ten shots in a row. The gun jerked, but improved with each shot.

"Put on the lock. Always hold the gun pointing down if you're not shooting." Mac removed the gun from her hand. "Not too bad. You need a lot of practice. Next, Maggie?"

Maggie stepped forward and Mac repeated the process.

Sara grabbed a bottle of cold water from the cooler under the lean-to structure at the back of the range. With a shaky hand she unscrewed the cap and took a long swig. Whether it was from actually shooting a gun, or from having Mac hold her so close, she wasn't sure. Most likely it was Mac. Damn him anyway.

Sara watched Maggie take her turn at the shooting range. She judged the distance between Mac's body and Maggie's. He stood close, but there was no blurring of personal boundaries.

Damn him to hell, he had moved in closer deliberately, and it had worked. She couldn't stop thinking about him.

Graham Hargreaves strode back and forth in front of the huge stone fireplace. His hands clenched and unclenched. *What the hell happened?*

His daughter was gone. She couldn't have left on her own.

Somehow, someone had managed to enter his property undetected, avoid the guards, disarm the security system, break into the house, remove his daughter and disappear without a trace.

First he needed to get his daughter back. She had control of the estate and the money. His father had left everything to her, the stupid bastard. He'd assured Graham he would inherit everything. Then he'd gone and left Elizabeth control of the business, the house and the old man's fortune.

He had to get his daughter to write her will and leave everything to him. Then he'd have her killed. He'd been working on getting her to sign the damn will, but she'd refused so far. If she didn't he had a back-up plan and a back-up will.

When he found her he'd find the organization that could arrange to take her. If he could control an organization like that he could control political power around the world. He would have ultimate power and money. Graham kicked the ottoman and sent it sliding into an antique end table. A porcelain bowl smashed to the floor.

Who gave a damn? It didn't belong to him, at least not yet. He had to find out who held the power to operate a plan extensive enough to kidnap his daughter. He wanted to find that out, almost as much as he wanted her back, or dead.

Whoever took her had screwed his plans royally. Depending on what they did with her, he could be out on the street without any source of income. If she ever suspected what he'd done she would kick him out and maybe sell the estate. He'd have no place to live. That would be the least of his problems, though, if he didn't get his hands on the money quickly. He had to get her back and make sure she wrote a will in his favor. The forged will wouldn't be any good if she was still alive.

Maybe if she died in testate he could also get the family fortune. He'd have to check with his lawyers.

Maybe that loser boyfriend of hers took her. Damn, what if they got married? But what's his name wouldn't have the brains to implement a plan this extensive, even as an elopement. No, someone else took her. He had to figure out who and where the hell she was right now.

He knew the person to call. It would cost him, but he had nothing left to lose. He punched in a number on his cell phone and waited.

# Chapter Twelve

Mac hurried around the corner toward his office and collided with a muscular body wrapped in soft curves. Fascinating gray eyes stared up at him.

"Damn." He'd been avoiding her for the last three days, except in a group setting.

"You seem to be good at running into people." She flashed a smile with those damn enticing lips.

"Apparently just you, good morning, recruit."

"Good morning, director." Sara looked directly at him. "Running into you, literally, is probably a good thing. We need to talk."

"About what, recruit?" Mac tried to keep it on a professional level, but knew he was losing ground rapidly. Heat ignited his body.

"Come on, Mac. Let's try a little honesty here. Because we've met before doesn't have to be a problem."

"It's not," Mac snapped. He took two steps back.

"Whoa, yeah, right. We had dinner. Nothing happened. Was I surprised, maybe even shocked, when I showed up here and there you were welcoming us to training? You bet? And from the expression on your face, so were you."

"Yes, you were the last person I expected to get out of that plane. I didn't think I'd ever see you again."

"And you felt guilty for that?"

*Hell no*, Mac thought to himself. *I felt guilty because I wanted to sleep with you.* "I guess you could say that."

"It's okay, Mac. I like you. You're the first man I've gone out with, even casually, since my husband died, which is probably why I found you attractive. I'm not upset you never called. I didn't expect you to."

"I see. So you don't have a problem working together?"

"None, I'd like to think we're friends, but nothing more than that. I don't think it's against the rules to be friends, is it?"

Mac smiled. "No, it's okay to be friends."

"Good, then maybe you can quit avoiding me and treat me like the other recruits. I like you, Mac, but I don't expect anything more from our relationship other than friendship, and you making me a crack shot."

"I will do that. You're a natural with a Glock. We'll see how you do with the other weapons. I'm glad we had this talk."

"Me, too," Sara checked in both directions to make sure no one was around before she gave Mac a peck on the cheek. "See you on the shooting range, buddy."

Without a backwards glance, she sauntered away toward the cafeteria.

Mac watched the slow, sway of her slender hips, still sensuous under the green camouflage pants, tucked into boots. Hell, she was one sexy woman and there was no bloody way they could be just friends. He wanted so much more.

He stormed off to his office. How he could be friends with a woman he visualized naked every night when he went to bed?

Sara sat cross-legged on her cot, a bottle of water in her hand.

Lydia stretched out, hands behind her head, feet at the edge of the cot. "You know trying to move objects with your mind is almost as hard as those ten miles runs in the morning. I'm exhausted."

"But you're improving." Maggie commented from the chair she occupied. "You moved the cup on the table tonight."

"Yes, but I need to get better control. He's right. It's a matter of practice. After all these years of non-use, it's going to take time to build up that muscle."

"I think we're all finding that. It amazes me that we've all had these talents since our childhood. For whatever reason we were all discouraged from using them."

"You're right, Maggie." Sara shrugged. "I wonder how many other people have lost the use of their special talents. I guess Mogee is right. For many people it's scary to have a relative who is different or unusual."

"It's terrifying for everyone, me included and especially when you don't understand it or can't control it." Lydia sat up. "For a lot of people, they don't want you to know about their private stuff so they threaten you, so you don't use your gift."

"What about the other day when Diane said you were afraid?" Maggie looked at Sara.

"I was surprised that you could read me." Sara flashed a look at Diane, who shrank down in the second chair that came with the tent.

"Don't worry about it, Diane, like I said, it surprised me. No one has read me before. I'd just read you, so all's fair. Besides, I decided if we were going to be a solid team it meant we needed to share. No secrets."

Diane glanced up and shifted in her chair. She took a sip from a can of soda.

"So what are you afraid of? You mentioned your daughter." Lydia swung her feet to the floor.

"I got a letter from her the day we arrived. I asked to have my mail forwarded through The Foundation. She said she had met this wonderful man. He had invited her out to dinner. She hadn't even gone out with him yet. I don't have any read on him, but I feel sadness and something bad. I don't know what yet, but I'm worried about her."

"Listen to your body, but let's hope she goes out with him once or twice and that's it." Maggie crossed her fingers.

"That works for me," Sara replied. "Hold that thought. Anybody want another soda or water?"

"I'll have a soda." Maggie got up. "I'll get it. Anyone else want one?"

"No, I'm good." Lydia took a sip out of her can.

"I'm not sure what you saw, but you were right. I had a very abusive childhood, plus I watched my mother being abused." Diane blurted out.

No one said a word for several seconds.

"It's what Sara said about honesty and the team, but I don't want any of your damn sympathy. And I'm sorry I called you all nut cases."

"I think that deserves a little more than plain soda." Lydia leaned over and pulled a small overnight bag out from under the bed. She fumbled around inside the bag then triumphantly pulled out a small bottle of vodka.

"Lydia, you're full of surprises. I'll get the glasses." Sara hoped off the bed, scooted across to the small cupboard that held glasses and a few other basic utensils and grabbed four glasses. She put them on the table.

Lydia added a little vodka to each glass. The other women topped the alcohol with their sodas.

"To honesty, sharing, and the team of the PI Nuts." Maggie raised her glass. "Here's to the Nuts."

Everyone laughed and clinked.

Sara silently made her own private toast to the salute, to Mac Langston and a strictly platonic relations ship, even though she dreamed about him every night.

She would not give up her freedom or her self-confidence for any man. Why did he have to be the director? Why did she have to see him every day?

Something told her the training might be the easiest part of the next few months. She had to see Mac every day, and she had a sensation of doom when she thought of her daughter and the new boyfriend.

Mac paced his office. This wasn't going well. Dammit, what the hell was that woman doing up here, learning to shoot and fight so she could go out and risk her life? Last night he'd agreed that they could be friends, but it wasn't going to work. She had a nice house and a dog, for chrissake. She should be baking cookies and taking a yoga class.

It was too early in the day, but to hell with it. He pulled open his bottom drawer and took out the half full bottle of Chivas Regal scotch whiskey. He hesitated and put the bottle to his lips. He jerked it away, stomped over to the cupboard and pulled out a glass. He poured two fingers into the glass and threw the whole thing back. It burned as it trickled down his throat.

Sara Peters needed someone to look after her. She shouldn't be trying to help other people. Didn't she have a clue about how she could get hurt?

There was a knock at the door.

"Come in."

"Reporting as requested, sir," Sara stood in front of him in her fatigues, her hair pulled back in a ponytail. She looked about twenty-five years old, not a couple of years older than him.

Mac resisted the urge to pull her into his arms and kiss those lips.

"You wanted to see me, sir?" Sara waited.

"Yes." Mac took a step back. Her spring scent floated through the air, wrapped around his head and dispersed the anger and all the arguments he had planned. All he could think about was how cute she looked and how good she smelled.

"Um, look, Sara, before you go too far with this training, I really think you should reconsider."

"Reconsider what?"

"You know, doing this. It's dangerous. You've got a great life, two kids and a great dog, why step out of your comfort zone and into such a risky job?"

"Maybe it's because I don't have a great life. Until now I've barely existed. Until my husband died I was an abused wife. Now I'm fighting to get back a life my husband stole from me twenty years ago. I've never felt so alive and in control of my life as I do now. I want to get stronger and help other women."

"You need someone to take care of you, protect you."

"Like hell I do," Sara snapped. "The last thing I need is someone who wants to take care of me again. Been there—done that. I can take care of myself just fine, thank you very much. I'll do it even better when I finish this training."

It might have been the scotch, or having her desirable body so close, Mac took three steps forward and wrapped his arms around her. One hand tipped her head slightly so his lips could brush those damn sensuous lips. He'd wanted to taste them ever since that first night outside her house.

She tasted of vanilla. He pulled her tighter and slipped his tongue between her lips. This was where she belonged, here in his arms; in his bed. She moved against his body. His breathing ratcheted up.

"Sara, please, let me take care of you. I'm thinking of leaving this position. I could get work in Seattle. We could be together."

She jerked out of his arms. "You're crazy. I don't know what you're thinking. It must be the alcohol. I've never been happier. I like taking care of myself. I never want any man to look after me again."

She spun on her heel and stomped to the door. It slammed behind her.

Mac poured another shot of scotch. He'd really screwed that up. He'd been blindsided by Sara's arrival at camp and his reaction to her. Except for the shooting sessions, he planned to stay as far away from her as possible for the next few weeks. Then she'd be gone and he'd never see her again.

Of course that had been the same thought he'd had when he'd left her house that night in Seattle. He hadn't slept all night thinking about her sexy gray eyes and that sultry, subtle scent that wafted around her.

He'd smelled it again at the shooting range yesterday, when he'd put his arms around her luscious, body. When he'd held her tonight he couldn't believe how she'd muscled up since she'd arrived at the camp. Damn, what the hell had happened to him?

She'd felt so good in his arms. Her lips sent fire to his belly and burned more than the damn scotch. He wanted her. He wanted to take care of her, but more than that he wanted to make love to her, all day every day. He'd never wanted a woman like this before. He'd give up his position to move to Seattle and get a normal job. He'd do anything to be with her.

And she didn't want anything to do with him. She wanted to become a secret agent and he wanted to quit being a secret agent.

CCB had won three contract bids in the last two days. Carly felt good. They'd immobilized Minnamar's attempt at a takeover, without alerting them to the fact they were on to their game. One problem solved, at least temporarily.

She hadn't heard anymore from Link on Percy York. Elizabeth Hargreaves was safely ensconced in a small hotel on a Caribbean island with two of The Foundation's teams guarding her.

The report on the new team in training said they were making excellent progress. Their skills had already been utilized with Graham Hargreaves. The recruits had picked up on the murder and how it had occurred. The police were beginning an investigation into his father's death. It was about time she flew up to the training center and made a personal visit and talk to Mac. She didn't want to do it over the phone in case there were bugs somewhere. Besides, she wanted to see how Mr. Mogee and his students were progressing. She picked up the phone and ordered her plane to be ready to fly in two hours. Then she buzzed her secretary.

"Anna, can you have Sam bring my car out front in thirty minutes, please?"

"Of course, is there anything else?"

"No, that's all. I'm going to be out of the office for the rest of the day. You can get me on my phone if anything urgent comes up."

"Very good, enjoy your day."

"Thanks. I'll see you in the morning." Carly checked her tablet to make sure the info she needed was there, grabbed her large lavender DKN bag, picked up Phoenix and placed her inside the bag. She checked her office to make sure everything was put away and locked before she hooked her bag carefully over her shoulder. She stepped into the private elevator.

In the lobby Carly headed out the door to her car.

She sank back into the soft leather upholstery. Her mind spun with all the new challenges that had appeared. The CCB take-over appeared to be under control, but they still weren't any closer to the person or persons interested in The Foundation. Carly tried to unwind during the drive to her private hanger, without much success. With Phoenix still in the bag over her shoulder she tramped across the runway to her plane.

Two hours later Carly clambered down the plane's steps. While circling for a landing over the camouflaged tents she'd seen the recruits at the shooting range. She walked up to the range where she found a seat on the small bleacher set up for students or new staff to observe. She pulled out a thermos and poured herself a shot of caramel mochacino. She took a sip, brushed her hair out of her eyes and leaned back to watch Mac demonstrate the appropriate stance for shooting an MP3 rifle.

He took each student, went over proper procedure on how to handle a rifle and talked them through their shoot.

Carly leaned forward as Mac put his arm around recruit Peters. The hairs on the back of her neck stood up. Her hand reached across to pat Phoenix. She continued to watch the shooting lesson.

What was she missing? There was something different in the way they both stood. Mac stood a little closer. Sara stood rigid. Both bodies appeared tense. One spoke. The other listened and followed directions. They avoided eye contact.

Carly observed for a few more minutes, finished her coffee and carefully descended the bleachers. She trotted across to Mac's office. They needed to talk.

When Mac strode into the office half an hour later Carly sat behind his desk, legs crossed, hands tented, fingers tapping. "So what's with you and the new recruit?"

Mac's mouth opened slightly and then snapped shut. "And hello to you too, Carly. I saw your plane land. Where's your mutt?"

"She's sleeping in my bag on the floor. Flying tires her out. Tell me about you and the new recruit?"

"Which recruit are you referring to?" Mac reached into his bottom drawer and pulled out an almost empty bottle of scotch. "Would you like a drink?"

"No thanks. I'm flying. I'll stick to coffee."

Mac refilled her coffee cup before he poured a shot into his own glass. "Sorry, it's not the fancy kind."

"Come on, Mac, the truth. Sara Peters, what's going on between you two?"

"Nothing, and that's the truth. Nearly ran her down with my bike a couple of months ago, and took her dinner to apologize." Mac folded himself into the chair across from Carly.

"That's it?"

"That's it, Commander. Nothing more."

"You didn't sleep with her?"

"Jesus, no, Carly, I didn't even kiss her good night. I left her at her door."

"So? There's nothing that could be a concern for the training session?"

Mac shook his head.

"I believe you, but I sense there's more between you than you're letting on. I saw the look that passed between you and the sparks were visible for several miles. I also saw a lot of tension between the two of you on the shooting range."

"Carly, you're an incorrigible romantic. There's nothing there. The sparks were probably sun spots."

"Nope and I'm not wrong, but I'll drop it for now. You're sure the both of you can handle this without a problem? Maybe I should talk to Peters?"

"Don't do that. It would upset her. We're both handling it professionally. Today I had my arms around her and we were both overcompensating, but other than that, we're handling it."

"Okay, but if there's anything that's going to compromise this team I want to know about it immediately. I don't want to be blindsided. Got it?"

"You got it, boss." Mac took a long drink of scotch. "You know me, I don't get involved with women unless it's strictly for sex."

His thoughts pulled him away and Carly watched, wondering what he was really thinking. "Hello, earth to Mac."

"Sorry, Carly, I was thinking about the introductory session this afternoon.

"Sure you were cowboy. The rest of the recruits look like their doing good. Are there any problems with any of them?"

Mac shook his head.

"Those items we sent up for them to check out pointed us in the right direction. We couldn't have done it without them."

"I'm glad it worked out, whatever it is they did. Why don't you hang around until tomorrow? I've rented a plane we're taking our recruits sky-diving."

"Sky diving? That's a new twist isn't it?"

"In this day and age they may have to jump from a plane if the plane can't land safely, in a jungle or for whatever reason. So they're going to learn how to jump, what to do if the parachute doesn't open and how to hit their target when landing. Come with us. I'll show you how it's done."

"No thanks. I'll pass this time."

"Aw come on Carly. It will be fun. It's a real rush when you pull the rip cord. You've never done it before."

"And I have no intention of doing it now. I'm not out in the field any more. I don't have to risk my life."

"No risk. I'll be there. You're not afraid are you?"

"Leave it alone, Mac. I have no intention of jumping out of an airplane—ever." Carly stood up. She'd never been able to overcome her fear of heights, most of the time she compensated. She could fly a plane, but froze at the thought of jumping out of it.

"Sorry, boss. I didn't mean to upset you."

"On a different topic and the main reason I came up here today. I mention my concerns before and I don't trust phones or even texting these days. I got your report on the background checks of your staff. It was thorough and cleared everyone. I didn't see any red flags."

"That's a relief. The staff is kind of like one big family."

"We've had a few challenges with bugs and not the animal version. It's more with the CCB end, but if you notice anything different or sense something not quite right, let me know ASAP, okay?"

"Sure, what's with the bugs? Do we have a new problem?"

Carly shook her head. "I don't think so, but I'm getting a few rumbles that someone may be trying to get information on our operation. My office was bugged, but I think that was from a competitive company planning a hostile take-over of CCB. I don't think it had anything to do with The Foundation, but you never know. It's better to be over cautious."

"That makes sense. Everything's normal here. Well, normal considering the new recruits. If I see or hear anything, you'll be the first."

"Thanks, Mac. Have you thought anymore about quitting?"

"Oh yeah, I've thought about it, but like you suggested, what the hell am I going to do, pump gas somewhere? I guess you're stuck with me until I figure out what else I want to do."

"Good. I don't want to lose you. If I can help in any way, let me know. Okay, I'm out of here. I'll fly up in another few weeks to see how our recruits are doing, unless something unusual happens." Carly took a last sip of coffee, clunked the mug down on the desk and strode out of his office, her high heels clicking on the wooden floor.

Something told her Mac was lying, either to her or to himself, about the recruit. She'd keep an eye on them both. She didn't want anything to cause a problem with the recruits.

"Don't you love living on the beach?" Phillip asked.

"Yes, the beach is nice."

"You love the house, right? You prefer it to your tiny apartment."

"It's a nice house, but it's a little expensive. I really can't afford it."

"Are you saying I'm sponging off you?"

"No, of course not, Phillip, that's not what I meant. I l know you're building your business and when it takes off you'll pay me back. It's just that, in the meantime, things are a little tight. I'm sorry. I didn't mean to say anything to upset you."

"Here." He held out a single yellow rose. "I know you like yellow. I saw this and it reminded me how beautiful you are."

"Oh, Phillip, thank you. It's beautiful." Amy took a deep breath of the rich fragrance.

"You better put it in a vase right away so it doesn't die."

"Of course." Amy scurried into the kitchen.

He smiled. He'd picked the rose off a bouquet on a grave close to the gym. It would probably die by tomorrow anyway and she'd feel bad that she didn't take good enough care of it. They'd been together almost six weeks now. Everything was going according to plan.

"I saw Verna at the office today. She asked if I wanted to go to dinner with a couple of the other girls from the office." Amy carried the rose in a tall, slender vase, back into the room, and placed it carefully in the center of the table.

"That would be nice but it's a long drive from there to the beach. Would you really want to drive it late at night?"

"No, you're right, of course. I'll tell Verna it won't work."

"Are you sure? I mean I don't want to come between you and your friends."

"No, you're right. I'd rather be with you, anyway. It's fine." Her head dropped. She didn't look directly at him.

"I'll help with dinner." He pulled his lips into a pout.

"No, that's fine. I'll do it. Why don't you go and check on your business. Dinner will be ready in an hour."

"You're sure, honey?"

Amy nodded.

"Okay, I'll check the office and see if any orders have come in. I'll be back in half an hour. I'll bring a bottle of wine." Phillip hurried out the door and slid into his Porsche. He'd convinced her he needed to keep up his image, for the sake of the business. Amy now covered the monthly payments for him.

He chuckled at her gullibility.

Tomorrow night he'd take the next step, the proposal. He had a well-used engagement ring and the matching wedding band that had served him well up until now and he'd made dinner reservations at a place up the beach. They'd stroll back via the beach and he'd propose on the large rock right before the house, under the light of the full moon. It was forecast for tomorrow night.

Then he'd explain that they needed to get insurance policies so the other person would be protected. She'd agree without even thinking about it. She'd be so happy at the thought of being married and having children. They all were. She'd want to call her mother. They always did. He might even have to talk to good old mom on the phone, or not.

Mom apparently was still away in training. She phoned when she could to chat and see how Amy was doing, but a phone call didn't have much influence. It sounded like good old mom might be away for another five or six weeks. She wouldn't be a problem. He'd checked her out and she was an older version of Amy. No issues there. In fact they might not even meet until the funeral.

Amy had mentioned a younger brother, but they didn't appear to be close, or see each other very often, so he could probably arrange a wedding before brother dearest managed to fit in a visit. He'd tell her they could visit him on their honeymoon.

So far everything had worked out exactly as he planned, but then all his arrangements did. He was smarter than everyone. Losers went to work nine to five for peanuts. They started at the bottom and worked their pathetic way up where they still had to suck up to their bosses and for what? He didn't have to worry about anyone telling him what to do. He was slowly building his income. Soon he'd be a millionaire. Thanks to stupid women.

His mother had showed him how losers live. The most she ever got from her tricks was more booze. She was too drunk and stupid to even take care of her kid. Mostly he was ignored.

He wouldn't rush Amy, but in a few months they'd be married and he'd be a little wealthier. In the meantime she'd support his present lifestyle from her pathetic little job where she worked her butt off every day.

He drove his sleek, black Porsche into his favorite watering hole and parked. He parked sideways and took up four stalls. No way was anyone going to put a dent in his car. He strode into the bar.

Inside he checked out the single women hanging out at the bar. He didn't see anyone worth his time. After he had a drink drop by Didi's for an hour or so. Amy would hold dinner and accept any excuse he offered.

Didi was always there for him. He had complete control over her. She'd do anything he asked. And he meant anything. Like all women, she was powerless where he was concerned.

# CHAPTER THIRTEEN

Link called Carly to let her know they needed to meet. The information he needed to share his information in person, not over the phone.

After that night in the gym he'd tried to stay away from her. He'd reported mostly by phone or computer. They'd gone for a drink after the workout. He'd surprised himself when he asked her and was even more surprised when she agreed. Surprisingly, it had been a fun night. She'd relaxed. They'd talk sports mostly. She was a Giants fan. He preferred the Jets. He was still waiting for another Joe Namath to show up and lead them to victory.

Even with the light chatter all he could think about was how her body felt against his when they had worked out. The way her soft skin rubbed over his chest. Her wild flower scent mixed with sweat haunted him all night. He still remembered it. He'd had a hard on all evening until Carly called Sam to pick her up and drive her home. After a couple of more beers he'd gone home, taken several cold showers and dreamt about her all night.

He'd never wanted a woman this much. If he stood next to her again he knew he'd kiss her. He had no control when she walked into a room. His forbidden goal was to find out if her lips were as soft and warm as they looked.

He'd tried to stay physically away but today he had no choice. He punched in her number and considered meeting over a drink.

Two hours later Carly strode into the gym, wearing jeans and a loose yellow sweatshirt.

"Good idea, meeting here." Link commented. "I did a quick sweep for bugs, in case, but I don't think anyone knows about this place or even if they did, would never think of having it bugged."

"What have you got, Link?" Carly hopped up on an exercise bike and pedaled slowly.

"I think I've put the chain together, with a few twists."

"Go on." Carly kept pedaling.

Link paced. He focused on his thoughts. "Frank was sneaking into our main computer when he worked in the computer lab. He fed Uncle Freddie some of the easy accessible financial information and the list of bids CCB were planning. Also the maximum and minimum amounts of the bids CCB was contemplating. Uncle Freddie took the information, reviewed it and decided which ones were most lucrative for him and which might cause you the most destruction."

"We'd guessed that much."

"Yeah, I know but I do have the proof now. The bugs, Frankie planted, Anna Lee let him into the Board room."

Carly stopped pedaling. "No, you must be wrong. Anna is a protégé. We rescued her sister from being put to death. I'm paying for her education."

"I know, but Anna is dating Frankie. She has been for a few months. He stays at her apartment most nights."

"Damn. I hate that. I thought she was trustworthy. It never occurred to me...What else?"

"Anna has been funneling some of the information from your office to Frankie, whatever on your computer that isn't password locked."

Carly sighed. "I guess you can't trust anyone. Mostly it was letters on there, but there is some financial info and maybe a few legal documents. Nothing that could bring us down, but if you add it to the rest of the information, it could help. Did you find anything else I should be aware of?"

"I'm not sure. Since you found out about the bugs and now only the information you want Rempler to know is passed on and you got Arnie to have our Frankie work on historical stuff and non-essential CCB work, they've lost the last two bids to you. It looks like they're losing the other bids they've got out. They lost those to you as well. I think Uncle Freddie is frustrated. His company isn't doing well. They don't have much credibility and from what I've been able to find, his money is running out."

"So he needs to kick it up a notch. What do you think is his next move?"

Link hesitated. "There's not much more factual information, but there are rumblings."

"Go on."

"He's looking at taking out someone in the company."

"You mean like a hit?" Carly's eyes shot open.

"Yeah, that's the word on the street. And he's using whatever money and credit he's got left to find the best hit man out there."

"So the hit would be on me. No one else would be worth the cost. If I'm out, our stock tanks and if he plays it right, he'd get our contracts. Then eventually take over, or dissolve the company. The man is desperate. Who has he hired?"

"Again, the rumor has it he found the Groundhog."

Carly shook her head. "Sorry, that means nothing to me."

"I don't know him either, but I checked him out with the cops. He's considered the best hit man out there. He never misses, although, since no one knows who he is they can't say for certain. He's never been seen. There's no description. They don't know where he lives. He slips in, fulfills his contract, takes the money and disappears."

"Hence the name the Groundhog. He's never seen out of his hole."

"It's something like that. Carly you need to leave town for a while."

"Don't be ridiculous, Link. I'm not going into hiding. Besides, if he's that good he'd find me wherever I went. We need to make sure he doesn't kill me."

"That's all?"

"Simple, isn't it? Hit men seem to be big these days. He's the third one I've heard about. Maybe he's keeping busy and I'm way down on his list. Okay, I'm going home for dinner. I need to mull this over. In the morning I'll fire Frank and Anna and let the CCB Board know the situation."

"I'm taking you home and checking out your apartment."

"That's not necessary."

"Yes ma'am, it is. You may be the boss, but I'm head of security. Call Sam to take us to your apartment. He can drop me back here after, if that's okay with you."

"It doesn't look like I have much choice does it."

Ten minutes later Carly sat in the back seat with Phoenix in her arms. The dog glared at Link and growled most of the ride. Carly didn't even try to shush the dog.

"I thought she liked me."

"I guess she's territorial when you get in her car." Carly smiled.

At the apartment Link let Carly unlock the door and then went in first. A large German shepherd barked and charged at him, teeth bared, a smaller sesame red dog that looked like a fox watched him from a doorway.

"Watch out. Petey's here."

Link backed up.

"Maybe I should go first. Down, Caesar," Carly pushed in front of Link and rubbed the dogs ears." It's okay, boy. He's a friend. Sit."

The shepherd put his butt on the floor and nuzzled Carly.

"I knew you had a few pets but I wasn't prepared for this. Is it safe to check the rooms?"

"Watch out for Petey." The voice came from another room.

"That's my parrot. He won't hurt you."

Link shook his head and walked through the open door past the foxy dog. He stomped through all the rooms, dogs at his heel. A marmalade cat appeared and joined the procession.

"Watch out for Petey."

Carly waited by the door.

"Okay, you can come in. I can't believe how many animals you have in here. I knew you collected them but I thought you gave them away. Aren't there regulations about animals in apartments?"

"I only have three dogs." Carly stomped into the room.

"And a parrot and a cat."

"Two cats, actually. Now you can go home and leave me alone. I have things I need to do."

"Sorry Carly, you do need to be careful. This man doesn't play around."

"I got the message." Carly started toward the window.

"No! Stop, Carly. Stay away from the windows."

"I'm just going to close the drapes. I'm in the penthouse for heaven's sake."

"No, let me do it." Link raced toward the window.

The window cracked. A small hole appeared. Carly grabbed her shoulder.

Link shoved her down. She crumpled to the floor.

"Carly, oh God, Carly," Link had his gun out. He bent down to check for a pulse. A sigh of relief escaped. It was strong and steady.

Phoenix raced across the room. She growled at Link and then licked Carly's face. She whined between growls. Caesar and the third dog raced to the crumpled body. Caesar whined.

"It's okay, girl, she's going to be fine." Link patted Phoenix. He pulled out his cell phone in one hand and dialed 911. He crawled away from Carly to the window.

"This is Link Stone, head of security for CCB Enterprises. There's been a shooting. I need an ambulance and the police." He gave the address while he carefully closed the blinds. He hurried back to Carly and gently rolled her on to her back. Blood seeped from a wound near her left shoulder. He checked her pulse again, still strong and regular.

She moaned.

He confirmed the address for the operator. "It appears she's been shot in the shoulder. There's a fair amount of blood, but her vitals are strong. Yes, I'll hold until the paramedics get here."

"Phoenix, get off my face. I can't breathe." Carly groaned. "Damn, that hurts. Caesar, you have bad breath."

"Glad to see you're back with us."

"Was I out for long? What happened? I can't remember."

"You were only out a few minutes. The paramedics are on their way. The operator's holding on the phone until they get here. You've been shot."

"It burns like hell. Now I know how it feels to get shot. I don't plan to let it happen again. I'm in the damn penthouse, across from the park. How did he do it?"

"I don't know. Climbed a tree? Found a spot where he could get a good shot with a telescope on his rifle? I'll check it out after we taken care of you."

"Okay, so you were right, but he's not that good. He only hit my shoulder."

"Will you lay still and quit talking until the paramedics get here? If he was shooting from a distance and through glass, the glass probably deflected his shot. He could have planned a quick second shot through that same hole, but I shoved you to the floor." Link unbuttoned his shirt and yanked it off. He used it to apply pressure to the spreading stain on her left chest and shoulder.

"Ouch, that hurts more than the bullet. Do you have to push so hard? He didn't kill me."

Sirens screamed closer and closer and then quit.

"Thank, God. And yes, I need to apply pressure to slow down the bleeding. Thank you, operator." Luke clicked off. "She says EMS is pulling up out front. It looks like I'm going to be attached to you until we can catch the guy or buy him off."

"What? You're planning to move in here?"

Link grinned down at her. He continued to apply pressure. "Looks like I'm not going to have any choice if we want to keep you alive. Use your right hand and keep the pressure on."

Link stood up to let the paramedics in. "Call the dogs off so they don't attack the medics."

Carly shooed two dogs off to one side. "Down you two, Cesar, Yoshi, down."

The dogs looked at Carly and slowly slid to the floor. They lay there and watched Carly and the strangers.

The paramedics pushed stretcher into the room in the direction Link indicated. Phoenix didn't move. The medics immediately started to check vitals and asses the wound.

"So do you have two bedrooms, or are we going to have to share?" Link asked.

Amy held out her left hand. The light hit the facets of the diamond. "It's beautiful, but can you afford it, with starting your new business an all?"

"For you my darling, only the best and yes I can manage it. The business is starting to pick up." Phillip filled the fluted champagne glasses with an inexpensive sparkling white wine.

"Here's to the most wonderful woman in the world, and my future wife."

*And here's to a short relationship, with lots of money at the end, you stupid cow.*

The last few weeks of the plan always started to irritate him. Once they were engaged he wanted to get it over. He knew how brilliant he was, but right now, no one else really appreciated his superior intellect, except Didi. He'd have to see her tomorrow. His ego needed stroking, as did something else. He smiled at the thought. Didi was subservient, but she'd do anything to please him. He'd keep Didi around for his pleasure.

Amy raised her glass and then took a sip. "It's my turn. Here's to the handsomest, smartest man in the world, whom I adore and who makes me feel so special." She giggled.

Phillip clinked his glass to hers. "You're too flattering, but I love you so much. Let's not wait too long to get married. I want the world to know you as my wife."

"Okay, silly, but I'll have to let my mother know and see when she can make the wedding. I think her training finishes in a couple of weeks. We can wait that long. Besides we need to make a few plans. I need to find a dress and a bridesmaid."

"Yes, of course, darling, whatever you need."

They also needed time to get the insurance policy. He'd suggest it in a few days, then it wouldn't sound related to the marriage. If they were married she should also be insured for the business, in case anything happened to one of them. Like, nothing would happen to him. He was too clever. She'd buy it. He had her so wrapped around his finger she did everything he suggested. She never questioned anything he said. He had her right where he wanted her.

All the women he used were wrapped around his finger. It didn't take much work to make it happen. He knew all the tricks.

Growing up he'd had no power or control, first with his drunk mother. Then there had been a chain of foster homes. If he didn't behave they moved him. Originally it had left him powerless and with no control over his life. Gradually he'd learn to use his behavior to gain a little control in his life and over other people. He'd learned and now had power and control over women. Not only that, but he hadn't had to take any formal training or preparation for a job. He used his skills to get all the money he needed.

Maybe the mother wouldn't be able to make it. It would be a wasted trip anyway. From what he learned about the mother she wouldn't be much of a problem anyway. She didn't have a job or much of a life. Whatever training she was taking wouldn't make any difference. He'd be able to handle her—no problem.

# Chapter Fourteen

Carly entered the office, her left arm in a sling, carrying her coffee in her right hand. Phoenix trotted at her heel.

"Good morning, Anna. How are you today?" Carly forced a smile.

"I'm fine." Anna's eyes widened. "What happened to you?"

"I was shot. Someone tried to kill me last night." Carly continued to smile.

"Oh my gosh, are you all right?"

"No, but I will be. Apparently someone in my company has been feeding information to the competitors. When that wasn't enough for them to take over CCB Enterprises they hired someone to kill me."

The color drained from Anna's face, leaving it a chalky color.

"Yes, that's right, Anna. Your information wasn't good enough. Take your purse and get out, now."

"But…I mean… I had no idea they'd try and hurt you."

"I trusted you. You hurt me by being unfaithful. You went behind my back and gave information to a competitor. What did I ever do to you that you would try to destroy me; except rescue your infant cousin; bring her to this country, provide for her, give you a well-paying job and trust you?"

Anna refused to look at her.

"Don't worry, I'll continue to make sure your cousin is taken care of and educated. Hopefully she won't turn on me, too, when she gets a little older. You're on your own. Don't ask for a letter of reference. Now get out of my sight. Security is on its way up to escort you out of the building." Carly passed by the desk into the boardroom, Phoenix trotted to keep up.

In The Foundation board room she had to put her coffee down before she closed the sliding panel bookcase.

"What happened to you?" Nadia jumped to her feet.

"Oh my goodness, Carly, are you okay?" Julie rushed around the table.

"Don't touch." Carly held up a hand to stop them. "I was shot last night."

"Where?"

"How?"

"In my shoulder, someone shot through my window."

"But you're in the penthouse," Nadia commented.

"Yeah, don't take anything for grant. And let me tell you, being shot is damned painful so I don't recommend it for anyone. I can really empathize with Fareeda now. Apparently when Rempler couldn't manage a takeover of the company by cheating, he thought he could manage if the owner and CEO were out of the picture."

"So it's for CCB you got shot, not The Foundation?" Julie's face registered surprise.

"Shocked me too, but it's the legitimate company that's causing me problems. And I fired Anna on the way in. She's been working with the enemy, and also sleeping with him"

Nadia shook her head. "It keeps getting better and better. So what happens now? How do we protect you? Are you going into hiding for a few weeks?"

Carly shot Nadia a glare. "No way, I need to get some work done. Link has this brilliant idea, that as head of security he plans to join me at the hip. He's also looking into seeing if he can pay the hit man more money not to shoot me."

"I like that idea." Julie chimed in.

Nadia shrugged. "It might be worth a shot."

"Somehow I doubt that it's going to work, but we'll see. Okay, let's get back to work. I noticed an item on the morning news before I left home. Elizabeth Hargreaves married Todd Weber, an up and coming artist. They mentioned something about her filing a new will now that she was married. The newsperson said it looked like the money went to her husband and a few of her mother's relatives. They speculated on why her father wasn't mentioned."

Nadia smiled. "That pretty much covers it. When Todd found out that he could save Elizabeth's life by marrying her, he didn't hesitate. It trumped his concern over money and they are very much in love. If the media does some digging they'll realize her father is bankrupt. He owes millions of dollars to bookies, bank loans, car dealers and other creditors."

"And the police? Are they looking into the grandfather's death?" Carly asked.

"Yes, but I don't think Mr. Hargreaves is aware of that, yet. Elizabeth and Todd are honeymooning in Paris. Todd's going to talk to a few galleries about his paintings. Once Elizabeth finds out what her father's plans are now, and it's safe for her, they plan to return to New York."

"That is so cool." Julie grinned. "Another perfect romance, we do good work."

"Is there anything pressing at the moment?" Carly asked.

Julie shook her head. "I'm working on The Foundation budget. I'm also checking to make sure no one has managed to hack into any of our programs. I'd like to bring in an expert at detecting hackers. I know someone who I trust and I won't tell him anything about The Foundation, or even mention you guys."

Carly glanced at Nadia. "What do you think?"

"If Julie trusts the guy, I'm okay with it. You'll be with him the whole time, right?"

"Oh sure, I wouldn't leave him alone."

"Who is it?" Carly asked.

"His name is Trevor Williams. He went to college with us. He was two years ahead and really smart."

"Hmm, so is he cute, too?" Nadia glanced across at Julie.

The red flush started at the base of Julie's neck and raced up to her cheeks.

"I think the answer to that might be, yes." Carly laughed.

"That's not why I suggested him."

"Right, I think maybe we need to interview him, to make sure he's not going to lead our girl astray," Nadia suggested.

"No, please. He doesn't even know I'm alive. It's strictly business. Trevor is someone I had a crush on in school. He didn't know. I haven't seen him for years. I ran into him the other day at a computer exhibit."

"Oh, a computer exhibit, that sounds exciting. And you recognized each other?" Nadia asked.

"Well, I noticed him first. I guess I was staring because I couldn't believe it was him. He's even better looking than in college. He noticed and then came up to me. We started to talk."

"That's so cute. And now you want to give him a job." Nadia grinned.

"Come on, I don't bug you guys if you're interest in someone."

"That's because we never are. Go ahead and hire him, Julie. I'd like to see his resume if you don't mind. I'd like in t in my file." Carly commented.

"No problem. I'll ask him for it."

"Good, let us know when he starts. Any other loose ends we need to tie up? Link is checking on Percy. He's been a little busy but I'm hoping to learn a little more about him today. I guess my next task is to hire a new secretary." Carly sighed. She'd have to screen extra hard. They couldn't afford to have another spy at the company.

"That's it for today. Take a break. Let me know if anything comes up."

Nadia and Julie waved and left the office. Carly followed behind and closed the bookshelf door.

At her desk Carly moved her shoulder slightly and grimaced. It was going to take a few days to heal. She'd let Link know she'd be working in the office and maybe see how he was doing with the hit man. She should at least be safe in her office.

Roger sifted through the stack of papers in front of him. He had enough information to hone in on four North American organizations. Two helped victims of crimes, one helped women in abuse shelters and one helped women on the street and women who had been abused. None fit the exact profile but it was a place to start.

He riffled through information on the managers and staff of the organizations. He came up with several possible positions for infiltrating the organizations. Street social workers, computer whizzes, tax accountants and financial advisors. Any of these occupations should be able to get on the staff of these agencies.

He reached for a second pile of papers, thumbed through them and checked occupations and references. Who would make the best spy? Who could he trust to get the information and bring it directly back to him? Who wouldn't sell out to a higher buyer? Who did he have the most pressure on?

Whomever he hired Roger would make sure they knew if they sold him out, the Mafia would take care of him. That should assure the person's loyalty.

He began a computer search of the agencies and the staff, looking for any vacancies or potential job openings. It would take a few more days of research but he was getting closer to finding out more about these organizations.

And that meant one step closer to finding his cheating wife. She'd probably taken a lover by now. In fact she'd probably taken several, laughing at him behind her back. That slut would pay for leaving him, but first she'd suffer. He chuckled at that thought. It was what kept him going. The thought of finding her and making her pay—before he killed her.

Julie brushed her hair back with her fingers. She tried to think of something witty to say.

Trevor sat across the gleaming white linen table cloth. He looked deliciously handsome in a navy blazer, white shirt and red tie. His dark brown hair had been recently cut and the hairline laid clean and crisp against his neck His glasses emphasized his rich, chocolate brown eyes. When he smiled, she noticed gold flecks dancing in the brown.

"You're staring."

Julie put her hand to her cheek. She felt the heat rise up her throat. "I am, aren't I? Sorry about that."

"I'm glad you invited me out tonight."

"I'm glad you came." Julie squirmed in her seat. This was disastrous. She'd hoped they might have a romantic dinner while she brought up the idea of him doing some work for The Foundation.

"I've wanted to ask you out for a long time, but was too nervous."

"Why would you be nervous?" Julie asked.

"You're pretty, wealthy and smart. I've always been intimidated by you, even in college."

"I didn't think you noticed me in college."

"Oh yes, I noticed you, but I was too scared to do anything more."

Julie felt the warmth throughout her body. She took a sip of the wine he'd ordered. "Then I'm glad I asked you. I do have an ulterior motive though."

"You don't look like you'd have an ulterior motive bone in that beautiful body of yours."

Julie smiled and put the wine glass down. "Maybe I've had enough wine."

"And I was about to propose a toast to getting to know each other better."

Julie picked her glass up again and raised it to his. "I certainly have to drink to that. I would like to get to know you better."

The waiter brought dinner. Julie picked up her fork and speared one of the giant prawns in a white wine and lemon sauce. "Mmm, this is delicious. How's your steak?"

"Excellent. Good choice of a restaurant. The food at Maxim's is always good. You said you had a reason for inviting me?"

"Yes, I work for a small company. I guess you could say it's an underground company. I'm concerned that there may be people trying to hack into our computer. You're the best in the business on tracking down hackers."

"Thank you. I thought you were interested in my body."

"That too," Julie almost choked on a forkful of basmati rice. "We need someone I can trust to check our computer. Would you be interested?"

"Will you be with me the whole time?"

"Oh, yes."

"Then I'm definitely interested, although my fee might be a little steep."

"I'm sure we can cover it."

"I wouldn't be so sure until you hear my price. I want six more dates with you. I get to pick the places. I may also ask for special favors at the end of each evening." The gold flecks appeared to take over most of the brown. A dimple appeared at the corner of the left cheek.

Julie licked her lips. "I see. That is a little more than I thought, but I'll have to agree and take one on the chin for the company."

"Terrific. We can start Monday. I have tickets to the New York symphony."

"I love the symphony. I've gone many times with my mother. I'd love to go with you."

"I may expect a small down payment later tonight."

"I think that can be arranged." Julie had never felt so excited. Her whole body sang with electricity. Trevor liked her and wanted to spend more time with her.

Carly and Nadia would tease her, but maybe, just maybe, the attraction to Trevor was more than just a fling. She'd see how it went when he checked for the hackers and they spent time together.

⁂

Link entered the office without knocking. He'd moved some of his stuff into the bedroom next to Carly's her apartment. Under the circumstances he felt formalities were a little redundant.

Last night she'd refused to go to the hospital. The bullet had gone right through her shoulder so the paramedics had cleaned and bandaged the wound. They'd given her a strong sedative and five minutes after they left she'd been out cold. She'd slept right through the night.

Link had carried her into her bedroom, removed her shoes and covered her. He'd slept on the floor beside her bed, three dogs curled up around him.

"I checked out the area and talked to the police. The general agreement is he was at least two hundred or three hundred feet away on the roof of one of the apartments in the area. He could see the penthouse through a powerful telescopic lens on his rifle. They're combing the area but haven't found anything yet. Chances are if it was the Groundhog he'd pick up any shells or anything from the area. It will be clean. They think he might have used an M-40, or USMC sniper rifle, or the AR-15 with a 5.56x45 round. They're looking for the bullet in your apartment, but haven't found it. They're concerned one of the animals might have found it and taken it somewhere."

"That's possible. Even Petey might have spotted it. I'll see what I can find when I get home."

"They said he could have waited there for several hours, before you came home. He's a patient killer."

"He fired from that far away? Damn. So what do we do now?"

"We know who he is. I told the police what I suspect. I've put out feelers to see if we can talk to him about outbidding whoever contracted the hit."

"Do you think that might work?"

"It's hard to say, probably not. He's a professional. He's going to want to protect his reputation. He could lose clients if they thought they could be outbid. I don't hold out a lot of hope. I'm surprised Remple can afford the guy. If Remple can't make the final payment, that would cancel the contract. Then we might have a chance to work out a deal."

Carly stood up and began to pace. Phoenix whipped in behind her feet. "Okay, see what you can do. Maybe recheck Remple's financial state. Get Julie to help if you need. If we can show the Groundhog that Remple doesn't have the money to pay him that might help."

"Good idea. I still think we should consider you leaving town, maybe even the country for a week or two."

"Not going to happen."

"Fine, then the inside of the windows in your penthouse and this office will be tinted so no one can see through them."

"These ones already are."

"I'll check and make sure they're dark enough. Your limo also needs to have tinted windows. In fact, I'm going to get a second limo so we have a decoy car if we need it."

"Isn't that a little over the top? It's beginning to sound like something out of The Godfather."

"Make fun if you like, but take a look at your shoulder. He hit the left side because it's closest to your heart, assuming you have one."

"But he missed."

"The next time, he won't miss."

"You're so optimistic. Okay, do what you have to. On a brighter topic, have you found anything about Percy York?" Carly dropped into her chair and waved at Link to sit.

"He's a society hanger on. His mother left him a small among of money, in a trust. I guess she didn't think he could manage his own money. He has a ten year lease on a one bedroom apartment in Soho. He doesn't work, but lives on the money from his mother. He wangles invitations to society functions, none of the important ones. He finds somebody who gets an invitation, buys them a drink, does some small favor for them and convinces them to get him in to the event. He has no friends that I can find and no girlfriends. I don't think he dates at all."

"Probably not, from the general impression I've got from a few females. Do you have any idea how he gets invited to our fundraisers?"

"Graham Hargreaves is the person who gets him into the affairs. Hargreaves pulls in favors from business associates or his bookies. I know where Percy hangs out. I'm going by there tonight. I'll see if I can find out why Graham gets him the invitations."

"Graham Hargreaves? He's the man who killed his father and has a hit out on his daughter, which he has no money to pay. Do you think everyone is hiring the same person?" Carly asked.

"That's an interesting thought. And if the Groundhog is coming to town he might as well make the trip worthwhile and do several jobs all at once. If that turns out to be the case it will be interesting when he finds out neither one of his employers can pay him."

"Why would Graham Hargreaves want information on our company?."

"I'll try and find out tonight."

"Thanks, Link. I appreciate that. And thanks for…last night." Carly struggled over the thank you. "I guess if you hadn't yelled at me and I stopped, his shot would have been accurate."

Link refrained from comment.

"Anyway, I owe you. I'll write you a bonus."

"I don't need a bonus. I'll think of some way you can repay me." Link stood up and moved across to Carly. He stopped a foot or so away. Her wonderful wild floral scent wafted across the space between them.

"I'll be back later before I hunt down Percy, to take you home. Do you cook?"

"Of course," Carly replied.

"Good, you can cook dinner tonight, before we go to bed."

Her breathing became more rapid. "What do you mean? We aren't sleeping together."

"We'll see" Link whistled and headed for the door. He didn't look back.

"Wait there." Link opened the door and stepped in front of Carly.

"Oh come on…"

"Wait. Hey, Caesar, good dog." He patted the shepherd on the head and bent down to the other dog.

"Watch out for Petey."

Link grinned to himself. After doing a check of all the

rooms and closing the drapes he returned to find Carly on the floor outside the door. She sat with her back against the wall, her arms hugged her knees.

"You took so long I got tired."

Link shook his head. "Give me your good hand."

Inside the apartment Carly headed for her bedroom. "I need to change into something more comfortable. Why don't you pour us a glass of wine?"

The door closed. Link moved to her liquor cabinet. He'd seen it last night after Carly was shot. "Do you like white or red?"

"White for me, please." The voice came from behind the hand-carved wooden door.

His imagination started to work over-time. He thought about her undressing. She'd step out of off the turquoise pants from the suit she wore. Her long legs would look muscular and shapely in a lacey thong. He pictured her nicely shaped breasts covered in pieces of lace.

This wasn't going to work. If he had to be in her apartment he needed to stay professional. If this kept up he'd have to leave her alone to take frequent cold showers.

He picked up a couple of wine glasses, opened the fridge bar and removed a chilled bottle of Chablis. Sports, he'd think about football. He could plan his fantasy football team for the next season.

He opened the drawer, pulled out the cork screw and opened the wine.

"I would have thought you'd have it poured by now."

Link looked up and gulped. Carly had put on a loose, but clingy floral lounge outfit. The soft yellows and greens brought out the highlights in her hair. Caesar and Phoenix trailed along behind her.

Link handed her a glass of wine. "You look beautiful."

"Thanks. It's one of my favorite outfits for hanging out around the house. It's loose and light weight, almost like not wearing anything at all." Carly took a sip of wine.

Link felt his body heat up again when she mentioned not wearing anything. Maybe he should assign one of his staff to look after her, but he was the best and he wanted the best to keep her alive.

"You look odd. Is everything okay?"

"I found good old Percy York last night at one of his favorite drinking places."

"What did you find out?"

Link found another glass and filled it with red wine. "He said it's Graham Hargreaves, who gives him his invitation. I'm guessing because Hargreaves doesn't have the money for a donation but doesn't want anyone to know. He tells Percy to hang out and listen to what people say. If he hears anything that sounds unusual or someone talks about doing something international, Percy's supposed to tell him. He never hears anything interesting, so there's nothing to report back to Hargreaves."

"He never hears anything because he never leaves the bar." Carly said.

"That's about it. Why Hargreaves keeps giving him tickets, I have no idea."

"I wonder what he hopes to find. He's not in competition with me and we hadn't rescued Elizabeth until a short time ago. Weird."

"Maybe he's doing it for someone else?"

Carly took a sip of wine and thought about it. "I think he may do business occasional with Fred Remple. Maybe Fred has more than a couple of spies and bugs out there."

"We've immobilized them and Percy doesn't have a clue about anything, so I think we're good. Maybe make sure Graham's name is taken off the invitation list. That should eliminate Percy." Link took a drink of his wine.

"I'll talk to Julie and make sure she does that."

The medium size reddish dog walked across to sniff Links' pant leg.

"What kind of dog is that one?"

"Yoshi? She's a Shiba Inu, a Japanese hunting dog. Someone turned her into the SPCA. They can be a little difficult to train at times. They're runners. They are the closest thing to a cat."

"And all the dogs and cats get along?" Link asked.

"Amazing isn't it, but they do. I hate to leave them alone all day, but it's better than what they had before I found them."

Link took another sip of wine. Carly was a very complicated woman and a very desirable one. "So what's for dinner?"

"My special Spaghetti Bolognaise, right after I feed all my critters."

"It sounds good."

This was going to be so much more difficult than he'd thought.

❦

Link woke early.

Carly's spaghetti had been delicious. Shortly after eating she'd gone to bed. The day and the pain had worn her down. He'd been up every hour to check on her and make sure the apartment was safe. All three dogs had accompanied him every time he made rounds.

If she'd been killed Link didn't know what he would do. He knew his feelings for her went beyond a one night stand or even a short relationship. The thought of losing her had devastated him. He needed to figure out how to work with his feelings. He couldn't go on like this; she the wealthy employer and he the penniless employee. Except he wasn't, but until now he hadn't consider touching his inheritance.

He slept in the second bedroom and dozed off and on. His mind worked hard to figure out a solution. First they had to make sure Carly was safe from the Groundhog. After that Link needed to find a way that he could ask Carly out.

He needed to meet her on her own ground and not as an employee. That meant he had to resign and find someone to replace him at CCB. He could work on other stuff for her on a contract basis where he owned the company, but he couldn't be her employee any more. It had hit him when she was shot. He loved her.

Link alternated between dozing and checking Carly. He tucked the quilt under her chin and kissed her forehead. "I love you, babe," he whispered in her ear.

He didn't know how Carly felt, but there was definitely a spark between them. If he wasn't her employee they could explore that spark and maybe he could ignite it. A beginning of a plan started to emerge. Tom Gerow, a retired cop, would be a good replacement for head of security for CCB. He'd talk to him tomorrow.

Then Link would open his own security company. He had made a lot of contacts and Carly could contract with him on special projects. It would work. He needed to work out the details and then he had to tell Carly.

# Chapter Fifteen

Sara picked up the photo. Faces careened around her. The photo slipped from her fingers.

"What?" Lydia asked. "Are you okay? You're dead white."

Sara picked up the picture again and sank to her cot. Her fingers gripped the paper.

"Sara? Are you all right?"

"No, not really, Amy sent me a snapshot of her and her boyfriend. Unfortunately they haven't broken up. They're engaged. She thinks he's Prince Charming, everything she's ever hoped to find in a man. He treats her like royalty. Damn."

"That does sound terrible." Lydia smiled at her.

Sara shook her head. "I know, he sounds perfect. I should be happy that my daughter is in love."

"But…?"

"Every time I pick up this photo of my daughter and her boyfriend these faces of dead women race around me. How do I know they're dead, because they're ghosts? I'm terrified it means my daughter is in danger."

"You haven't met the boyfriend?"

"No, Amy met him about the same time I came up here. When training is over I'll to go down and visit, but that's another few weeks. Once I learn all this knowledge and the fighting techniques I'll be in a better position to fight this man, if it comes to that. I'll also be in a better position mentally."

"That makes sense. What do you know about him?"

"Only what my daughter has told me, and she's in love with the man. He has his own development business; whatever that is. He's good looking and smart. He thinks she's a princess and worships the ground she walks on, or so he says. That's about it."

"Name?"

"Phillip, Phillip de Beares."

"Sounds impressive," Lydia responded.

"Sounds damn ostentatious and phony, if you ask me." Sara snapped.

"Hey, I was being facetious. I agree. It sounds like a phony name, like he's trying to impress her. It looks like it worked. Maybe you could talk to the Director." Lydia suggested.

"Mac?"

"Director Langston? Yes. I'm not on a first name with him. Is there something I should know here?" Lydia smirked.

Sara felt the heat rise up her neck. "Not really," she mumbled.

"Sorry? What was that?" Lydia asked.

"I met him once, before I knew anything about The Foundation. He almost ran me down on his bike and took me to dinner as an apology. That's it, nothing more. Our relationship is strictly platonic, like his with any of you."

"Sara, my friend, you have unfathomed depths."

"No, I don't. I don't have any depths, but Mac might help me get some background information on the impressive Phillip. Good idea, thanks Lydia."

"You might want to talk to Maggie as well." Lydia suggested.

"Maggie?"

"She talks to ghosts. Maybe she can talk to the ones you see and provide more information that way. We're a team, remember. That's why we're here."

"Lydia, you're a genius. Why didn't I think of that?"

"I have no idea. Maybe you're too close to the whole thing. You might want to make this a team project, off the record of course."

Sara had never been part of a team before. It felt good. She wasn't alone. She might not have to handle this alone. If the other members of the team helped, they wouldn't be a bunch of helpless women. They'd be a skilled group of paranormal warriors by the time they tackled him. Amy might be a lot better off and a lot safer, especially if Sara's concerns were valid.

"I can't think of anything I'd like better right now than to talk to my team about my problem."

"Good girl. Why don't I go and see if they've got a few minutes to come by and listen to your concerns?"

"Thanks Lydia, I'd appreciate that."

Lydia stuffed her feet into a pair of slippers and opened the yurt door. "I'll be back in five minutes."

Sara lifted the top of her foot locker and pulled out a bottle of red wine she'd smuggled in the first day. They said all the great wineries like Wolf Blass were using screw caps so she hoped that meant this was a decent wine. She unscrewed the cap and dug out four glasses.

"Here we are." Lydia shoved the flap back, hopped into the tent, and dropped down on her cot. Maggie and Diane followed. They sat in the extra two wooden chairs.

"Next time we meet in our tent. You guys can sit on the chairs." Maggie grinned.

"Ah, but we have wine." Sara poured the wine into the glasses and handed one to each women. "I hope you're okay with plastic. I sent the crystal out to be cleaned. Cheers."

"Cheers! And plastic is perfect for the occasion." Maggie responded.

"Cheers," everyone clunked their glasses.

"Lydia said you had a problem and needed our help." Maggie took a sip of wine. "Not bad. I won't even ask where you got it."

"What's the problem?" Diane asked.

Sara repeated the situation and the information she'd shared with Lydia. "Lydia suggested you guys could help."

"Hey, we're a team, right? Kind of like the four musketeers. To us." Maggie raised her glass. Everyone clunked again, and took another sip.

"If we can get through all this crap they throw at us in training and we're supposed to learn to support each other, then we can certainly support each other if anyone has a problem. There are computers in the classroom where we learn about computer white collar crimes. I can see if I can borrow the use of a computer and do a search and see what I can find out about this guy."

"Thanks, Diane. I'd appreciate that."

Maggie took a sip of wine. "I guess this is where I need to see if I can talk to the ghosts you see."

"It might help. I don't want to push you into anything you don't want to do."

Maggie managed a half smile. "Mogee doesn't hesitate to push, but he's right. If this damn gift can be used to help other women, then I need to use it. I have been more open. I've picked up a few things, but nothing too noticeable. I'm not sure there are a lot of ghosts hanging around out here. What do you suggest?"

"Sara, why don't you hold the picture? When the women appear, tell Maggie and she can see if they'll talk to her." Lydia suggested.

Sara and Maggie looked at each other and shrugged.

Sara hesitated. She hated the images that crowded into her life, but if Maggie was willing, they'd both manage. She grabbed the photo. The forces pummeled her. A gasp slipped out.

"They're here?" Lydia asked.

"Yes. There are three women. They look sad and angry at the same time."

Maggie took a deep breath. She gripped the wooden arms of the chair. "My name is Maggie. I know you're here. Sara can see you. I can hear you if you speak. Can you hear me? Can you tell me your names and how you died?"

"Good," Maggie nodded. "Tell me your names."

Diane, Lydia and Sara watched Maggie carry on a one-sided conversation. Her head bobbed up and down in reply to their answers. Ten minutes passed. They sipped wine and waited.

"Great. I mean I'm sorry about what happened to each of you, but the information may help to save Sara's daughter. Thank you, ladies. I appreciate you talking to me. We'll do the best we can."

Sara topped up Maggie's glass and waited.

Maggie took a sip. After a few minutes she spoke. "Sorry, that actually takes a lot of energy. I'm a little tired. I guess it's like what Lydia said about trying to move objects with the mind.

Anyway, the three women that Sara sees are May Long-Bernstein, Genesis Waters-Bailey and Ann Taylor-Banks. All three of them married the same man. They didn't know this until after their death. They've come together to try and prevent any more victims. They'd like to help the police catch him. He used three different names, Paul Bernstein, Patrick Bailey and Palmer Banks. After going together for two to three months he asked them to marry him. Once they got engaged he got them to sign large life insurance policies, with him as the beneficiary, at his suggestion. He had logical explanations for each of them as to why they needed the policies. They were all murdered by that man on their honeymoon, immediately after they were married."

"But if he's killed three women why aren't the police looking for him?" Sara asked.

"Under normal circumstances they would be, but he is clever. May disappeared on their honeymoon to Catalina, in California. She fell overboard and her body was never found. Genesis fell from the balcony of their honeymoon hotel in Spokane, Washington. She died immediately."

"I'm seeing the pattern. A man by different names has his wife die in different states. They're entered into the computer data base, but no one's connected them yet." Diane said.

"Bingo." Maggie responded. "Ann Banks disappeared on a ski slope in Idaho. Her body has never been recovered."

"And Amy will disappear in Oregon and still no one will connect the deaths." Sara swallowed a sob. "What am I going to do?"

Lydia moved across to Sara's cot and wrapped her arms around her. "First thing, you're going to do is keep in close contact with Amy. They just got engaged, so you have some time yet. We'll use all the time we can get to find out more information and to hone our skills so we're prepared to take him on. He sounds like a very dangerous serial killer. He's smart and plans well. We need to be smarter."

"You're right. I've got my cell. I'll call her frequently and make sure they don't get married before we get there."

"Good." Lydia squeezed her shoulders. "Diane, what else can we do?"

"I can make a few calls to some of the contacts I have at the police departments. I can pass on the information and see if we can get them to tie the cases together. If we can convince them we really have a serial killer they might bring in the FBI, because it's happening across state lines. He's not so smart there, but he doesn't think anyone will ever connect him to all the murders."

"Phillip de Beares, PB, he's still using the same initials. A phony name like we thought. I wonder why he keeps the same initials," Sara commented.

"I have no idea, but it helps tie the murders together.

Maybe he's trying to legitimatize his name and history by keeping the same initials. Who knows? If we get the FBI involved they might come up with the profile of the serial killer."

"That sounds good, thanks Diane. Let's see what we can come up with by tomorrow night and meet back here."

"How about we meet in our tent?" Maggie offered.

"Fair enough, tomorrow night in Maggie and Diane's tent. You and I get the wooden chairs." Sara grinned at Lydia.

"It may not be official but I think we have our first mission. I can't think of a better one than to save Sara's daughter. To our first mission," Maggie raised her glass.

"Lights out ladies." Agnes Normand knocked on the door.

Everyone finished their wine. Lydia turned out the lights. Maggie and Diane cautiously lifted the canvas door, checked to make sure the area was clear, and crept back to their tent. An occasional giggle punctuated the night stillness.

Sara climbed into bed. Amy was in danger but at least it wasn't the old Sara, who wouldn't be able to help her daughter. She was trained and she had a team who would make sure Amy survived.

Carly paced the length of the Boardroom. Julie said she had something to share. So where was she?

"Sorry." Nadia hurried into the room, her long black hair pulled back into a clip. Her face was flushed. "I just got back and checked on our last project."

Julie trailed in between Nadia, her eyes focused on her tablet. "I need to let you know I've been working on the budget and it looks like someone has been trying to hack into our account. I've been working to divert our signals and bounce them a few more times. I'm also looking at a new jammer that's in the trial phase."

"I have Link tracing Groundhog, who's trying to find me, but other than the fact he works underground and never sticks his head out so no one knows what he looks like, it's difficult to get anything on the person. He's dangerous, we know that. He can track almost anything and he's a killer. We need to be extra careful. I also think we better get the Rempler kid out of the computer room. He could be an additional complication. I'll talk to Arnie and get him transferred to scheduling."

"Who do you think hired him to find out about us?" Julie asked.

"You mean hired him to get hired by us? That would have been his father, Fred Rempler who may have hired the Groundhog. If not him then Graham Hargreaves comes to mind. He has the most to lose and Groundhog showed up a few days after we took Elizabeth."

"That would be my guess, too," Nadia replied. "But we don't have any proof. We need to get everyone to work on this to protect our teams. Then maybe meet again to discuss and coordinate what we're doing. If anyone ever finds out about The Foundation our teams are in jeopardy and all those women who need help will be on their own."

"I know Nadia. I'm as concerned as you. And all those women we have already helped could also be back in danger, if anyone ever cracked our records on relocation. We've never had anyone even consider that we're an organization that helps people, let alone get this close. Graham has been upset because he's lost his daughter and his source of income. He'll do anything to find her. He's probably promised the Groundhog a large financial amount once his daughter is found dead." Carly paced the room. "I think he wants to find us or whoever rescued his daughter almost as much as he wants to find Elizabeth. Since Elizabeth has written her will and married her boyfriend, we could ask her to send Graham a message and tell him to leave the house and the business. That might shut him down, hopefully."

"I'll talk to Elizabeth."

"Thanks, Nadia. We should schedule another meeting to check on our progress on both our latest projects and whoever is trying to find us, later this week. What works for you two? Would a breakfast meeting on Thursday work?"

"Works for me." Nadia made a note on her phone.

"I'm good on Thursday." Julie entered the meeting date into her tablet. "That's my emergency for today."

Carly looked at the message in front of her. "I have one more, it's in Palestine. There's a young woman, early twenties who has been caught and accused of passing information to Israel. Because she's a woman they're going to have a quick trial and then kill her. I even heard they were considering stoning her to death. If it had been a man he'd get a couple of years in jail."

"That's why we try and save the women." Julie shook her head.

"We need a team who can get in there right away and get her out. Once she's safe we can work out her relocation and new identity. We can't negotiate with anyone on this and we probably only have a few days, maybe a week, max, before the trial and they make her an example. Do we have any teams ready to go?"

"I've got the Hammond team. They're already in the Middle East. They finished their mission a few days ago. They were hoping for a little R&R, but I'm sure they won't mind taking this on. We can add another week of R&R on after they get back." Nadia covered the distance to the secure phone in two strides. "I'll call them now and we can work out the details."

"Perfect. Thanks, Nadia, and thank your team. Julie, we're going to need money for this. Since its short notice and we're going to be bribing a lot of influential people, both for information and to look the other way, we'll need a lot of accessible cash."

"No problem. I'm on it. Is there anything else?"

Carly shook her head. "Not right now. I need to talk to a couple of people and work out a plan. Then I'll run it by you two."

"We'll be here when you need us." Nadia punched in a number, "Jasmine's florist?"

Carly left the room and made sure the bookcase was in place before she hurried downstairs to the CCB tactical division. They would make it work. With luck the woman would be out of Palestine and safe by the weekend.

After a strenuous hike up some of the cliffs and rappelling down in temperatures in the high nineties, the four women headed off to their Krav Maga class. Sergeant Golding paired them off.

"First thing we're going today is review situational awareness. You always need to be aware of your surroundings and potential threats. How you handle them could vary from personal life to being on a project. Learn the difference and attack only when necessary. Remember to use simple, repeatable strikes. Use any object at hand and target the body's most vulnerable points, such as the eyes, neck, throat, face, solar plexus, groin, ribs, knee, foot and fingers. Put on your pads and let's do a little demonstration."

An hour later the team pulled off the pads. Their bodies covered in sweat.

"Good work, ladies. You've all improved. Remember that your life or someone else's could depend on how well you can fight and disarm a male guard. See you tomorrow."

"Yeah, well I hope when we have to do that it's at night and a whole lot cooler than today." Maggie moaned.

"You got that right, lady. And maybe it could be inside with air conditioning." Diane added.

Sara laughed. "With my luck it will be in Alaska in the middle of winter. Come on let's grab an ice water before we start the class on drugs and how to survive an interrogation."

"The poisons I had no problem with. In fact, I'm working on how I might use one on my son of a bitch husband. Its basic electronics class, my head doesn't wrap around. I'm not techie." Lydia shrugged.

"I think the whole point is that we all have a basic knowledge of everything. Then we find our strengths and we develop them so together we have a solid knowledge of everything and make a strong team. You can be strong in poisons and Diane goes to the head of the class in computers. If we get cases where either might be involved, Lydia works on the poisons and Diane the numbers stuff. The interrogation survival we all need to understand— worst case scenario."

"Sara's right." Diane chimed in. "I'll figure out the patterns, and take out the guard and then Lydia can poison him."

"That works for me." Maggie saluted with her water bottle.

Their bottles of ice water in hand the women headed into the air conditioned class room to learn survival techniques.

Several hours later they finished their day with Mr. Mogee.

"Since Sara and Maggie have already managed to successfully combine their skills and work together, let's pair Sara with Lydia, and Maggie with Diane. Sara and Diane have similar skills in that they are both sensitives, although in very different ways. In this situation I'm going to have you enter a dangerous situation and see how you handle it." Mr. Mogee nodded to Lydia and Sara. "You two go first."

A man in a brown delivery uniform entered the room. "I have an envelope for Peters and Chapman"

"I'm Peters." Sara stepped forward.

"Sign here." He handed Sara a pen and an electronic signature pad.

Sara felt a jolt. She could see the man in fatigues with a gun pointed at her.

At a look in her eyes he immediately reached behind him.

"Gun." Sara screamed.

Diane and Maggie hit the floor.

Lydia scrunched her eyebrows together, focused on the dark metal grasped in his hand. He pulled it from his belt. The gun lifted toward the ceiling.

A surprised look on his face, the man grabbed at the floating gun, before it crashed to the floor.

Lydia took a deep breath and closed her eyes. The gun slid across the floor to her feet, and hit her foot. She bent down, picked it up and held it on the man. "Is this our situation or did this asshole really mean to kill us?"

The man raised his hands over his head, "Whoa there, no one said I might get shot."

"You can put the gun down, Lydia. It's not loaded. Yes, this is the assigned situation. You two did admirably. Lydia, I'm very impressed. You've been practicing, excellent. That could save a life one day." Mr. Mogee smiled.

A grin slid across Lydia's face. "That's the first time anyone's complimented me when I did something like that."

"I'll add my thanks as well. Great job, Lydia, if it hadn't been for you and it had been the real thing he would have killed me before I could get to him." Sara gave Lydia a hug.

"Thanks, roomie. I wouldn't want anything to happen to you, but you saw what he was going to do and warned me so I could go into action."

"That's the team approach. George, can I get you to help us out again?" Mr. Mogee addressed the man in uniform.

The man frowned. "No more shooting?"

"No, but I may ask the little brunette to throw you to the ground."

"Do I let her?"

"Of course not, George. You can stop her."

"Okay, I can do that."

"Good. Next up is Diane and Maggie. There's nothing as dramatic for you two, this time. Maggie, I don't have a ghost handy today so I want you to listen very hard and see if you can pick anything up from George. George, I want you to concentrate hard on throwing Diane, the dark haired lady to the floor."

George grinned and exposed a gap in his front teeth.

Maggie stood very still. She watched the tall man look at Diane.

Everyone held their breath.

Maggie shook her head. "Sorry. No wait.... he's thinking this could be fun. I can throw her to the floor, but gently so I don't hurt her and grab a feel at the same time."

George's face went beet red. "I didn't...I mean..."

"Too late, George, I should have warned you to keep your thoughts pure. Diane, Maggie has told you this man is going to grab you, throw you to the floor and cop a feel at the same time. What are you going to do about it?"

A huge grinned spliced across Diane's chubby cheeks. She stepped forward. "George, give it your best shot because you're going down, boy."

George grinned. He lunged forward. Diane stepped to one side and threw out a right hand. It hit George on the jaw.

A shocked look registered on George's face. He spun around; fists raised and shot his left hand into Diane's gut.

Diane staggered back with a grimace. "Damn."

One hand on her stomach, she pulled her body into a fighting stance. The two squared off and slowly circled counter-clockwise. Diane watched George. He jabbed in her direction. It was a weak, misdirected punch Diane easily avoided.

She followed through with a barrage of punches, grabbed his right arm and tossed him to the floor.

George lay on his back and stared up into Diane's laughing face. The others chuckled around him.

"That will teach me to think about a woman's body around this group. Sorry about that, Diane." George shook his head.

Diane offered him a hand to help him up.

He hesitated.

"It's okay. The exercise is over. You're safe, at least for now. Come back tomorrow."

"No, thanks, I think I'll let Mogee find another volunteer." George brushed off his pants and hastened to the door.

"Bye George, see you around." Diane cooed after him.

The women high-fived Diane and chortled at the retreating back.

"I bet he doesn't think about copping a feel from a woman for a while now." Sara said.

"Poor George, maybe we were too hard on him." Lydia suggested.

"Lydia, he's a man who thought he could throw a woman and touch her inappropriately at the same time. No quarter given, he deserved it." Diane stated.

"You're right. I've got to get over that. I guess it's part of the reason I put up with Harry. I kept giving him the benefit of the doubt. Now I know what he's planned for me, there's no doubt in my mind. I will take care of him when we leave here."

"We will take care of him." Sara squeezed Lydia's arm.

"Great work today, ladies. I think you can begin to see what your talents can do, both on your own and together. Keep working on them. Maggie, that's something new for you to try. It might not work all the time, but it will get stronger. See you all tomorrow." Mr. Mogee turned toward the door and disappeared.

No one even commented.

"Whew! One more day down, let's shower, change and grab dinner. Then meet back in Maggie and Diane's tent and see if we've come up with anything to help Sara," Lydia suggested.

"Works for me, come on Diane, race you for the shower. See you guys at dinner."

Sara trudged out the door after them.

"You okay?" Lydia followed her.

"I think I'm getting physically and mentally stronger. Another few weeks and I should be a match for the scum ball that's threatening my baby, but will it be soon enough?"

"Hey, don't forget tomorrow we change roomies." Maggie yelled over her shoulder. "Lydia and I switch places."

"Right, it's hard to believe it's been a month already. So does Diane snore?" Lydia shouted back.

Graham glanced nervously over his shoulder. He'd been told to meet the hit man here, at the edge of Central Park, by the Lennon memorial. Nine o'clock at night was not a good time to be here, alone. He paced up and down, looked over his shoulder. He jumped at the slightest sound. The man would want money. He'd been working for Graham for four days without receiving a penny. Good name and assurances only lasted so long.

Damn Elizabeth. She and that loser boyfriend had disappeared. Someone said they'd got married. If it was true he had more problems on his hand.

Could he convince Groundhog to kill both of them, on credit?

"Mr. Hargreaves? Don't turn around." A gravelly voice came from somewhere off to Graham's left.

Graham tried to glance over his left shoulder.

"I said—don't turn around." The voice shot like a knife through the night.

Graham stopped.

"You owe me a great deal of money. So far it's over a million dollars. I haven't received a down payment yet."

"I told you when my daughter is dead you'd get your money. Have you found her?"

"Yes. I know where she is. She's out of the country."

"Is she with that loser boyfriend?"

"I believe so, yes."

"Damn. When she's dead I'll get the money. In a few weeks I'll pay you everything I owe you, plus a bonus."

"Sorry, Mr. Hargreaves, I don't work that way. I've already found your daughter without any show of gratitude from you. I want half the money now and half when I do the job."

"I'll get it. I'll mortgage the house. It will take a few days."

"The house does not belong to you."

"I'll borrow the money."

"I've heard your credit isn't good these days. In fact, I've learned quite a bit about you. I think I've been conned by a man who has no money and no way to get any."

"Once my daughter is dead I'll have access to a fortune."

"That's not what I hear. In fact, I hear she's written a will and you're not in it. Also the police might be looking at you for the murder of your father."

Graham froze and held his breath. *No, no one knew or even suspected.* "You're bluffing."

"I never bluff and I never work for free. I will not complete my part of the bargain until I get half the fee. If I don't receive the money you owe me in twenty-four hours, I will have to protect my reputation."

"What does that mean?" Graham's voice barely managed a whisper. Terror crowded through his body.

No reply.

"Mr. Groundhog?"

Dead silence greeted him. Graham turned slowly.

The man had gone. Graham had the distinct feeling his own life might be in danger if he couldn't raise the money by tomorrow night. If Elizabeth wasn't dead he knew he had no way of getting cash. He already owed his bookies and other creditors more than his limit. And if she'd made a new will… Everyone was threatening his life. He had no place to go and no place to run.

What if the police were looking into his father's death? He had no place to hide.

# Chapter Sixteen

Loaded with bottled water, another bottle of bootlegged red wine and a brick of cheese Lydia had scored from the kitchen using her powers of telekinesis, she and Sara dumped the stuff on the table.

"I didn't think I'd get it all the way to the door before it dropped," Lydia laughed. "I've never lifted anything so heavy before but I managed to carry it directly to me. I grabbed it and hid it under my t-shirt. Laura does the dinner menu and clean up and I was gone before she noticed anything."

"That talent of yours is definitely becoming very useful." Diane dug out an army knife and sliced of four pieces. "Maybe next time you could get a few grapes?"

"Don't push it, but I'll see what I can do."

"I think I'm going to like having you for a roomie." Diane handed Sara and Maggie a slice of cheese. "I managed to get a call through to one of my contacts in the California police department. Interesting thing, a body had just been washed up on shore; an unidentified woman. Apparently she'd been weighted down but something, perhaps a storm had damaged the weights and they broke off. It left the chains around her wrists and ankles. They didn't weigh enough to keep her weighted down so she got carried to shore. She's been in the water for several months so identification is difficult. I suggested it might be the missing bride of Paul Bernstein, May Long-Bernstein. I also mentioned the other missing wives in Idaho and Washington. Harvey was very appreciative about the information."

"I bet Paul or Phillip or whatever his name is will be upset when he hears about the body washing ashore and being identified. That wouldn't have been part of his plan. He thinks he's smarter than everyone and feels he's superior to cops and even FBI. He doesn't believe the laws apply to him. He's above them. He hates women and chooses them usually because they're young with specific weakness, so he can control them and feel the power he never had in his life. If and when he finds out one of his wives has been found and messed up his perfect plan to stay under the radar, by moving from state to state to avoid FBI, it will affect his sense of control." Lydia commented.

"He'll be furious." Diane grinned.

"Maybe he'll back off Amy," Sara said hopefully.

"Not likely. He still thinks he's above the law and smarter than everyone. Do you notice he always uses the same initials? If we had anything more to go on, like his birth date, birthplace or parents or something we might track down his real identity." Diane sipped her wine.

"That's not going to happen. Okay, we have the police working on it in California, thanks to Diane. Maybe they'll get Idaho and Washington involved. What do we do next?" Lydia asked.

"We need to develop a plan. I can't visit him until boot camp is over, but I'll phone Amy and see if I can get any more information. It will all be lies but I can try. He might let something slip. I can also talk to the Director and see if he can point us in a new direction. We need DNA or fingerprints to run through the data base. Diane, could you contact the police departments where the deaths occurred, or the women went missing, and see what they found in the hotels or on the body? Maybe a fingerprint, or semen in Genesis; they were on their honeymoon. Maggie, maybe you could talk to the women again and see if they remember anything from their relationship, or their death, that might help us? Lydia, can you start drawing up a chart we can post our findings on so we have a visual picture?"

"Great idea, I can do that. On TV they call it a murder board. I think that qualifies here. I'll get some paper from the classroom tomorrow."

"Anybody have any other suggestions or questions?" Sara looked around the room.

Everyone shook their head, except for Diane. "I have one question, who gets to bring the wine tomorrow night?"

Everyone erupted in laughter.

"I think I've got a bottle or two hidden away," Maggie said.

"If you bring wine, I guess I'll try and sneak food out of the kitchen." Sara contributed.

"Let's see what we can accomplish tomorrow between and after classes. Any chance you could tap into what Phillip or whatever his name is, might be thinking?" Diane asked Maggie.

"I don't know. I've never tried something like that, but then I'd never read anyone's mind before today. I can work on it. Maybe I can use the photo Sara has of him. It's worth a try. If I need help I'll ask Mogee."

"I'll call Amy again. As long as they haven't set a date we'll be good, time wise. Unfortunately, she's head over heels in love with this perfect man, which we know he isn't. But so far he's the perfect serial killer."

Sara crawled through the mud. She tried not to move the long grass. The seagulls screamed above her. Lydia would be waiting for her when she got to the hut. She used her elbows to pull her along. She slid snake-like toward the small grove of trees. Diane's assignment was to get up the tree over the hut without being seen. They all had paint guns. If anyone got hit they were out of the game.

Sara spotted the hut and stopped. She scoured the area through her binoculars. One guard stood near the door. Sara reached into her army style boot and pulled out a knife. Taking aim she threw it into the guard's chest. He fell to the ground when the bladeless knife hit his chest.

Sara continued to crawl slowly toward the hut, constantly scanning the area. A sound hit behind her. She twisted in time to see a guard fall to the ground with red paint stains on his chest. She gave thumbs up to Diane in the tree.

Lydia waved her in from her position near the door. Sara rose to her feet and raced across the opening in the trees, to the door. Together, guns in hand, they kicked the door open, and rushed inside. A doll had been tied to a chair. Lydia cut the rope. Sara tossed the doll over her shoulder.

At the door they paused to check the area was clear. They stepped outside. Another shot hit a guard creeping up from around the side of the hut.

Good old Diane.

Lydia and Sara ran toward the waiting vehicle, Diane slipped down the tree and followed them. She ran backwards to cover their retreat. Seconds later they jumped into the waiting vehicle and Maggie hit the gas. They tore down the road. Sara and Diane kept an eye out for anyone who might follow them.

Minutes later Maggie raced the car into the camp garage. Diane and Lydia jumped out, shut the doors and locked them.

The four women high-fived each other, then, holding the doll high over their shoulders they marched into the classroom where the instructors waited, not a splatter of paint on any of them.

"Might as well get it over with," Sara mumbled.

"What?" Lydia looked up from the text book on electrical circuits she was studying.

"Nothing, I'm going over to see Mac and find out if he has any suggestions. It's not that late. I'm sure he'll be in his tent."

"Good idea. I'll be here." Lydia went back to the book.

Sara pulled on a thick, fuzzy gray sweatshirt. The evenings in the mountains got chilly. She tied the pink laces in her running shoes. "Come on, Gloria, we're going visiting."

"You're taking the dog? You can leave her here, unless she's your chaperone."

"It's okay. Come on Gloria."

Outside she breathed in the rich, scents of late spring and the fresh cool air. If they had time she'd love to explore the area.

There were no lights except the glow in the different tents. On their first day they'd been given a tour of the camp. There were six smaller tents, the cafeteria and one larger tent, all hidden under trees and shrubs. Mac's tent was closest to the cafeteria. She chose her path carefully. She patted Gloria on the head while she walked towards his yurt.

"Okay girl, this looks like it and the lights are still on." Sara tapped on the door.

No answer.

She tried a firmer knock.

"What?"

Sara swallowed. "Excuse me." It came out a whisper.

The door opened. Mac stood there, shirtless. He held a beer in his hand. His dark eyes stared down at her.

"Sara? What the….?"

"I'm sorry to bother you, but I need to talk to you. I need your professional opinion." She didn't meet his eyes but stared at the fascinating dark curls that trailed down from his chest. Heat permeated her body. The night felt hot and oppressive.

"Come in. Hey, Gloria," he bent down and rubbed the dog's ears.

Sara stuck one toe through the door way. She looked back over her shoulder.

"If you were going to run you should have done it before you knocked. It works better that way. Sit." He waved to a chair. "Want something to drink?"

Sara stepped inside. "They would be good."

"All I've got is beer."

"Beer's fine." Sara couldn't remember the last time she'd had a beer, but she needed something to help her through this meeting. Gloria was no help. She'd gone over to Mac and kept nuzzling his thigh.

Mac popped the cap and handed it to her.

She took a long sip. It felt icy cold as it slid down her throat. The hoppy taste left a slight bitter taste on her tongue, but not unpleasant. She took another swallow.

"Sara, what's this all about?"

Sara met his eyes. Those damn lightening arcs exploded between them. She had to get past the enormous physical attraction she felt. He was her boss. She was here because she had a problem.

"I don't know if I mentioned my daughter, Amy, when we had dinner."

"You did. She's living in Oregon somewhere."

"Yes, well she met a man. I believe he's a serial killer and she's going to be his next victim."

Mac choked on the last swallow of beer. He kept coughing.

Sara started to stand up but Mac waved her off. He

shook his head. It took a few minutes before he quit coughing. He took another sip of beer.

"Do I dare ask how you know this?"

"You know my team has an extra class every day. We're a little different from your other teams."

"Carly mentioned something and they sent that stuff up for you to do something with. I didn't pay much attention, something about psychics."

Sara grimaced. "Something like that, anyway with the four of us working together we've determined he's killed at least three other women. He uses different names and operates in different states, so no one is looking for a serial killer. I think he's quite a bit older than my daughter, but he told her he was twenty-five. His luck may be about to change because one wife who he weighted down and dumped overboard, just floated ashore. This man is now my daughter's boyfriend. If they get married he will kill her."

Mac shook his head.

"Look, I don't care if you believe me, I need some guidance. We're working the police angle. Diane is going to ask about prints or any DNA. Maggie's going to see if she can find anything more about the man or the murders."

"What does Maggie do again?" Mac finished his beer and stood up to get another one.

"I bet if I asked you'd have all our grades from the shooting range and how we're doing in martial arts right at the tip of your tongue, wouldn't you?"

Mac had the grace to at least look sheepish. "Um, well, you scored an eighty-eight average today which is very respectable and you took George down one out of three times, which is a good start."

"See, I knew it." Sara threw up her hands.

"You're right. I should be paying more attention to the other unusual thing you're all bringing to your team."

"That would be a start. You don't even have to believe in them but you could at least acknowledge that maybe we have something others don't. Maggie talks to ghosts, although it also appears she can read some minds. That's something new for her."

Mac slapped his forehead. "Terrific, someone who can read my mind. That's just what I need."

"Ah, but if it's the enemies mind it could prove very useful." Sara countered. "Anyway she's talked to the three women we know who were murdered."

"And you want what from me?"

"I honestly don't know. We're trying to work out a plan. Diane and Maggie are getting more information. I'm going to talk to Amy and see if I can get any more information, but I'm sure they'll all be lies. He's not going to tell her the truth about anything, especially if he plans to kill her. What else can we do?"

Mac stroked his chin. "So you're looking for a plan to catch this guy and prevent him marrying your daughter?"

"Yes, and we'd like to have everything in place so we can make this our first project and take care of it as soon as we graduate. We'd been multi-tasking and doing it on our own so we don't take anything away from The Foundation's plans."

"Hmm," Mac took a swig of beer and leaned back. "We may need to send someone down there to assess the situation, meet whatsisname and try for a fingerprint or DNA sample. It might not help anyway if he's not in the system."

"But if anything was left at the other scenes it could tie him to them and get police more interested."

"It could. Let me think on this, okay? I need to wrap my brain around it."

"No problem, I realize it's not what you normally do. I appreciate you listening to me. Thanks for the beer. Come on, Gloria."

The dog raised her head from Mac's feet where she'd been dozing.

"Great guard dog you are."

Mac followed her to the door.

"Anything you can think of to help would be appreciated." Sara swung around.

The heat between them could combust at any moment. His male scent mixed with something that smelled like saddle soap sent the heat pooling between her legs. No man had made her feel like this before.

"Oh hell let's get it over with and try again. That last time was sort of a bust."

"You think?"

Mac bent his head and brushed her lips. They fused together with the heat. He slid his arm around her waist and pulled her already sweaty body against his. She wanted to resist but her bones felt like mush. She felt his maleness press against her.

Her arms slid around his neck. She leaned into him.

"Damn," Mac muttered. "I didn't expect that."

"Me neither." She managed to whisper.

"I thought we'd get that kiss over with and realize there was nothing else to it."

"Kinda backfired, huh?"

Mac allowed his lips to twist in a wry grin. "Kinda."

"We can't let that happen again."

"I agree. It's bad for moral."

"Whose?" Sara smiled at him.

"The teams, The Foundation and mine, if the Commander ever finds out."

"I won't tell if you don't," Sara replied. "We'll need to make sure we're never alone."

"That's what we've been trying to do since the last time. If we need to talk we'll make sure it's in my office and you bring one of your team with you."

"No problem. I did bring Gloria with me, but that didn't work. Night Mac."

Sara stepped outside and paused. She lifted her arms, brought his head down, and kissed him hard on his thick, lips.

"One for the road." She grinned. "Come on, Gloria."

She hummed all the way back to her yurt. Mac Langston was the sexiest man she'd ever known. He made her body hum like a well-played guitar. If she couldn't see him alone again she damn well wanted something to remember. That last kiss would have to do, for now anyway.

What was even more important than her feelings for the man was could he come up with a way to help save Amy?

Roger drove down the highway heading for Los Angeles. He had a meeting at the studio, a lunch with a hopeful starlet. He had figured out which organizations to target. All his spies were in place, hired by various organizations. Now he had to wait for their reports.

Anticipation flowed through his blood. He thought about the nubile, young starlet, eager to do anything to break into the business. He was also sure in the next few weeks he should be able to narrow down the organizations that might be responsible for kidnapping his wife.

He pushed down on the gas. Everything was going his way.

Graham Hargreaves parked in the shadows of the deserted warehouse. Most of the buildings down here were slated for demolition. The police didn't even patrol the area, which is probably why it had been selected as a meeting place. He crawled out of his black Mercedes and paced up and down outside the warehouse. Was it a trap?

Everyone wanted to get him these days. The Groundhog

had been right. Between the letter from Elizabeth and the copies she'd sent to everyone including the press, his life was pretty much over. Everyone knew he had no money. His creditors were all after him and the Groundhog…who the hell knew what he would do when he found out he wasn't going to get paid, not a penny.

He'd been hiding in the house since yesterday. Sweat trickled down his back pooling below his belt. His breath came in rapid spurts. He ran his fingers through his graying hair. He had to figure out how to get out of town, without any money.

Why had Fred told him to come to this warehouse? He'd done a few dealings with the man, but nothing very big. He approached the side door and paused with his hand on the door knob. Graham slowly turned the knob and peered into the darkness of the deserted warehouse.

"Fred?"

No answer. Maybe he hadn't arrived yet.

He stepped inside, pulled the door almost close. He left it open a crack in case he needed to make a hasty escape. His eyes adjusted to the darkness, he noticed a faint light down near the end of the main floor. He edged toward the light. Two men stood together, talking quietly. He recognized one of them as Fred Remple, the man who had recommended the Groundhog to him.

They had done a few shady business deals together in the past.

"What's this all about Fred?"

"Graham? What are you doing here?"

"You sent me a note asking me to meet you."

"Me? No. I got a note from Frank, asking me to meet him in this warehouse. You've met my son."

Graham shook his head. "No, I haven't had the pleasure. If you didn't ask me to come, I don't understand."

Fred's tall, geeky son shook his head. "I didn't send you a note, Dad. You sent me one. You said we needed to change plans for CCB and you didn't want anyone to see us together."

Graham felt the hairs on the back of neck stand at attention. Something was definitely wrong. He needed to get out of here.

"My mistake, I'll leave you two alone." Graham almost ran toward the side door.

It was tightly closed. He'd left it open. In a panic he twisted the doorknob. Nothing happened. The door was locked. He heard Fred and his son pounding on another door at the other end of the warehouse. They screamed and yelled in hopes someone would hear them and open the door, but there were no security checking a deserted warehouse and no one in the area unless some homeless person had found himself a place to crash.

What was going on? Why had they all been lured here? Did it have something to do with Fred? Had he hired the Groundhog, too?

What was the point of locking them in a deserted warehouse? Graham stared up at the windows just below the roof. If he could get up there he could break a window and get outside. Then he'd have to find a way down from the roof outside. After that he'd need a plan B.

Outside a shadowy figure stood beside an older model, non-descript compact car. The warehouse erupted into flames, quickly engulfing the whole building. He listened to the screams from inside. After several minutes they ceased. He could hear sirens in the distance. Someone would have reported the flames. He slid into the driver's seat and started the engine. The sirens drew closer.

You didn't double-cross him. People knew better. If you didn't have the money, you didn't contact him. Two people had hired him for similar purposes, neither had the money to pay for his services. They had made promises based on wishes, not facts. He had eliminated both at the same time.

This should emphasize the message to anyone else who thought they could bargain their way out of a deal or make promises they couldn't keep.

The envelope lay on the floor inside the door.

Carly spotted it when she stepped into the room, about the same time Link saw it.

"Don't touch it." He pulled on plastic gloves, picked it up and turned it over carefully.

"Did someone shove it under the door?" Carly asked.

"I don't think so. I think he was in your apartment."

"Well, shoot. What about the dogs?" Carly staggered to the closest chair and collapsed. She put a hand out to protect her injured arm.

On cue two of them trotted out from the bedroom.

"It looks like they slept through the visit. Great watch dogs you have there. Stay where you are while I check the apartment."

"Watch out for Petey."

"Another voice heard from, who didn't scare the bad guy away. What a group?"

The marmalade cat stalked out and swished her tail around Carly's legs.

"Get out of here, you mangy animal. You could have at least scratched the guy."

A few minutes later Link returned. "No one here and nothing looks like it's been touched." He glanced around at the menagerie. "Next time maybe pick up a guard dog who would bark if someone enters the place."

"Let me see the letter. It would be meant for me, in my apartment."

Link handed her plastic gloves. "Put these on first."

Carly pulled on the gloves and took the envelope. She turned it over. It was a standard white business envelope, blank on both sides. It was tucked in to close. Not licked, so no DNA.

"We should probably give it to the police."

"Why? If it is the Groundhog there won't be anything on it they can trace. Let's see who it's from, then we can decide what to do with it." She opened it and withdrew a single sheet of standard stationary.

> *Ms. Brazil,*
>
> *This is a courtesy, to let you know your life is no longer in danger.*
>
> *The contract has been terminated due to non-payment.*
>
> *Both the termination of a contract and this letter are a first for me.*
>
> *As a business man I felt these things were necessary to my professional reputation.*
>
> *G*

It was typed on cheap, dime store stationary, probably on a computer at a library or coffee shop.

"How about that? He's an honorable killer." Carly shook her head. "You don't have to worry about me anymore. There's no longer a hit on me."

"This is the first time I've seen anything like this. I wonder how he terminated his contract. This is probably untraceable." Link muttered. "Have you got a baggy we can put it in?"

"Try the kitchen, left drawer, under the sink."

Link returned, put the page and envelope in it and sealed the baggy. "I'll take this to the police."

"You don't need to stay here any longer. You can go home. Not that I haven't appreciate everything you've done. Thank you. And I have my animals to protect me." Carly laughed.

"I can see how well they do that. You'd think a shepherd would have scared him." He patted Caesar on the head. "It could be a distraction you know, to get you to let your guard down."

"I don't think so. I don't think you do either."

"No, I think you're safe, for now. I'll see if I can find out how he terminated the contract. It should be interesting."

"Let me know. I'm interested in that, too."

"I will. I'll get my stuff together. You should still be careful."

"Sam will be with me in my car. You tinted the windows. I should be fine. I don't need a body guard twenty-four/seven anymore."

"Now that crisis is over, we need to talk. I'll pour you a glass of wine." Link poured her a glass of chilled Chablis.

"You're scaring me. What do we need to talk about that's so serious I need a drink? My hit man just resigned."

Link handed her the glass of white wine. "I'm quitting. I have hired a replacement, for your approval. I plan to leave almost immediately."

Carly stared at him. "Wha…Why…?"

She grasped the stem and downed the whole glass.

Link cracked open a beer and paced the length of his living room. Thoughts of Carly penetrated his every thought; her cute butt, her penchant for picking up stray animals and taking them home. It looked like someone was trying to find more about Carly. She hadn't said anything but there had been a few clues. He had nothing definite. The Foundation held fund raisers and had some lofty goals about providing assistance to women in their fancy brochure. She had a plane she flew up into the mountains somewhere, frequently. He had no idea what she and her girlfriends were doing but it was probably a lot more than the purpose the brochure stated. One thing for sure, when he left CCB he still needed to keep an eye on Carly. Her activities with The Foundation, whatever they were, could probably make her a target.

Shit. She needed him but didn't know it. He loved her and couldn't tell her until he got his life on track and he could tell her as an equal.

*Okay Stone, get your ass in gear and get your security business off the ground and profitable. Swallow your damn pride and use the money that's been sitting there gathering interest.*

His grandfather had left him the money to use as he wanted. Until now Link hadn't wanted to touch it. He felt if he spent it, it should be on something very special. There was nothing he wanted to do with it until now. He took a long slug of beer and almost choked as an idea hit him.

He'd get his business up and running, He'd get Julie to invite him to the next function they organized. He'd meet Carly on neutral ground and on his terms.

He grabbed his cell phone and punched in a number.

"Hey, Joey. What you doing these days? I'm looking for someone to work for me. Great, meet me for lunch at the Diner, noon tomorrow and we'll talk."

There was a sharp knock. He hurried over and checked the peephole before he slid back the lock and opened the door.

"Jimmy thanks for coming."

An older man with a short, graying crew-cut, wearing jeans and a plaid, short-sleeved cotton shirt marched into the room.

Link gave him a slap on the back. "It's good to see you, Sarge."

Taller than Link, but at least fifty pounds lighter, the dark-skinned man slapped Link back. "It's been awhile, Link. What are you up to?"

"I'm making some changes in my life. I guess it's time I grew up."

Johnny shook his head. "Son, you grew up in Iraq. You all did. I'm sure if you'd wanted you could have bought your way out of going."

"Maybe, but I don't believe money should divide one man from another. Besides, if someone is lucky enough to have money it should be used for something of benefit to people."

"I figured that out, man, during your stint over there."

"We had a good crew. You kept us in line and saved our sorry butts. I just contacted Joey to see if he might be interested in working with me."

"How is Joey? I felt bad about the bomb. I hate it when one of my men gets hurt. He had a rough go for a while after losing his leg."

"He's making it. His wife stayed with him. That made the biggest difference. They have two kids now. He's working mall security."

"I'll bet he jumped at the offer to work for you."

Link grinned. "Something like that. But it's not charity. He's good at his job. He was good in Iraq. I can use him."

"Sure, but it's nice to remember your buddies. See any of the other guys?"

"Nope, Leroy and Buzz are still over there I think. Marty's married and living somewhere in Florida."

"At least he doesn't have to freeze his balls off up here. Enough reminiscing, you said you're giving up that security job to start your own business?"

"Get you a beer?"

"About time you offered."

Link returned with two beers and handed one to Johnny. "I need an office and top of the line equipment."

"That's where I come in, right?"

"You've always been the technical person. I need cameras, listening devices, recorders, scanners, even weapons. Can you handle it?"

"Can a fish swim?" Jimmy grinned. He dropped into a recliner, his long skinny legs stretched out in front of him. "What's the budget?"

"Whatever you need?"

"Man, this is going to be fun." Jimmy pulled a pad and pencil from his pocket and started to make notes.

"I'll need some training on the newer computer stuff. CCB has top line but I'm sure you can find me the latest."

Jimmy kept writing. He didn't look up. "It'll take a week or two. I'll get back to you with a list of what I can find and the cost. No problem with the training. Joey will need to be trained too."

"Uh huh."

"Okay, let me get back to you. As for the office, have you checked with Charlene, Eric's wife? She's a real estate agent, specializing in offices and businesses." Johnny closed his pad.

"Good idea. I'll call her in the morning. I want some place central."

"She can set you up and probably get you a deal. I've got your number. I'll call you when I get everything put together. Good seeing you again." Jimmy extended his hand.

Link grasped it tightly. "Thanks for coming, Sarge. I want the best and only you can get it for me."

The door closed. Link shot the inside bolt. Everything was in progress. He had enough contacts from working CCB he should be able to get a few contracts right away. He'd send out information on the new security firm. He wouldn't take any away from CCB.

Now he needed to tackle Julie. Hopefully she wouldn't be too upset with him because he quit CCB.

# Chapter Seventeen

Sara held her stomach. Someone was hurting. She could feel it. It had to be Amy. She decided to phone Jason first and check on him.

"Hi Andy, it's your mother. I haven't heard from you for a while so I thought I'd give you a quick one minute to call to see how you're doing."

"Hey mom, I'm sorry about not calling. I'm doing great. How are you?"

"I'm okay. How are your classes going?

"They're good so far."

"Good. Will I get to see you during summer break?"

"I got a summer job with a big computer firm but I'm hoping to make it home for a couple of weekends."

"That will be nice. I'd love to see you. Have you heard from Amy?"

"No, she hasn't called for months, why?"

"She's getting married next month."

"Really, I wonder why she hasn't said anything or invited me to her wedding."

"They seem to want to make it a very small affair. I'm not even sure I'm invited."

"That's odd, but I'm sure you are. Who's she marrying?"

"Phillip de Beares. He's supposed to be a business man, but I don't think he works. I think he's a lot older than Amy and he's living off her."

"Sounds like you don't like him."

"I don't." Sara decided to be honest. "He's moved her from her friendly condo to an isolated place near the beach, away from any of her friends. He expects her to be with him twenty-four/seven when she's not working."

"From what you're saying, he doesn't sound like an ideal match for my sister. I'll call my sister and see what I can find out."

"Thanks, Andy, I appreciate that. He's also had her take out an insurance policy on her life."

"And they're not even married yet? That's a little odd. I'd wonder about him, too. I'll call her tomorrow."

"Thanks again and please call me after you talk to her. I'd love to know what you think." Call me later."

Amy hadn't even talked to her brother or told him about the wedding. She used to be close to her little brother. What had that killer done to her daughter?

Sara punched in the phone number. She kept one hand on her stomach.

Amy picked up the phone. "Hello?"

"It's your mother, how are you, darling?"

There was a long pause.

"I'm doing fine, Mom." Amy finally squeezed out.

"Good. How's Phillip?"

"He's fine too," Amy replied. "You called last weekend."

"I know. I miss you. I wondered if there were any more wedding plans."

"Mom…"

"I'm not trying to interfere. I just wondered if you two were going on a honeymoon after the wedding, or if you were going later."

Amy's voiced perked up. "We're going to stay in Las Vegas for a few days and then take a trip about a month later when he can get away from his business for a longer period of time. Phillip booked the honeymoon suite at the top of the Platinum hotel in Las Vegas. It will be very exciting. We're also going to see a couple of the big shows while we're there."

"That sounds wonderful. Las Vegas is a great place for a honeymoon. You'll have a wonderful time."

"Thanks. I think so."

"I should be able to get there the day before the wedding. Maybe we can get together for a few minutes."

"Maybe, I'm not sure what our plans are."

"That's okay, we'll see what works. Did you invite your brother?"

"Uh, no, Phillip wants to keep it a small ceremony, with just us, oh and you. He said we could visit Andrew later."

"Oh, well, what about a wedding gift? What would you like? Or what do you need?"

"You don't have to buy a gift. That's not why we're getting married."

"I know, sweetie, but it's traditional. I want to get you something."

"I'll talk to Phillip and see what he says. I'll get back to you, if that's okay?"

"Of course, it's okay. Let me know later. How's work?"

"It's good. I think they're going to give me a promotion at the end of the semester."

"Oh Amy, I'm so proud of you. You've made a wonderful career for yourself. Daddy would be very proud of you, too."

There was a catch in Amy's voice. "Thanks, Mom."

"You take care of yourself. I'll call soon. Love you." Sara hung up and stared at the phone. He'd hit her in stomach and given her a black eye, Sara felt sure of it. There was just enough time before the wedding for the black eye to heal. She was surprised he hit her in the face.

They were staying in a high rise hotel in Vegas. Only three weeks until her daughter's life could be over.

Her team's graduation was almost here. They had a plan in place. Would it be enough? Could they take down a serial killer and save Amy?

They gathered in Diane and Lydia's tent. Diane flipped open a manila folder. "Okay, he's real name is Peter Burns. He's thirty-two and has a criminal record for assault."

"How did you get that?" Lydia asked.

"My contact found finger prints from his case. They were the husband's so no one checked them out. He ran them through the data base and there was Peter. He's the husband, but now he's also a person of interest."

"That's a start. What do I do now?"

Diane held up her hand in a stopping motion. "Wait, there's more."

Maggie chewed on a finger nail. "We should be checking insurance policies. He had policies on each wife. If I can pull that information we can also feed it to the police."

"Can you do that?" Sara asked.

"I can do it. It's what I did when I worked at the bank, before Brad got me fired. Does he have a policy on Amy?"

"Yes, she said something about having to take a physical. He told her they needed to get them because of his business."

"From what I've been able to find he hasn't worked for the last seven or eight years. I think he lives off the insurance money when a wife dies and when it gets low he finds another victim. I think he's a serial killer for the money, maybe the power." Diane continued to read from the folder. "I've sent requests to the various police departments. I don't think anyone has linked the cases together to make him a serial killer. So far I think they all investigated their cases separately. If you can get information on the insurance policies, when he took them out, how much they were for, I'll shoot the information off to the various police departments."

Sara sank her head into her hands. "I can't believe it. There's only three weeks to get him before they get married. Then he plans to kill her. I've got to save her."

The other three women reached for her.

"We'll protect her, Sara. We'll get him. We're finished training in under three weeks. We'll talk to the Commander about making it our first assignment."

Sara shook her head. "I don't know…"

"Let me check out the insurance policy angle." Maggie offered. "I know how to check that and if I need any help, there are a few favors I can pull in. Diane can use her sources to follow up with her contacts."

"I'll dig into his background and see if I can find anything. Peter Burns' birthplace is listed as Deer Creek, Montana. If we get more information from there we might be able to profile him, and figure out how to get him arrested and convicted."

"Can you get me a sample of Amy's signature?" Maggie asked. "That way we can check if the signature is a forgery, if there is an insurance policy."

Sara slumped in her seat. *I could go down and bring her back to Seattle with me. Maybe tell her I'm sick and I need her to stay with me and help me.*

"Come on, Sara, you can't give up. If you go down and bring her home he could kill both of you." Diane thumped the table.

"How did you know…?"

"…what you were thinking, it wasn't that hard," Diane replied.

Sara's mouth twitched. "You've been practicing. You're getting good at it, aren't you?"

Diane shrugged. "Maybe, but we're not talking about me."

"I wish I could do more." Lydia commented. "But, I am working on my talent."

"Keep working on it, Lydia. You may need to move another gun soon." Diane grinned. "You may need to make this one fly a few feet away from him."

"I'll head over and see if I can get into the computers and start working tonight." Maggie moved to the door.

"Hold on, I'll go with you and start working on his background." Diane tucked her folder under her arm.

Maybe I can talk to Nadia and tell her about Amy. Mac suggested someone go to Oregon to follow the guy. We could find out what he does every day. It might help figure out how to catch him. I'll ask him if he can contact Nadia."

"Maybe I could hire someone. Nadia might know someone. I'll ask Mac when she's coming up again."

"We've got a lot more information now. Mr. Phillip de Beares doesn't know it yet, but he's not that smart. We're closing in on him."

⌘

"Mac said you wanted to talk to me." Nadia waved Sara toward one of the hard-backed chairs in Mac's office. "What's the problem? Are you having trouble with the training? It's almost over and I understand you've been doing very well."

"No, nothing like that, it's personal."

"I'm listening." Nadia stretched out her legs.

"I have a daughter."

"I know. She lives in Oregon."

"She's involved with a serial killer. I think he plans to kill her in the next few weeks, after they get married. I've asked them to postpone the wedding until I can get there, right after training. He's not happy about it, but Amy insisted because she wants me there, so he's agreed. It's a small ceremony and no one else will be there. They're getting married two days after I graduate, in Las Vegas, where they plan to honeymoon. I believe he will kill her there."

"And you know this, how?"

Sara hesitated. She didn't want to get anyone in trouble, but this was her daughter's life. "We've been working on it for a few weeks."

"We?"

"Maggie and I used our paranormal skills to see the ghosts of his three dead wives, talk to them and get information about their deaths. Diane used that information to check up on him and to notify the various police departments. Maggie checked into insurance policies on each of the women, including the amount and the waiting period until he can kill them and collect. Amy took one out about four weeks ago. If anything happens to her he's the beneficiary."

"You've been a very busy team."

"It's my daughter."

"So what do you need to talk to me about?"

"Two things, I want to hire a private investigator to follow this man for a few days and see what he does and how he spends his money. It might help to figure out how to catch him. And the team would like Amy to be our first mission after graduation. We'll do another one right after for The Foundation."

Nadia sat quietly for several minutes.

Sara wriggled in the chair. She forced herself not to say any more.

"If we allow Amy to be your first mission, it would have to be because The Foundation also wants to save her. Show me copies of all the information you've gathered so far. She certainly qualifies as a victim. If it becomes a Foundation mission, we would hire an investigator, do the necessary ground work and come up with an appropriate plan for the mission."

Sara almost bounced out of her chair, but forced herself to simply nod.

"I need to make a phone call. Could you wait outside, please?" Nadia asked.

Sara hurried outside and closed the door behind her. She had her fingers crossed. If it was a Foundation mission it would be so much better for Amy. She paced back and forth.

Nadia opened the door. "You can come back in."

Sara perched on the edge of the chair.

"Yes, Sara, we will save your daughter. That's what The Foundation does and we certainly will do it for a team member. You can let your team know that it is now an official Foundation project. Immediately after graduation we'll fly you to Las Vegas where you'll be briefed on your mission." Nadia stood up, a smile played with her mouth. "Dismissed, Recruit Peters."

"Yes sir, ma' am, thank you, ma'am." Then unable to resist she stepped forward and hugged Nadia before she rushed out of the office.

Outside the main building she watched Sergeant Bush demonstrate attack to Gloria in an enclosed area. She had Gloria sit and stay.

A volunteer approached. They pulled out a gun and aimed at the trainer. When they pulled the gun Gloria charged the volunteer. She bit into the padding on the volunteer's arm that held the gun. The volunteer dropped the gun.

"Good dog." The trainer praised Gloria who plumped her bottom on the ground. She looked quite pleased with herself.

Even her dog would be ready for this mission. Phillip or Peter or whoever he pretended to be, was going to get a surprise this time when he tried to kill his next, and last, victim.

The graduation ceremony was short and private. No family or friends were invited. Mac called them into the dining area. The four women sat behind a dining table.

Gloria lay at Sara's feet. Mac strode to the front of the room.

"Ladies, congratulations, you've managed to survive the ten weeks of training. Each of you has excelled in different areas and together you will make a strong team.

I wish you success in your missions. Remember to always be on alert. Continue to practice the skills you've learned in all areas, particularly self-defense. Work out and stay in top condition. There are no certificates and there is no record of your training, so no grad party."

The team sneaked a look at each other.

"Your group worked on special talents during this time. I'm not a believer, but I have seen how your talents could benefit both the organization and people in general, so good luck with those too. And last, but not least, Gloria, you've been a joy and surpassed the expectations people had about training an older dog. Tell Sara to give you some extra treats."

Gloria's tail thumped against the floor.

"The plane will be here to pick you up within the hour, so grab your bags and be ready. It's been an honor to know you all. Good luck and good luck on your first mission." Mac strode out the door.

"I guess the lack of ceremony goes with working undercover." Maggie gave a lopsided grin. "Now we're about to find out how much we have learned."

The women trailed outside and shuffled toward their tents, to give it one last check over. Sara and Gloria brought up the rear.

Mac grabbed Sara's arm and pulled her aside. "Look Sara, you know how I feel about you. Won't you consider doing something less threatening with those skills?"

Sara shook her head. "We've been through this, Mac. This training gave me back my life and taught me to be strong and respect myself. I don't need anyone to take care of me. I don't want anyone to take care of me. I want control over my choices. And I want to save my daughter."

"Sara, listen, I understand. I want to try…"

"No Mac." Shaking her head she pulled her arm away. "You want to make my decisions, like asking me to quit what I was trained for. You don't understand. I'm an equal now, not a pathetic woman who needs a man to take care of her. I'm sorry. I like you, but I don't plan on seeing you again. Come on, Gloria." Sara stalked off to her tent, blinking rapidly.

"Didn't go well, huh?" Maggie stood up after she checked under the bed.

Sara shook her head. She didn't trust herself to speak.

Maggie hugged her. "It's okay, sweetie. You've got the team. I think I hear the plane. Let's blow this joint. Grab your pack."

Sara followed the order and staggered outside behind Maggie. The plane landed on the small runway. The door opened.

Lydia and Diane were already half way up the steps.

Sara pulled her shoulders back, didn't glance toward Mac's tent and marched across the runaway. This was what she'd trained for. She and her team were going to save Amy. The plan was to fly straight to Vegas and arrive before the wedding. The Foundation would explain the full plan when they arrived. Would it work? They would save Amy. It wasn't an option. She's kill him herself if all else failed.

A private car and driver picked them up at the Las Vegas airport and drove them to the hotel. Nadia met them in the lobby and handed them their room keys.

"Ladies, you're already registered. Sara, dogs are allowed, so Gloria is in your room with Diane. Unpack, check your equipment and meet me in the King of Diamonds conference room in forty-five minutes."

Forty-five minutes later the five women huddled together around a small conference table. Nadia sat in the middle, an open folder in front of her. She surveyed the group.

"This is the first rescue we've done for family. Carly questioned whether we should let you take the lead because of the emotional involvement, but we figured you'd probably go rogue if we didn't give you this assignment. So, you will keep the emotions in check and follow the plan, precisely. Got it?"

All the women nodded.

"Good. We have checked the man out, thoroughly. Diane did a good job as far as she got before we took it over. Peter Burns was born in Deer Creek, Montana. His mother got pregnant by a white, travelling salesman, who left town and never knew about Peter."

"Probably wouldn't have taken responsibility, anyway," Maggie muttered.

Nadia pulled her pencil thin eyebrows together and shot a glance at Maggie. "His mother tried to look after him but a female social worker from the state took him away and put him in a foster home when he was three. He fought with the other children, stole their toys and lied. The foster mother asked the state to remove him when he was four and a half.

He went through fifteen foster homes. He stole money. When he got older, he threatened and intimidated the mothers, until some of them actually feared for their lives. There's a history that family pets and some of the neighbors pets were killed."

"Ohmigawd," Lydia gasped.

"This is not a nice man we're dealing with. He is intelligent. He designed this plan to get women to sign insurance policies for him, each with a different company and in a different, state. At one point he worked as a maintenance man in a police station. He was fired after three months because of his attitude and poor quality of work, but it gave him access to police procedures and how they worked.

He's a patient man. He stalks and takes time to pick his victims. His plan is similar in all cases, except the manner of the murder changes to fit the setting. From what we've been able to put together he spends at least a month and sometimes longer, stalking the victim every day, until he knows everything about her and her routine."

"Let me guess, they were all women with poor self-image."

"Correct, Sara."

"If I'd been a stronger mother and role model, my daughter might not be his next victim."

"That's possible, but when you look at the bigger picture, if he hadn't picked Amy, you wouldn't have caught on that he was a killer. No one would have linked the killings yet and dozens of other women might be killed until someone finally figured it out.

Like I said, keep those emotions in check, remember this man likes to kill and will keep doing it if we can't stop him. We didn't have enough proof to get him arrested. Now the plan is to capture him alive and turn him over to the police. It would look better that way, but if he threatens anyone and their lives are in danger, we take him out." Nadia continued.

"We sent one of our private team members to Oregon to watch him for a few days. He spends his days working out at the local gym, socializing with the wealthier clientele, and occasionally going out for drinks with one of them. We know physically he's in good shape so remember that if you need to challenge him. He has a stripper bar where he hangs out after the gym. He plays poker there and bets the horses. He also sleeps with one of the strippers. Didi O'Malley. Occasionally he gets invited to play golf.

That's pretty much his days. He usually visits Didi every

day or every other day. We've talked to her. She's afraid of him so she listens, strokes his ego and hopes he doesn't kill her when he leaves. He's told her about Amy and that he's coming into money soon."

Sara gripped the table until her knuckles turned white.

"Didi will even help Amy if she can. She'll testify against Peter if we catch him. He asked her to go to Los Angeles with him, so I'm guessing that's where he plans to find his next victim. He'll put Didi up in a room while he trolls for that person. When we save Amy and take him out of circulation, we'll also be saving that next victim, including Didi, and any other future ones. Remember that."

"I hope I get a chance to punch this guy's lights out. I want to cause him pain like he's never known." Diane snorted.

"Sorry babe, he's mine. At least until I've beat him to a pulp and chopped his balls off," Sara retorted.

"Ladies, please, remember about the personal emotions. Here's the plan. The wedding is the day after tomorrow at a small chapel here in Las Vegas."

"He convinced Amy to switch from the University chapel in Tillamook, where several friends were planning on attending. That was Amy's first choice. They plan to honeymoon in Vegas for a few days so he's arranged for them to get married in one of the small chapels on the strip, the Chapel of Love. He made the change in plans at the last minute so her friends can't get off work or arrange to make the trip. He's pissed that I said no problem I'd be there tomorrow." Sara interrupted.

"Sara gets to meet him, see if she can get a reading off him when she spends time with him and Amy. Diane is going in with Sara as a close friend and Amy's godmother's sister. We're hoping Diane can get into his mind and find out exactly what he's planning. Then the next day, depending on the information we receive from Sara and

Diane, they will attend the wedding. Sara will treat them to a special dinner. Gloria will also attend.

Lydia and Maggie will wait in the honeymoon suite he's reserved and where Peter and Amy are staying for two nights. It's on the twenty-ninth floor. Sara, if you get a chance, go up there and scout it out. We have the blueprints of the suite. I had someone go through them and compare them to the physical room, but it's always nice to know if they've rearranged the furniture or added anything. That should do it. Sara, go meet your new son-in-law. The rest of you, make sure you know exactly what you'll be doing and don't lose too much money at the casinos." Nadia strode out.

"Wish me luck. I'm going to have to pretend to be excited about my daughter's impending wedding and my wonderful, new son-in-law." Sara stuck her fingers in her mouth and made a gagging sound.

Maggie gave her a little push. "Go, give an academy winning performance and tell us all about it tonight."

"Before we leave here, I have a spell of protection I'd like to do. I figure every bit helps."

"Good idea, Diane." Lydia responded and sat back down. "What do we need to do?"

Diane lifted the cloth bag she'd been carrying on to the table. She pulled out four black cotton pouches with drawstrings and handed one to everyone. She also gave them each a piece of parchment.

"I need you to draw a pentagram with this ink." She put a bottle of India ink on the table and four pens.

Everyone dutifully scratched away on their pentagrams.

"Good, now roll them up and put them in your pouch. You can see the other items I've placed in the middle of the table. You each need to take one of the small, clear crystals, a pinch of the sage, a pinch of the wormwood, one of the lead fishing sinkers and a strand of your own hair in the bag. The scissors are to cut the strands of hair."

It was quiet for the next few minutes. Each of them followed Diane's instructions.

"All done." Sara sat back.

"Almost," Diane responded. "Now tie the bag with three knots and when you're finished, make sure you carry that bag with you until we catch that man."

"Thanks, Diane." Maggie finished her knots, popped the bag in her pocket and stood up.

"I'll join you for dinner. I'll pretend I couldn't make the same flight as you and arrived late this afternoon from Tacoma. I'll bring the pictures that my sister, Ellen, has of Amy as a baby. I'm sure Phillip/Peter will be thrilled." Diane twisted her lips into a grimace.

Sara headed up to her room in case Phillip or Amy might drop by. Until Diane officially arrived it was her and Gloria. Sara picked up the phone and asked for Amy's room.

"Hi, darling, it's me. I've just arrived. Are you free for drinks or I can come up to your room?"

"Hi, Mom, I'm glad you made it. I can't wait for you to meet Phillip. He had to go out for the afternoon. He's trying to make some business contacts while we're here."

"Sounds like a very busy man. He should be successful, working this hard."

"Oh, he will be. Why don't you come up? We can have a good chat until he gets back."

"Sounds perfect, what room are you in?"

"It's the penthouse. Can you believe it? He reserved the penthouse for our honeymoon."

"Wow, the penthouse. I can hardly wait to see it. Gloria and I will be right up. Love you."

"Gloria? Oh I don't...."

Sara hung up the receiver. Perhaps Phillip didn't like dogs, especially after all the ones he'd killed. Too bad, but, Gloria needed to check out the room too. She was part of the plan.

Sara checked the wire Nadia had put inside her bra and

then signaled Gloria. She took a deep breath. She needed to act normal and be excited for her daughter.

Link saw Carly enter her private elevator. He needed to catch her, tell her about her new head of security and arrange a meeting. He exited from the regular elevator and strode to her office door. He knocked.

No one answered.

*Odd, she had to be in there.*

He turned the knob and entered. The bookshelf on the back wall was closing.

*I'll be damned. There's a secret room back there. What does she need a secret room for?*

He took a seat and waited.

Half an hour later the book shelf opened and Carly walked out. She stopped and stared at him.

"What the hell are you doing here?

"Sorry, Carly. I saw you come up here and I needed to talk to you. When you didn't answer I came in and saw the bookshelf closing. I could have left but I didn't want to sneak out. I thought you should know what I saw. What's the room for?"

"It's none of your damn business. Obviously you weren't supposed to know about it."

"Is this something to do with The Foundation you hold fund raisers for?"

Carly dropped into her chair. She stared at Link. "You can't tell anyone. There would be too many people at risk."

"I would never do anything to put you, or anyone else at risk. My lips are sealed. Come on Carly, you know me. I'm sorry I found out something I wasn't supposed to. I came up to inform you about your new security head."

"I trust you, but the less you know is probably for the best."

"That's fine. I won't ask any questions. I didn't mean to upset you."

"I know. I need to be more careful. I should have locked my door if I was going in the back room. If anyone had to see it, I'm glad it was you."

"Thanks. I've finished security clearance on CCB employees and doing a recheck on a few. I didn't find any flags. I'll have Tom take it over. It will give him a little familiarity with the employees."

"Tom?"

"Tom Gerow, he's going to be my replacement, if you approve."

"I'm still having a problem digesting the fact you plan to leave. No way I can change your mind?"

"No, I really need to do this. You'll understand sooner or later, I'm starting my own security business. You can hire me on a contract basis if you need something special done. And I won't be undercutting CCB business."

"I didn't think you would. You're opening your own security business?" Carly shook her head. "I don't get it, but I wish you luck."

"One day you'll get it. In the mean time you need to meet Tom and officially offer him the position."

"If you've picked him and screened him, I'm sure he'll be fine. Bring him up tomorrow morning and we'll do the formalities."

"That sounds good. I'll stay on part-time to train Tom and he can call me anytime if he has questions."

"It sounds like someone you know well."

"He is. You'll like him." Link opened the door. "And if you need anything in the security way for that back room stuff, you could contract me to help. I'm very trustworthy."

"Get out of here." Carly waved her hand for him to leave. "I need to sit here and process a lot."

"Oh, and I think the Groundhog closed his contracts with a fire in an abandoned warehouse. I heard it was a mysterious fire, not sure how it started. Three bodies were found inside. They haven't released the identification yet, but I'm guessing two of them were Hargreaves and Remple. And Frank Reed hasn't showed up for work for a couple of days. He's probably the third body."

"When he breaks a contract he really does it with style. I guess he's sent a message to anyone who wants to book him."

"I think that was the point." Link closed the door behind him.

Carly stared at it. She knew she liked Link, but she hadn't realized how much she trusted him. Now he knew about the secret room. She wasn't too worried but she was getting careless. She needed to smarten up. With everything that was happening these days The Foundation could be in trouble. She stared at the closed door. Emptiness seeped inside her. How was she going to manage when he left? How was she going to handle it, not seeing him again? The depth of her feelings for link Stone hit her hard. Emptiness seeped through her.

Amy opened the hotel room door and threw her arms around Sara's neck. "I've missed you so much."

Sara hugged her daughter. She held her close and tried to pass on strength and positive energy. Finally, she stepped back.

"You look lovely, very happy and excited."

"I am. He's the perfect Prince Charming. He could have any woman he wanted and he wants me."

"Of course he does. He knows a good thing when he finds it." Sara stepped into the room and closed the door behind her.

"Mom!"

"What?" Sara glanced around.

"I've never seen you look like that."

Sara glanced down at the emerald green silk, sleeveless top she wore, over white linen Capri's. She'd chosen a matching pair of green sandals and earrings.

"This outfit, yes, I'm wearing brighter colors and more up-to-date things these days."

"No, it's not just that. You've cut your hair. I love the red highlights by the way. Look at you. You have muscles and a great body. You look amazing and you look happy."

"That's right; you haven't seen me for a while. I've been working out. I want to get back into the shape I was when I was in University, before I met your father." Sara spun around. "Not looking too shabby for an old lady, huh?"

"You're not old and you look fantastic. Maybe I should take a few lessons." Amy looked down at the faded jean shorts and yellow t-shirt. "I really need some new clothes, but we can't afford a lot of extras right now with Phillip starting up this business. I can't believe he spent the money for a penthouse."

*All the better to kill you with. That bastard is spending all Amy's money on his clothes, the gym and some stripper. Oh, he was going down.*

"Come on, sit down. Hey, Gloria." Amy knelt down and nuzzled the dog. She wrapped her arms around her furry neck. "I've missed you, too. At least you haven't changed."

Gloria's long tongue came out. She lapped Amy's face.

"Gosh, it feels good to have you two here. I haven't talked to anyone for ages."

Sara glanced around the room. It looked much the same as the blueprints. Three doors lead off the room, two on one side and the other at one end of the room, off from the balcony.

"Oh, a balcony, I bet you can see all of Vegas from this high up."

"Not quite, but there is a good view of the pool and the gardens down below and at night you can see a lot of the lights from the strip."

Sara leaned over the balcony. "Be careful out here, that's a long way down and you'd land on the cement deck by the pool."

"Don't worry, I'm careful and if I go out, Phillip is with me, so I'm safe." Amy smiled.

Sara came back in and sat down on the couch. Gloria curled up at her feet.

"I'll make tea." Amy went to the coffee tray in the room.

"So how is work? What have you been doing besides preparing for the wedding?"

"Work is good. I like the library. It's interesting. I can use both my computer and administration skills. I'm working on my degree online. I think I told you, the head librarian is retiring. Her assistant will move up and I've been told I'll get her assistant's position while I finish my degree, so that's exciting." Amy poured the tea and brought Sara a cup. "Still just milk?"

"Yes, please, that hasn't changed. Congratulations on the upcoming promotion. Phillip must be very proud of you."

"Actually he hasn't said much. We'll see if it actually comes to fruition."

Typical serial killer too wrapped up in his own importance. He'd resent any success by Amy. They could use that against him.

"So do you see many of the people you work with at the library?"

Amy sat next to Sara and carefully balanced her mug. "Some, but it's a long trip from the beach to the library so I don't have a lot of time to talk, except at lunch."

"I wondered about that when you said you'd given up your apartment and moved out there."

"Phillip likes the beach. He felt it looked better, business-wise, to live out there, rather than my tiny apartment."

"I see, but what about you and your social life, the friends you've made?"

"I sort of gave it up, for now. Once his business is

established we can move back into town and we'll be able to see people occasionally."

"We'll be able to see people? What about just you and your friends?"

Amy took a sip of her tea. "Is yours all right? I don't usually get things right anymore."

Sara bit her tongue. She'd heard those words enough times for almost nineteen years and recognized them immediately. Damn Gordon and damn her for letting it happen. "The tea is perfect, much better than I make."

"Really?" Amy perked up.

"Yes really, you have a knack for it."

A key turned in the knob. Gloria growled and stood up.

Amy put her cup on the table, stood up and raced to the door. "It's Phillip," she whispered over her shoulder.

Sara put her cup down, one hand on Gloria's back, and waited.

"Hello, my darling. Do I hear a dog?"

"It's Gloria, I've told you about our dog, and my mother's here. She got in early and I invited her up for tea." The words tumbled out of Amy's mouth.

"I'm surprised they let a dog in this hotel." Phillip strode into the room. He reminded Sara of a greasy, penguin with his chest puffed out.

Sara didn't move. She made him come to her. "You must be Phillip? Amy has told me so much about you."

He stopped and glared at Gloria. "I didn't realize you could bring dogs in here."

"Oh yes, they're very dog friendly. Isn't that nice? This way Amy gets to see her dog, too." Sara stood up, only inches away from him.

He immediately backed up.

*Doesn't like people in his space; make a note.*

Sara put out her hand. "I'm Amy's mother, obviously. Congratulations on your upcoming wedding. I can hardly wait to get to know you better."

Phillip reluctantly took her hand. He barely touched it and dropped his hand. "Yes, well, we'll see how much time we can manage. I'm busy making business contacts."

"Amy mentioned that. I'd love to hear all about your business venture." He hadn't let go quite quickly enough. The anger and hate rushed over her. He really didn't want her around. She also sensed confusion. She wasn't what he'd expected.

Phillip stared at her. "Yes, well, I'm sure you wouldn't understand."

"You might be surprised," Sara pasted her smile on her face. "I studied Business Administration in college. I might be able to offer a few suggestions."

Sara touched his arm. He jerked it away.

He had expected her to be an older version of Amy. He'd done his research and hadn't expected any problem from Amy's mother. Unfortunately his research had been outdated. Even Amy hadn't known how much her mother had changed until today. He'd made a mistake. Sara made a note of that, too. They could use that to rattle him when the time came.

"I still want to hear about the business, especially when Amy is also investing in it with the move to the beach and all."

This time he couldn't hide his anger. He glared at her. "We'll see."

He stomped off into what Sara assumed was the bedroom.

"Phillip, don't be rude, please."

"That's okay, honey. He's probably had a bad day. We can talk over dinner. Diane, your godmother's sister is joining us. Ellen couldn't make it to the wedding so she asked Diane to come instead. She should be arriving soon. We can all have dinner together. I made reservations in their dining room downstairs for six-thirty. Does that work for you?"

"Uh, six-thirty, should work. I have to check it with Phillip."

"You do that. I need to use your bathroom is that's okay?"

Amy nodded and shuffled toward the bedroom.

Sara tried a door. It was the second bedroom. She closed the door and tried the next one. She could hear Phillip talking to Amy.

"What do you mean, someone else is coming? You never mentioned a godmother."

"I never thought about Aunt Ellen. I haven't seen her for years, although she always remembers my birthday."

"Well get out of it. I don't want any damn family dinner the day before the wedding."

"Phillip, she's already made reservations. We have to go. We don't have to stay long."

Sara stepped into the bathroom. The room was the size of her bedroom at home. A black marble tub with double jets for two people stood on the gray marble floor. There was a shower with a clear glass door, a vanity with two sinks next to the toilet and a bidet.

Very impressive. She washed her hands before she walked back into the main room.

Amy shuffled back into the room.

"Come on, Gloria, we need to go and see if Diane has arrived yet. She'll be sharing a room with us."

"Six-thirty will be fine." Amy didn't look at Sara.

Sara hugged Amy. "Good. We'll see you then. It will be fun. The reservation is under my name. Come on, Gloria."

Sara closed the door.

"Tomorrow can't come soon enough," she said into her bra.

Phillip and Amy entered the dining room. He said something to the maitre d'. The man led him to Sara's table.

Amy scuffed her shoes, trailing a few feet behind. She wore a simple gray, cotton dress with a high neckline trimmed in white.

Sara recognized the style. It was one she was familiar with and had been for nineteen years. She and Amy needed to go shopping tomorrow, before the wedding.

Sara took a sip of her Mojito and elbowed Diane. Sara stood as they approached the table. "Thank you, Antoine."

"My pleasure, Madam Peters, enjoy your evening."

Phillip frowned at the interchange, which pointed out that it was Sara's evening.

"Phillip, it's so nice to see you again. This is Diane, Ellen's sister. Wasn't it lucky she could join us on such short notice? It's too bad your brother couldn't make it." Sara pulled Amy from behind Phillip and hugged her. "You look nice, honey. This is Diane."

Sara moved so Diane could hug Amy. Then she beamed at Phillip who stood awkwardly beside the table, his lips tightened together.

"And this is Phillip, my soon to be son-in-law."

Diane put out her hand. He ignored it.

"Amy, sit between us so Diane can talk to you. She's brought pictures from Ellen."

Phillip sat beside Sara and motioned for the waiter. "Bring me a scotch and soda, Glenlivet, twenty year old, and a glass of house white."

"Don't be silly. Amy, do you still like Manhattan's"

Amy bobbed her head. She shrank back in her seat.

"Good, then bring her a Manhattan. I'll order wine later."

Phillip crossed his arms and said nothing.

*He doesn't like anyone taking charge except him, especially a woman. Make another note. He also has poor social skills.*

Sara smiled and picked up the menu. "Since this is sort of the rehearsal dinner I'll order if no one minds."

Without looking at Phillip she proceeded to order for Amy, Diane and herself. Phillip, since we've just met what would you like? Steak? Rare?"

"Medium rare," Phillip growled. He motioned to the waiter for another scotch.

Sara closed her menu with a smile. "Now, Amy, tell us all about the wedding tomorrow."

Amy sipped her Manhattan with an occasional glance at Phillip. She hesitated. "There's not much to tell. We get married in the Chapel of Love down on the strip at one o'clock. We need to be there by at least twelve thirty."

"What are you wearing, honey?" Diane patted Amy's arm.

"It's a plain, cotton dress with a little lace around the sleeves."

"Oh my, that won't do. It won't do at all, right Sara?"

"Absolutely." Sara allowed another grin to sneak across her face. She watched Phillip get redder as he tried to hold his anger in. "Most stores in Vegas are open late. If we can't get everything tonight we'll find the rest first thing in the morning. I'll talk to the concierge right after we finish dinner."

"Her dress looks fine." Phillip snarled.

"It's her wedding. A woman only gets married once. Don't worry, Diane and I will pay for the dress. Diane, have you got time to arrange a reception luncheon after the wedding, if I take Amy shopping?"

"Of course, I'd love to." Diane took a sip of her drink and winked at Sara.

A very long hour later, Phillip excused himself and Amy. He grabbed her arm and almost dragged her from the table.

"Be careful Phillip, we don't want any bruises on Amy for her wedding day. We're hoping to find something sleeveless with a low cut front. I'll be up in about half an hour to steal Amy away and take her shopping." Sara blew a kiss at their retreating backs. Amy tried a weak wave with her free arm.

"Here's to taking care of that creep tomorrow." Diane clinked Sara's glass.

"Let's go meet the others and finalize our plans. I will be so happy when he's in jail and Amy is safe. I can't believe how ignorant and rude he is."

They headed for the elevators. Sara glanced into the bar and stopped. "You go ahead. I'll be up in a minute. I have something I have to do."

"Need any help?" Diane offered.

"Not this time, thanks. I can handle it." Sara strode into the bar and climbed up on a stool. "Hi, sailor, come here often?"

Mac swung around on his stool, his brown eyes widened in surprise. "Sara? I wasn't expecting you."

"I'll bet you weren't. What in hell are you doing here and don't lie to me?"

Mac stroked his chin. "Can I buy you a drink? Dry white wine?" He motioned to the bartender.

Sara sat in silence, her eyes focused on his face.

"Uh, I guess you caught me."

Sara stared at him in silence.

"Okay, dammit, I followed you. Now are you happy?"

"Why?" Sara took a sip of the Chardonnay the bartender placed in front of her.

"It's not what you think—well, not quite." Mac rubbed his chin again. "I came down to help if you needed any and to make sure that if you did get hurt, I'd kill the bastard who hurt you."

"That's it?"

"I got it, I finally did. The light bulb got turned on. You want to be independent and not have someone take care of you. I'm not sure I completely understand, but I am trying. I know you're an equal. I got that part, no problem. You are afraid someone will try and change you and take away the person you've become. I know that's from your previous marriage to an abusive jerk. You have to realize that everyone isn't like that. When you truly love someone you want to protect them."

"Yes, but…"

"If you love me, you'd want to protect me, too. But I'm not here to protect you. I'm here to support you, act as a resource, be there if, and that's a big if, you need me."

Sara stared at him.

"And when it's over and you've got the killer and your daughter is safe, I'd like to be there to celebrate with you, after you and the team are finished celebrating of course. I'd also like to meet your daughter and tell her what an awesome mother she has."

"I'd like that. You're right. I'd want to protect you, too. You're not interfering with our plan?"

Mac held his hands up in front of him. "No ma'am. I know when I've lost. It's your mission. Tell me about it after."

"I think I love you, Mac Langston." Sara leaned over and kissed him, tasting the warm, burn of good whiskey.

"Good thing. So will you marry me?"

"No. Ask me again after the mission is completed."

"Don't trust me, huh?"

"After the past few months, let's say I need to be convinced. Besides I think there are a few things we need to talk about, like what Mac Langston did before he became a director."

"Fair enough, I guess there some things I should share."

"I know you were in a jungle and shot."

His mouth dropped.

"You should have been paying more attention to those special talents my team and I have. We need to talk about that, too."

"It looks like there are a few things we need to talk about. Okay, but still be prepared for the question again tomorrow night."

Sara slid off the barstool. "We'll see how things go between now and then. I need to go over the plan with the team one last time. The wedding is at one o'clock in the Chapel of Love tomorrow, if you want to slip in at the back and watch my daughter marry a serial killer."

# Chapter Eighteen

Sara and Diane sat in the first pew of the Chapel of Love. The building held four chapels; one for large weddings of over a hundred people; on for those for twenty-five to fifty people and two small chapels for about twenty people.

Phillip and Amy had chosen the smaller one. It was done in peach tones with artificial peach and white flowers at the front.

"Thank God they didn't pick one of those places with tacky red velvet," Sara whispered.

Diane grinned. "Does it really matter? Even if Amy doesn't know it, the wedding is a sham. She'll be single again tomorrow or as soon as the wedding is annulled. One day she'll have a real wedding."

"You're right."

The music started. Amy walked slowly down the short aisle. She wore a lovely, knee-length, white lace dress with a low décolletage and small pearls in an abstract design on the white satin. They'd found matching shoes and a short veil in a frantic shopping spree with help from the hotel concierge.

Sara had even managed to get an appointment with the hairdresser who piled up Amy's dark blonde hair and fitted in the veil.

Tears crowded the corners of Sara's eyes. Her daughter looked like a fairy princess gliding down the aisle. It might not be real, but her beautiful baby was getting married.

Over her shoulder she saw Mac slide into a back seat. He caught her look and gave her thumbs up.

Phillip stood by the altar, in a dark suit, looking glum and angry. Amy looked beautiful and she upstaged him.

Sara knew she and her team had changed his plans. He wasn't happy.

*Wait until he finds out he won't be a widow tonight.*

After the wedding, two taxis took everyone back to the hotel where Diane had reserved a small private room and a caterer.

"We really want to go up to our room and celebrate our wedding." Phillip snarled.

"Sorry, Phillip, she's my daughter and Ellen's god child, we want to be part of the celebration. You understand." Sara squeezed Phillip's arm.

The deep blackness and goo from inside sucked into her body. She learned she needed to be careful who she touched and for how long. She would have to figure out how to cleanse all that ugliness from her body. It was going to take more than a day or two to eliminate. Even Gordon had never caused her this much distress.

The luncheon finished late afternoon. Sara saw Lydia in the doorway. Lydia gave a quick nod and hastened to the elevators.

"Okay, Phillip, a toast to the bride and groom and you two can take off for the rest of the day, but I insist on meeting Amy for breakfast tomorrow morning before we fly out."

"No problem." Phillip smirked.

Sara lifted her glass of champagne. "To my beautiful daughter and her husband, may your life together be a new start for both of you."

Phillip clinked glasses, took a sip and grabbed Amy's arm. "Come on honey; let's go up to our room."

"Okay." She followed Phillip out of the room. "See you in the morning, mom."

"Yes, darling, you will." Sara raised her champagne glass as they exited the room.

Seconds later she and Diane rose and strode to the elevator. It was quick trip up to the penthouse floor.

"Before we continue, even though he doesn't work for The Foundation, I need to let you guys know that Link has resigned to start his own business."

"No, really, when?" Julie asked.

"He resigned immediately but will stay around part-time to train his replacement. We've hired Tom Gerow, a retired cop."

"What's Link going to do? I mean what business is he starting?" Nadia asked. "And why is he resigning and so quickly? What did you do to him, Carly?"

"I didn't do anything to him, Julie," Carly snapped. "And I don't know why he suddenly decided to quit. He just did."

"He doesn't want to be your employee anymore." Julie grinned.

"What do you mean by that?"

"He's probably in love with you, but you can't ask the boss out."

Heat rushed up Carly's neck and across her cheeks at the thought of Link being in love with her. "Don't be stupid. There's nothing between us."

"Maybe there wasn't, I'm not sure about that, but let's see what happens in the next few months, now you don't employ him. And from the becoming pink on your cheeks, I don't think you'd be averse to dating hunky Link Stone. If you are, let him know I'm available."

"You've got Trevor. I'm showing Tom around the

building and introducing him to some of the department heads in about half an hour. I'd like you two to meet him so he knows you by sight and vice versa."

"Sure." Nadia responded.

"We'll move into my CCB office so we're all there when he arrives, if that works for you two. I want the bookshelf in place so he sees the office as it should be."

"It's going to be different without Link around." Julie commented.

"Yes, it is." Carly knew it was going to feel very different. She felt like she was losing a friend and maybe someone even more important.

Lydia watched the newlyweds enter the room from a slot in the closet where she was hiding. "Suspect has arrived," she whispered into her wire.

"I love you, Mrs. de Beares." Phillip wrapped his arms around Amy and kissed her long and hard.

"And I love you, Mr. de Beares," Amy whispered into his ear.

"I had champagne sent to the room. We'll have a few glasses and then I'm going to show you things you've never imagined." Phillip moved to the ice bucket on the coffee table and removed the champagne bottle. He smiled at Amy and popped the cork. It flew across the room and landed by the closet door, inches from Lydia.

Lydia held her breath.

Amy giggled. Phillip strode across to pick up the cork. "I hear women save things like this." He returned to Amy and handed her the cork.

"Absolutely, I want to remember every minute of our wedding and our wedding night."

"Me, too." Phillip almost sneered.

*Damn, she really loves this guy and we're about to ruin her marriage and break her heart. But he doesn't even like her and he plans to kill her.*

Phillip poured the champagne into the two glasses. "To my beautiful wife, may our marriage last forever."

Amy giggled again and touched her glass to Phillip's. She took a drink.

Phillip put his glass down without tasting it and hugged Amy. "Finish your champagne. I'm going to slip into something more comfortable."

Phillip closed the bedroom door. Amy perched on the couch. She took a few more sips of champagne.

"Now," Lydia whispered.

From her hiding spot she saw the door open. Sara, Diane and Gloria slipped inside the penthouse. Diane raced for the bathroom. Sara and Gloria edged along the wall to the spare bedroom.

Phillip was gone quite a while. Lydia thought she heard him on the phone, probably making a date with Didi.

Phillip returned, wearing a dark green sweat suit. "More wine, honey?"

Amy stood up and held her glass out in front. "If I have too much more I'll probably just fall asleep tonight. I don't want to miss our wedding night."

"Are you starting to feel drowsy?"

"No, not yet, but I know what happens when I drink too much."

Phillip frowned and filled her glass almost to the rim. He gripped his glass by the stem and attempted a smile. "Here's to us, down the hatch."

"Don't be silly, you can't drink champagne like that. The bubbles tickle your nose. I think I'll go in and change into something more comfortable, too."

Phillip put his glass down on a corner table, still untouched. "Don't change yet. You look like a fairy princess in that dress, my fairy princess. I want to keep looking at you as my princess."

He put his arms around her and kissed her lightly on the lips. "Let's finish the champagne first and maybe check the hotel gardens from the balcony. The lights should start coming on soon. Then you can change."

Amy sipped at the clear, golden liquid. "Wait until you see what I've got for the wedding night. It's a surprise."

Lydia shook her head. They were going to break the kid's heart, but at least she'd still be alive.

"Let's go out on the balcony and enjoy the gorgeous view."

"Okay." Amy swallowed the last of her glass. "I think I'm getting tipsy."

"But you're not sleepy?" Phillip frowned.

Amy shook her head. She linked her arm through Phillip's. "No, not sleepy."

"I don't get it," Phillip mumbled.

"What, dear?"

"Nothing, we'll do it the hard way. Sorry Amy." He grabbed her arm and dragged her toward the balcony.

"Phillip, stop, you're hurting me."

"Not for long. You're not going to feel anything in a few minutes."

"What are you talking about?" Color drained from Amy's face. She tried to pull back into the room. "Phillip, you're scaring me."

"No you're not getting away from me, you bitch. I haven't put up with you this long for nothing. You're about to go for a little fall."

Amy froze. She stared into Phillip's contorted face. "What do you mean?"

"I don't know what happened, but the champagne was drugged. You were supposed to be unconscious for this part. It makes it easier for both of us."

"You're not going to throw me over the balcony. Oh migawd, you can't be serious. Phillip, I thought you loved me. We're married." Amy jerked loose. She tried to run to the door. Phillip quickly grabbed her arm.

"Yes, we're married, and I have an insurance policy on you."

Amy scratched his face. She drew blood.

"Bitch!" He reached for her waist and attempted to throw her over his shoulder.

"I don't think so." Maggie stepped into the room through the balcony door. "Let her go, and gently. The reason she didn't pass out was we switched the bottle of champagne that you had drugged with a new bottle."

Phillip held on to Amy's wrist and swung back toward the balcony. "Who the hell are you?"

Amy struggled to pull her arm loose.

"Let's just say I'm a friend of Amy and Sara."

"Yeah, well back off or I'll kill you too." Phillip yanked a 9mm from the waistband of his sweatpants. He pulled Amy in front of him.

"You're going to have to do better than that, Phillip." Sara stepped out of the spare bedroom, her Glock aimed at his head. Gloria stood at her side. She let out a low growl. Sara put her hand on Gloria's head.

Phillip spun around to face her. "What the hell is going on here? Amy and I want to be alone."

"Is that right, Amy? You want to be alone, with Phillip?" Sara asked.

Amy shook her head, her eyes wide, terror reflected in her enlarged pupils.

"Sorry, Phillip, she doesn't want to be alone with you. Drop the gun."

"Go to hell. Even if you shoot me, I can kill Amy first. You don't want that, now do you?"

"The odds are stacked against you. Three guns are aimed at your head. Which one of us do you think is going to pull the trigger first?" Lydia pushed open the bathroom door and stepped into the room, her Glock held steady out in front of her, a smile on her vivid, red lips. "I've never actually killed a person before so I'm looking forward to finding out how it feels."

"What the hell is going on? Who are you?"

"Another friend who doesn't like serial killers." Lydia continued to smile. She moved closer.

"Back off bitch." Phillip pressed his gun against Amy's forehead.

Sara continued to smile, but only with her lips.

Diane watched the scene. Her body tensed every muscle ready to attack. "I might as well join the party." She emerged from her hiding place in the closet. "That makes it four to one Phillip. How do you like those odds?"

"I don't understand. It's my honeymoon. What do you want from us?" He attempted to sound confused, but his eyes remained hard and bitter. He searched the room for his options.

Lydia stood in the doorway. She focused on his gun. All four women held their guns on Phillip and Amy. They waited.

"What? You're just going to stand there? Move to one side and let Amy and I pass."

Sara shook her head. "I don't think so. We're at an impasse, at least for a minute or two."

"And then what are you stupid bitches going to do?" Phillip snarled.

His gun started to leave his hand. His mouth dropped open. He grabbed at it, but it continued to float upward. It drifted across to Lydia. She grabbed in and tucked it in her waistband.

"Now it looks like the odds are all in our favor." Diane grinned.

Phillip pushed Amy into Diane and raced toward the door. "You're not going to shoot an unarmed man."

"Don't think I wouldn't like to, and in the back too." Maggie mumbled, loud enough for everyone to hear. "However, I'm giving Sara the privilege. Take him, honey."

Sara tossed her gun to Diane and stuck out her foot.

Phillip tumbled to the floor and landed face first. He rolled over quickly and jumped to his feet.

Sara took up a fighting stance. She bounced a little to center her core.

A snarl curled across Phillip's face. He shot his right hand out toward Sara's face.

"Too easy," Diane muttered.

"Mom!" Amy screamed.

"It's all right, honey, don't worry about your mom." Maggie squeezed Amy's shoulders.

Sara grabbed the fist and with a sharp swing Phillip landed on his butt.

He growled in anger and humiliation, struggled to his feet and charged Sara. She stepped to one side and with her hands clasped together smashed him on the back of the neck. He landed on the floor, his breath knocked out of him. He stared at Sara.

"You bitch, now you're asking for it!" He screamed and struggled to his knees. He pushed himself upright, his face red and his eyes bulging. His left hand pawed into the air.

"Go for it, Phillip or Peter. It must be frustrating to find a woman who actually hits back." Sara grinned at him.

Phillip clenched his fists and attempted to stagger into a boxer's stance. "You'll be sorry you ever interfered," he spit out. Blood dripped down his chin from a split lip. He swung again, and again, and again. They were all misses.

Maggie and Diane laughed.

"Oh, I don't think so." Sara chuckled. She weaved and ducked, danced to one side, then back in front. She raised her right leg and kicked him in the groin.

"Oww," he screamed, doubled over and grabbed his balls.

Sara moved in for the kill. She kneed him in the balls one more time and threw a right upper cut to his chin. He doubled up even more, his scream reached ear piercing tones.

Sara grabbed his hair, pulled his head up and jabbed at his chin. She hit him again and again. Phillip's head resembled a bobble-head doll. With one final whack across his head, he fell to the floor, face first, arms outstretched.

This time he didn't get up.

Maggie, Lydia and Diane clapped. "Nice going, lady." Diane chortled. "You did us proud."

"Mom, where did you learn to do that? I thought for sure he'd kill you." Amy rushed into Sara's arms.

"No, baby, he was going to kill you."

"I can't believe it. I thought he loved me." Amy sobbed into Sara's shoulder.

Sara tightened her grip around her daughter's shoulders. She stroked Amy's hair. "I know, baby. That's why we are all here. He's done it before. He's a con artist, a psychopath and a serial killer. He studies people and then plays to their weakness to get them to fall for him."

"I feel like such a loser." Amy sniffled.

"No, baby, you're not a loser. Phillip is. You're a winner, and my beautiful daughter."

Amy's sobs slowed and gradually turned to gulps. Sara continued to hold her and touch her hair and face. She kissed the top of Amy's head.

"I've called the police and hotel security." Diane came back into the room from the bedroom. "He was all packed and ready to leave after he reported Amy had jumped."

Phillip groaned and started to roll over.

"I wouldn't do that if I was you." Diane lifted her hand and placed her Glock at the base of his neck.

"It won't work. I'll say you all broke in and tried to rob us." Phillip shouted. He reached for Diane's gun.

Gloria charged and bit his arm.

"Ouch, get the damn dog off me." Phillip grabbed his arm.

"Gloria, come," Sara called. The dog trotted over to Sara and Amy.

"You broke in and that vicious dog attacked me. I'll charge all of you."

"Except we have it all on tape." Maggie pushed the button on the mini-recorder she'd been wearing inside her bra.

*"Nothing. We'll just do it the hard way. Sorry Amy."*

*"Phillip, stop, you're hurting me."*

*"Not for long. You're not going to feel anything in a few minutes."*

*"What are you talking about?"*

*"I'm afraid."*

*"No you don't, you bitch. I haven't put up with you for this long for nothing. You're about to go for a little fall."*

A sharp knock on the door announced the arrival of the police. Hotel security charged in followed by three LV police. They paused and took in the scene. They stared at Diane holding Phillip on the floor.

Two officers moved toward Diane. "We'll take him from here. Is that gun registered?"

"He's all yours. And yes, the gun is registered."

The older, third officer strode over to Sara and Amy. "Sergeant Lacey, ladies, we'll need a statement."

"No problem, however, my daughter was almost killed tonight, on her wedding night, by a serial killer. Would it be all right if you got statements from the other witnesses and I brought Amy down to the station in the morning, Sergeant?"

The Sergeant regarded Amy. She still wore her wedding dress and tears drifted down her cheeks. Sara's arms were wrapped protectively around the younger woman.

"I think we could work with that. Ten o'clock?"

"Thank you, ten o'clock will be fine. Come on Amy, we'll let the rest of then explain everything to the police. I want to go down and explain what happened to a friend of mine and let him know we're all okay. You need to meet him. And then you'll sleep in my room with Dine and Gloria."

Sara shepherded her out of the room. Gloria trotted along behind.

"Ladies, you know where to find us when you're finished here. We'll be in my room." Sara called over her shoulder. She passed by the hotel security man at the door. "My daughter needs to change and lie down. I'm going to call the hotel doctor to give her something to sleep."

Her arm around Amy, they descended the elevator and headed for the bar. Mac swung around before she got through the door.

"Thank God, you're all right." He jumped off the stool and raced to Sara's side. "You're not hurt?"

Sara shook her head. Gloria wagged her tail and nuzzled Mac.

Sara felt him quickly scan her for any injuries before he turned to Amy. "You must be Amy?"

Amy shrank back against her mother.

"Amy, this is Mac Langston. He's a friend of mine, a very close friend of mine. He followed me here to make sure we both came out of this."

Amy slowly extended her hand a few inches, "pleased to meet you, Mr. Langston."

Mac gently took the extended hand. He quickly let it go. "It's a pleasure to meet you, Amy. It's been a rough evening. I think you need to go lie down, maybe soak in a bath. I'd like to get to know you better, but after all this is over."

"I'm taking her up to my room. I'm going to call the doctor and have her checked over and give her something to sleep because she's still in shock. We still have to give statements, but they said we could do it in the morning. I just wanted to make sure you knew I was okay."

"I appreciate that." Mac gave Sara a quick kiss on the cheek. "Call me when you can."

"Thanks, Mac. Come on Amy, we're going to my room. I'm putting you to bed. Gloria's going to keep you company."

Amy's eyes widened and she had a deer in the headlights look.

"It's okay, honey. You won't be alone. Gloria and I will both be with you. I'm not going anywhere and Phillip won't be going anywhere for a very long time, if ever. You're safe."

The elevator doors closed. Sara could see Mac watching them. He blew a kiss and mouthed the word, "later."

# Chapter Nineteen

Mac stood outside Sara's hotel room door, his hand raised but frozen in mid-air. It was almost midnight. Sara would probably be asleep. He didn't want to wake her, but he needed to talk to her, to feel her soft skin and smell her intoxicating floral scent.

Damn, he wanted her, but he didn't want to disturb her and Amy.

He lowered his arm and tapped softly against the door. If she was asleep she wouldn't hear him, but…

The door opened. Sara stood there in a nightshirt of floral cotton. "Mac, what are you doing here?"

"I'm sorry if I woke you. I wanted to see how you were and how Amy was doing?"

"You didn't wake me. I was on the balcony thinking about you. I wondered if it was too late to call."

"Put on something decent and go talk to the man." Diane's voice reached their ears. "I'll take care of Amy and Gloria."

Sara hesitated for a second. "I'll be right back."

She closed the door. Mac paced up and down the hallway. What could he say and how could he say it? He really didn't want to blow this.

The door opened a crack and Sara slipped out. She'd changed into something lemon with loose pants and a t-shirt. Without make up she looked about twenty one. "You look delicious enough to eat."

Sara took his hand. "I'm glad you came up."

"How about we take a walk around the pool and the gardens? They're pretty at night with all the different colored lights."

"That sounds perfect.

They rode in silence during the elevator descent to the lobby. Mac took her hand and led her out toward the pool.

Sara put her hand to her throat. She stared into the crystal blue water with rotating, colored lights from the bottom of the pool.

"Damn, I'm sorry. What a stupid idea." Mac whacked his forehead. "Come on, we'll go to the bar."

"No, it's fine, really. It hit me when I saw the pool that her body could be floating there. He didn't get her and she didn't end up in the pool. We saved her and caught him. They've arrested him and hopefully he'll get put away for life and won't ever be able hurt another woman." She took his hand. "Let's walk. The pool is actually a sign of victory."

"How's Amy?"

"I got the hotel doctor to give her something to sleep. She should sleep all night. We'll see how she's doing in the morning. She went into shock when she saw what he intended to do. I think she really loved him and believed he loved her, but then they all did."

"And how are you doing?"

"I'm, I'm handling it. Catching him was a real adrenalin rush. The team let me take him down and all the skills Gwen taught us in hand to hand combat came back. I got a high just being able to physically hurt him like he's hurt so many women. Afterwards came the letdown."

Mac smiled. "I know the feeling. I've experienced that same feeling many times."

"Then there was the realization of how close he came to killing Amy. He is truly an evil man with no conscience or remorse. He was furious that a few women could ruin all his plans. Once the shock started to wear off, Amy realized how close she'd come to being his next victim; his fourth as far as we know. She's going to need counseling for a while."

"Her mother recovered from a long abusive relationship and turned out pretty good. I think Amy will recover."

"I've asked her to move back home, but I'm not sure she will. She likes her job in Tillamook and she has friends there. She'd move back there. And be close to them."

"You'll be there for her. That's the important thing. You are one remarkable lady. I heard about the fight from Maggie and Lydia. They took pity on me and filled in some of the details. I'm proud of you." He leaned down and kissed her soft, pink lips. They tasted of something sweet.

Sara slipped her arms around his neck and moved her body closer to his. "You're pretty remarkable yourself, Mr. Langston. You really did leave me alone and let me handle it my way."

"Yes, ma'am, from what I've heard, I'm no match for you." He nuzzled her neck and inhaled her soft, floral scent.

Mac kissed her again and deepened it. He pulled her tight against his body and felt her nipples respond through the gauzy material. He slipped his tongue between her teeth, searching her mouth.

"Oh God, Sara, I want you, right now."

"I want you, too, but not tonight. I am exhausted. The whole evening has been emotionally and physically exhausting, but Amy's safe."

"What am I thinking, except that I love you and I want you? Of course you are." Mac jerked back. "Let's grab a drink in the bar to help you relax a little so you'll fall asleep when you hit the bed."

"I'm not sure I'll need a drink, but it will be a nice way to finish a busy day and evening. I want you too, Mac, but I'd like to be awake to enjoy it. You know where I live. Come visit me when you can."

"I'll be there in a few days. We get R&R after we finish every training session."

"I'll be leaving after tomorrow, so we should get there about the same time. Stay as long as you like. No one will be there to interrupt us."

"I may take you up on that and spend my whole R&R with you. One of the new benefits will be I can actually talk about what I do. I've never been able to share that before."

"I can understand that. I can't tell anyone about my training. I don't know how long I'll be there. I don't know when my next assignment will be."

Mac sighed. They entered the bar and found an empty table.

"I forgot you're part of The Foundation now. We'll have to work on that. At least if you're not working you can always come up and stay at the camp, or I can come and visit you. We won't have to keep secrets from each other."

"We'll work it out." Sara rested against the back of the chair and closed her eyes. Mac ordered drinks and reached across and took her hand.

"You look like you're almost asleep. I guess I better wait until later to ask you to marry me."

Sara lazily opened her eyes and smiled. "I did say you could ask after the project was finished, didn't I? But I also want to know a little bit more about Mac Langston."

"Mac Langston, Angus Devin MacMillan Langston was born in Seattle, thirty-nine years ago. And I know you're a couple of years older but it's irrelevant. I have a brother Gordon and two nephews. I joined the army and after three years I was recruited by special ops." Mac took a drink.

"How's that, too much information?"

"No, but it's a start. You know everything about me. When we first met I told you a lot about me. You told me nothing about you. All I know is you ride a Harley and have a brother. I want to get a feel for the man who now works for The Foundation. How did you get there? What happened when you joined special ops? I'm sure that's not still classified."

"Except for a list of injuries it wasn't that interesting. I got sent to the jungles in South America on various assignments. I did special ops for eight years. During the time I was shot in the shoulder, stabbed in the forearm and across my cheek. The scar is obvious. I broke my upper leg and ripped it open. It required a couple of surgeries. They inserted a metal rod during one of them so I set the arm off when I go through airport security. I used to walk with a limp before physio and still do sometimes if I'm really tired. When I was in the hospital The Foundation found me and recruited me to train for them." Mac waved for another drink.

"How long have you been there?"

"About five years. I was thinking about leaving but it's a great job and the money's good. The hardest part is the secrecy. But the one positive thing about you being an agent is there's no more secrecy. I've found a partner I love who understand me and what I do."

Their drinks arrived.

"I may not get up tomorrow morning and I have to take Amy to the police station to give our statements."

"I'll make sure you get there. I said I would ask you to marry me tonight, or maybe it's this morning."

"And I did say I would give you an answer."

"Yes, you did. I love you Sara Peters and I want to make you Sara Langston. I had a thought. We're in Vegas. We could be married tomorrow. Your team and your daughter are already here. I don't know who else you'd want to invite."

"Is that the proposal?"

"Damn straight and I even have the ring to make it official." He fumbled in his pocket.

"Then yes."

"Yes, you'll marry me?"

"Yes, Mac Langston, I'll marry you, but my son has to be here. There's no one else."

"That's wonderful." Mac pulled a small black box from his pocket and opened it. The small diamond set in a cluster of small emeralds twinkled up at her.

"Oh, Mac, it's beautiful."

"Not as beautiful as you, the future Mrs. Langston." He slipped the ring on her finger. He tilted her face upwards, his fingers slipped along her jaw line and bent over and kissed her gently. "I love you so much."

"I love you, too. What if I said I wanted to keep my last name?"

Mac sat back. "Seriously, you don't want my name?"

"I'm asking for your thoughts."

"If that's important to you, I'm fine with it. It's you I love, not the name."

"You have changed. No, I don't want to keep my name. It was Gordon's name, never really mine."

Mac slipped the ring on her finger. It fit perfectly.

Sara held it up and admired it on her finger. "I can't believe I'm doing this. I never planned on getting married again."

"Love triumphs over all." Mac grinned. "Phone your son tonight. Wake him up. I'll fly him out tonight or tomorrow, as soon as I can book a flight."

"He won't believe it. He had a hard enough time with Amy getting married. At least he'll be invited to my wedding."

"Whatever you want, I'll arrange it."

"I need to talk to Amy in the morning and see if it's okay with her. I don't want my wedding giving her nightmares so soon after her bad experience. If it's okay with her, then I'll call Andy. Classes and exams should be finished about now. Hopefully he'll fly down on short notice."

"I'm sure he will, to see his mother getting married. I want to be married to you as soon as possible. I've loved you since the day I almost ran you over."

"I thought of you a lot after that first meeting, too." Sara's head drooped. "I think I'm going to fall asleep here."

She stood up. "I'll call you in the morning after I talk to everyone and let me team know."

"Come on, lean on me. I'll walk you back to your room. Want me to carry you?"

"No." Sara chuckled. "I can still walk."

"While you and Amy give your statement, I'll book a flight for Andrew and see about booking a wedding and a reception."

"What about your brother?"

"I don't think he can make it, but I'll phone him."

"Is there anyone else you want to invite?" Sara asked.

"No, I'm good. I only want you there."

"That sounds good. Keep it small, mostly the people who are already here."

"Anything you want, sweetheart."

They reached Sara's room. Sara opened the door.

Mac bent down and gave her a quick kiss. "See you in the morning," he whispered.

Two days later the second wedding was held. It gave Sara the time to empty the blackness from Philip. She'd learned not to touch some people from that experience.

This wedding was filled with love and hope for the future.

Sara looked lovely in a short ivory lace dress. Mac looked handsome in a rented tuxedo. Amy was her maid of honor. Her team was her bridesmaids. Andy gave her away. Nadia was there and gave the team a week off before their next mission.

# Chapter Twenty

Julie held up the skirt of her sparkling red sheath dress with one hand. She carefully mounted the steps to the stage in the matching high heels. She took a second to glance around the ballroom before taking the mike. The crystal chandeliers, the white linen table cloths on the tables for eight, the crowd of tuxedos and designer evening gowns all spread out before her. It looked like another successful fund raiser. Trevor stood at a center table and smiled up at her.

"Welcome, everyone. I hope you're enjoying the evening. For those who may be here for the first time I wanted to give a little about the background of The Foundation. Back in college Julie, Nadia and I volunteered to help at shelters for abused women. We realized at that time how much more these women needed besides food and shelter for themselves and perhaps their children. The staff at the shelters did the best they could, but they worked with little money and few volunteers. We put our own money into hiring counselors, employment personnel and buying clothing for the women to wear on job interviews. We wanted these women to improve their self-esteem and move forward in their lives.

After graduation we moved in other directions but we continued to help in a limited way. We can only work with a few shelters. So we formed The Foundation and started to fund raise. All the money goes to helping women, and women and children, in shelters in seven states now. We'd like to make it even more. There are pamphlets on all the tables so you can see which shelters are being helped and the results and benefits your generosity provides. I'm going to turn the mike over to Nadia for a few words."

Looking like a glamorous super model and wearing a sparkling gold sheath, Nadia joined Julie on the stage and took the mike.

During Nadia's short speech Carly mingled among the crowd. She shook hands and stopped to talk with various couples that had been family friends for years. It had been a long time since they had started their volunteer work. Even when they all went in different directions they'd come together to help and support abused women. Six years ago it had expanded into spreading out their organization to help women before they got to the shelters. She chuckled to herself when she remembered the first mission they had gone on without any training.

Nadia and several other celebrities finished their speeches and requests for people to support The Foundation. Julie stood near the stage and collected the donations from the patrons attending the fund raiser. A well-known band had taken the stage and a few couples made their way to the dance floor.

"Ms. Brazil, it's nice to finally meet you."

Carly turned to see a middle-aged man, an inch or two taller than her, in a tuxedo, extending his hand.

She automatically shook it. She noted his short, sweaty, fingers. "I'm sorry…"

"Walter Garfield, I knew your father." His squinty, watery blue eyes stared at her, before his gaze roved up and down her body. It stopped at her breasts.

"I believe I've heard my father mention you." *My father was scum when it came to honesty and dealing fairly with people, but he had absolutely no use for you.* Carly pulled her hand away and took two steps back. *So help me, if you put your hands anywhere on my body I'll clock you, right in the middle of the damn function.*

"It's Garfield Industries."

"That's right." He reluctantly looked away from her breasts.

"You'll have to excuse me, Mr. Garfield. I have things to attend to."

"I'd like to get to know you better, honey, maybe do a little business together."

"Call my office and talk to my office assistant. See what she can arrange."

His eyes darkened. "I don't usually deal with…secretaries."

Carly shrugged and took a step to the side.

His pudgy hand shot out and grabbed her wrist. "I don't like your attitude, Miss."

Carly brought her knee up quickly, hitting him right between the legs.

He dropped her hand to protect his private parts. "You bitch."

Carly heard him and smiled. She moved away and disappeared in the crowd. *What a disgusting and evil man.* She'd make sure he never got another invitation, even if he did contribute to The Foundation. She decided to get a breath of fresh air and strode toward the outside patio. Maybe she could slip away a few minutes early. Julie had everything under control. They didn't really need her.

Nadia glided through the crowd of people on the arm of one of the league's top basketball players. She loved basketball and had box seats for the Knicks games. She knew a lot of the players and dated one occasionally, mostly because his or her agent arranged it or for events like this one. They approached the stage and she quickly did a head count of the people in line to open their check books and write obscene amounts to the foundation. Julie had arranged another successful money raiser.

Nadia posed for photos with those wanting to be seen with a super model after they had written a check. Some were media shots that would likely end up in morning society pages or on the late night news. She noticed something and whispered to her partner before she left him and strode purposely to the bar. Percy York was going to explain why he was still here. Julie said she'd taken Graham Hargreaves off the list, besides the man was dead.

Percy was at the end of the bar, alone. He was easy to spot because he didn't fit in with the crowd. She paused to observe him. He downed his drink and motioned for another one. A young woman, perhaps the mayor's daughter, but Nadia couldn't say for sure, passed by him. His hand snaked out to grab her around her waist. He said something to her. She responded with a disgusted look. She removed his hand with her fingers, as if he had leprosy.

The sooner they got him out of here the better.

"Percy York, how are you enjoying the party?" Nadia approached the pathetic young man with a pasted smile on her face.

Percy sat up straighter and looked around. "Me?"

"Yes, you." Nadia kept her distance between them She didn't want him to try to put his grubby hands on her. His cheap cologne wafted around her and caused her stomach to roil. Whatever it was it should be banned as a pollutant.

"They ran out of lobster balls." Percy responded.

"I'll have to speak to them about that." Nadia edged half a step back, to escape his cloying scent.

"Do that, because it looks chintzy when you run out of food. People expect better at functions like this."

"Do they?" Nadia's pasted on smile turned into an honest one. "It's interesting that none of the other patrons have said anything, but then they've been busy writing checks. Have you written yours yet? I can take it for The Foundation right now if you haven't."

"I... I've... I think I gave it to the blonde chick."

"I'll check with her. Who do you get your invitations from, Percy?"

"What? What do you mean?" He slid off the stool and edged away from Nadia.

"You're not on the guest list. You haven't been on the guest list at any of the fund raisers you've attended and so far you haven't donated a penny to our organization."

Percy's Adam's apple bounced up and down, his mouth moved, but nothing came out. He grasped his glass in a stranglehold.

"That's right Percy, we're on to you. Graham Hargreaves is dead and no longer on the guest list. Nadia's smile disappeared.

Percy looked desperately for a way out but he had the bar in front of him, a wall on one side and Nadia blocked a frontal escape.

Nadia reached across, swallowed her disgust, grasped his forearm and squeezed.

Percy's eyes opened wide.

"Come now, Percy, the truth."

"You sent one out to Graham after he died. I got it from his office. There must have been a time difference or something. I won't come to anymore I promise. That really hurts. Please don't." Percy whined.

Nadia released his arm and took two steps back.

"Make sure you don't ever try and get back in to any of our events. Now if I was you I'd leave and quickly."

Percy almost ran toward the nearest exit. He bumped into people in his haste to escape.

Nadia chuckled when she noticed the wet stains down the back of his pants.

He took a sip of champagne. The fund raiser was impressive. CCB didn't spare any expense. He'd known Carl Brazil, but never met his daughter.

Carl had been an unscrupulous business man. Why he would have left his empire to a woman was beyond his comprehension. Women were only good for one thing—well, two.

They needed to be kept subservient and in their place. It would be interesting to meet Miss Carly Brazil tonight. It didn't look like this organization would have anything to do with rescuing women out of prisons or out of their own bedrooms. They donated to shelters, which was generous and probably made them feel like they were accomplishing some good. He didn't see anyone here that would go into a foreign prison. But, it had come up when he'd inputted his information. He had to check it out.

He'd get a better feel for the group after he talked to Ms. Brazil. He'd seen her earlier but she had disappeared. If she'd already left this evening could turn out to be a waste of his time. He'd keep The Foundation on his list, but it would drop to the bottom.

Carly gave the room a quick scan, caught Nadia's eye and signaled she was leaving. Nadia waved good-bye. Carly moved toward the door. She'd be able to take her shoes off as soon as she got to the car.

"Excuse me." She slammed into a solid, muscular body, encased in a tuxedo. She looked up and met Link's twinkling gray eyes. Her stomach lurched.

"Carly, you're looking lovely as usual."

"Link, what are you doing here?"

"I'm on the guest list." His smile spread across his face.

Carly wasn't sure if he was laughing at her. "We have qualifications for our guests," she snapped.

"It's nice to see you, too." Link chuckled.

The warm sound caused Carly's heart rate to pick up speed. She realized how much she had missed him, but he'd chosen to leave the company, and her.

"For your information, I met all the qualifications. You can check with Julie and I already gave her my check. I didn't realize how long you three had been helping women. I'm very impressed."

"But…how… I mean on a security salary. We pay well but not that well."

"I have some family money that I haven't been using. I thought this would be a good place to put it to work. Besides, I wanted to see you. How are you doing?"

"Fine, thank you. If you hadn't left you'd know."

"If I hadn't left I wouldn't be here with you. Shall we join the people on the dance floor?" Link offered his hand.

Carly hesitated. She didn't know if she could handle being in Link's arms. The outdoorsy smell wrapped around her head and played games with her mind. She stepped forward. His muscular arms pulled her close. She tried to lower the heat of desire that shot through her body.

Link took her hand and slipped his arm tighter around her waist. They wended their way through the crowd. On the dance floor he pulled her close, his chin rested on the top of her head.

"I miss you," he murmured into her ear.

"Then you shouldn't have left."

"I had no choice. I wouldn't be holding you like this otherwise. Some things are more important than working for you."

"Like what?" Carly mumbled into his shoulder. She felt

safe in his arms, like she belonged there. Their bodies moved as one in time with the music.

"Like this, like my being able to relate to you man to woman instead of employee to boss. I couldn't wait any longer." Link guided her across the floor and out onto the patio. He placed a finger under her chin, tilted her head up and lowered his head so their lips met.

Carly drew in a sharp breath. Heat pulsed through her body. It touched every nerve and fiber. She felt her toes curl when she tasted the scotch on his lips.

He increased the pressure, slipped his tongue between her lips.

Her body temperature ratcheted up. She wondered if Link could feel it through his tuxedo. She wrapped her hands around his trunk. She moved her fingers up until she felt the soft curls at the base his neck. She twisted her fingers through his hair. She no longer thought. She could only feel and it felt so good.

He ran his fingers over her breast. A moan escaped through her lips.

Another couple burst onto the patio. They laughed loudly and headed down a dimly lit path.

Carly pulled back.

Link chuckled. "They're going to do what I'd like to do to you right now, but you're right. This isn't the place. I want the first time to be very special."

"You left me, walked out. What makes you think I want anything to do with you?"

Link leaned forward and touched her lips. "I think you just showed me you were interested. That's why I left CCB. I'm there for you any time you need me, but as your employee I could never make love to you. You know that."

Carly's mouth dropped open. "I…you…what makes you…?"

Link ran a finger down her arm. "Oh, I don't know… My wealth may not be equal to yours, but I have enough and I own my own company. I'm in your league now. Have you figured out why I left yet?"

"Uh, I'm beginning, to but…"

"Good. I will definitely see you later, Ms. Brazil. Link laughed and strode off into the darkness.

Carly stared after him. He cared about her. He wanted her. She remembered the workout and the cold one after. It wouldn't have worked, but now if there was something between them they could pursue it.

She watched Link stride back into the main room and disappear in the crowd. Anticipation filled her body. All those thoughts she'd try to keep hidden could be released. He hadn't left her. He'd left a job so he could be with her. A wide smile spread across Carly's face.

The CCB issue was solved and they were getting their bids accepted. Someone was still trying to get inside The Foundation's information but without any luck so far. Hopefully Julie and Trevor would be able to shut that link down. And Link wasn't her employee. He wanted to be with her. Life was good.

She took a last look at another successful fund raising, moved out of the room and toward her waiting car. The future, and Link, looked exciting ahead.

*Coming Soon*

# LIABILITY WIFE

Book 2 in The Foundation Series


by Beverley Bateman


*Excerpt*

Hidden in the shadows they watched the guards change. The heavy under growth prevented any sun shining through but keep the humidity locked in, giving the air a sauna-like feel.

"Ready?" Lydia whispered.

Sara nodded, moving toward the path. She got the assignment because she spoke fluent Spanish. With her dyed black and make up darkening her skin she looked Peruvian. Mac had helped her dye her hair and use the skin darkener. He really had come a long way. With a quick glance at her team she pulled a scarf over her head and sauntered towards the prison gate.

Maggie moved with her, sliding into the undergrowth near the guard.

The guard stopped her,

"I'm working in the kitchen today. Maria is sick."

He nodded and waved another guard to escort her.

"'Scuse," Sara bumped into him as she passed, pocketing his gate key. She dropped into Maggie's hand as she proceeded into the prison.

In the kitchen Sara removed her scarf and pulled on an apron. The head cook shouted at her in Spanish to make the soup.

Sara swallowed a smile. The soup was perfect. As she added bouillon and water she pulled out a slim container from her pocket and dumped a large portion of the powder into the cauldron. Continuing to stir, she hummed a melody from her childhood. This had been easier than they expected, but would the rest of the plan work as smoothly?

When she finished the soup Sara checked the coffee, adding more water and a generous dump of powder.

A few hours later, after finishing the menu for dinner Sara left the prison. Maggie returned the key to her form a hidden post in a bush near the gate.

Sara smiled at the guard, running her fingers up his chest s she returned his key. Then, smiling, she swaggered down the trail, hips undulating, as she headed toward town. Rounding the corner she slipped off the trail into the darkness of the jungle where her team waited.

"They should sleep well." Sara grinned as they crept through the underbrush to the temporary camp they had set up.

Several hours later, in the pitch black of night, the four women made their way back to the prison gate. Dressed in fatigues and black face the women waited outside the prison gate for the change of guards.

Lydia nodded and they crept forward to the gate. Inside a guard slumped to one side, leaning against the pillar, snoring loudly.

Maggie pulled out the key and opened the gate, just enough for the women to slip inside.

Once in the courtyard Maggie grabbed the guard's keys. Sara lead the way through the prison, at a fork she turned away from the kitchen and toward the cells. As they searched for Dr. Miguay a few inmates woke, shouting to be released. Most slept soundly.

Dr. Miguay had a cell to herself near the end. Opening the cell door, Sara found the woman sleeping soundly. "Damn, she must have eaten the soup. Quick, Maggie, the antidote."

Maggie dug into her pack and handed saran a syringe. Sara shot it into the doctor's upper arm and waited.

She remained asleep on her cot for several more minutes. Finally her eyes flickered open. She stared blankly.

In Spanish Sara said, "We're here to rescue you. We're Americans. We're taking you to the United States."

Dr. Miguay tried to sit.

Sara helped her reach a sitting position and swing her legs over the edge of the cot and stood up slowly, stilling staring at Sara. Sara grabbed the woman's hand and pulled her forward, slinging her over her shoulder.

Outside the cell Sara dropped the doctor to the floor. Maggie took the doctor's other hand and between them they pulled her down the corridor between the cells toward the front gate.

"This way," Sara said in Spanish as they charged into the underbrush. "We have about an hour until we get to our plane."

The doctor nodded. "I speak English. Why are you doing this?"

"We don't like to see women abused." Diane gave a curt laugh. "You do good work."

The doctor nodded as they plunged through the dense underbrush, Diane hacking away at roots when needed.

"Do you have water? They wouldn't give me any."

Sara nodded. "But you'll have to wait until we get to the plane. We can't afford to stop. they'll wake up any minute."

"What did you give them?"

"I put something special in their soup and coffee." Sara grinned over her shoulder.

As they raced through the darkness with only a flashlight illuminating the leaves and branches, the humidity clung to every pore. After almost an hour of skittering of animals as the woman passed and chattering of monkeys in the trees as their sleep was disturbed, they raced into the clearing. The pilot started the engine. Maggie climbed up into the helo and put her hand down to grab Dr Miguay. Sara helped push the doctor into the plane and hiked herself up.

# About the Author

Beverley Bateman is a Canadian author of several books who loves traveling, good wine and a mystery. She lives with her husband and Shiba Inu on the Canadian prairies during the summer and snowbirds to Arizona in the winter months.

She loves to hear from her readers. You can contact her at babateman@shaw.ca.